My Boss is the Devil

Ben Schenkman

CAFFEINATED TERRIER PRESS

ISBN 979-8-8712492-4-6 (Paperback)

ISBN 979-8-9905133-3-4 (Paperback)

ISBN 979-8-8766467-9-8 (Hardcover)

Cover design by GetCovers.com

Chapter art by Kat Gruhala (@KinTheCryptid)

CHAPTER 1

The aroma was intoxicating, almost enough to pull me forward into real consciousness. I sat at my kitchen table, eyes bleary, waiting for a small moment of joy before stepping forth into my hell of a workday. My best ceramic pour-over was slowly dripping a dark brew into my favorite, but sadly chipped, coffee mug. Some say that mornings are a time for meditation, contemplation, and getting up in the wee hours to have a good long look at your life. Others think that it's the time to get the blood flowing, get your steps in, and improve the temple that is your body. Me? I always believed that mornings were good for one thing and one thing only. Coffee. It was one of the few things in my life that was going well, which was a really depressing thought, but it was true.

I hated mornings almost as much as they hated me. The game of chicken I played with the clock, whether I'd leave for work on time or take my chances with being late and eventually fired, was getting old. Good habits were hard, but bad habits were so much easier. I eyed the LED display that glared at me balefully from the counter, narrowing my eyes and watching the time tick over to five-thirty in the morning.

My lifeline finished brewing just in time to pour directly into a travel mug. I drank my coffee black when I could control the variables and brewed it myself. Hail coffee, full of caffeine, blessed are you among beverages hot and iced. Pray for me now in my hour of waking the hell up, which I hope is soon. Amen. I took a long sip, feeling satisfied with the completion of my morning ritual, and started my trudge to work. I was probably going to be late again, but it was the third time this week. Maybe I needed to get up earlier, but every time I wondered that I also quickly accepted reality. I was far too lazy to make that kind of habit stick no matter how good it was for me. The dark sarcastic part of me, different from the light and funny sarcastic rest of me, wondered if I would already be fired.

I didn't have to wait long for a bus, which was one of the nice things you could say about my city. New Haven, Connecticut, is a weird place to live and work in. It's not exactly a major metropolitan area, but it's not a rural town either. I lived far enough away from "downtown," read: near Yale, that I had to take public transit to get to work. It's too expensive to drive and park all day, and too far to take a bike on nice days unless I wanted to arrive as a sweaty mess. I rolled out of the bus on the New Haven Green, which was one of my favorite features of the city. A lush park with old chapels, paths, and monuments that the city grew around, it provides a small oasis in the middle of downtown. Sometimes on my breaks, I just laid out on the grass and stared at the clouds scudding by.

One of the permanent fixtures of the Green was a shifting homeless population. A few people were panhandling for change when I got off the bus, and I took a few dollars that I kept loose in my pocket to drop into each of their outstretched cups. I was aspirationally middle class, despite see-sawing on the poverty line, meaning since I could pay my bills and had food in the fridge I still felt like I should help people who needed it. There wasn't much I could do for myself without a lot of time, effort, and loans that I was unlikely to afford long-term, but I could at least give a little bit to help folks who weren't even close to stable find something to eat. I didn't care what they did with the money, even though some people will tell you that you shouldn't give charity like that. "What if they use it for drugs or booze?" they would ask. Why should that matter? All I could do was trust that they'd use it to get whatever it was they needed the most, and hope it helped. My job paid me enough that I could get by, and that was enough for the moment.

What's my job, you ask? Have you ever worked in retail or food service? If you haven't, I suggest that you try it at least once. In a few short hours, you will find that your previous life was a utopia never again to be imagined. Me? I was a barista. My job was to sell coffee to people who thought it was cool to order by using as many words as possible. If I never heard, "I'll have a half-caff, double-shot, caramel, mocha latte with soy, no whip" again, I'd die a happy man. There were, however, a few good things regarding my current profession. First, I worked at The Fix. It was an independent local shop. That meant we invested in the good stuff— quality beans usually roasted locally, and the staff knew how to brew it. We offered all the bougiest methods of coffee consumption and even house-roasted small batches just so we could put that on the menu. Being independent we didn't have to deal with corporate overlords, so at least I had that going for me. Cold comfort, I know, but I didn't have a lot of other silver linings.

I unlocked the door to the shop and let myself in, locking it again behind me. Without looking up from his newspaper my boss said, "You're late again," the moment he heard the bell over the door ring. How did he do that? Sometimes I wondered if Mark had psychic powers, but then I realized he wouldn't be managing a coffee shop if he did. That or his psychic powers were so limited that he could only use them to know who was showing up late for work. Again. Was it my track record of tardiness that alerted him to my presence, moments before I walked through the door? I doubted it.

"Not as late as I could have been," I said confidently. Maybe I could bluff my way out. "You know what it's like getting through downtown. I had to run over two guys on bikes and a cluster of nuns just to get here when I did." I went into the back room to put my messenger bag in my locker and grab my apron.

"I almost gave your shift away again, Nick," Mark said while flipping to the sports section of the *Register*. "You don't want to keep this job, do you? I don't want to see you coming in late again, or it's your ass."

"Well, when you put it that way." I placed my hand over my heart. "I promise to reform my wicked ways and show up five minutes early for every shift. I'll have my shirts pressed professionally and have my hair styled once a week, twice if I'm feeling particularly scruffy."

"Very funny..." Mark tried to interrupt me.

"And I'll stay an extra five minutes every day," I continued, "just in case I am ever, in the future, late again."

"Shut up and open the store." Mark folded up the paper and walked into his office, slamming the door behind him. The reality was that Mark could have helped open the store, but we made enough money that he could pay himself a modest salary and "lead the team" instead of getting his hands dirty. Other than occasionally pulling shots when we had a massive rush, he spent most of his time sourcing beans, advertising, and managing our social media. He wasn't just my manager; he was the owner, so he got to make those kinds of decisions, and the rest of us could either take it or leave it.

"You know you don't need to antagonize him like that, right?" Declan moved over to where I was standing at the counter, giving me one of his classic looks. It was the kind of look that asked, *are you really that stupid all the time?*

"Yes," I huffed, setting out the daily baked goods while surveying the blends Mark was offering today, "but it's so satisfying. You realize that Mark stopped into a traditional Italian cafe once, saw all the white shirts and aprons, and decided that was his new definition of 'fancy coffee,' right? I think it's a perfect example of why he's so uptight."

Declan couldn't help but laugh. "You're kidding."

"I am one hundred percent serious. The craziest part? It wasn't even in Italy, it was in New York City! Even so, he decided that very day to give the pampered students of Yale a more upscale experience. Hence the dress code." I gestured at my mostly unwrinkled button-down shirt.

"Well let's get this fancy-ass place open, I guess," Declan said on his way past me to stock the to-go cups. Declan was a recent transplant from Boston. He moved to New Haven to stay with his sister while she was going through cancer treatment at Yale New Haven Hospital. If there's one thing that New Haven has going for it, it's top-notch hospitals with cutting-edge treatments. Unfortunately, if you ask Declan it's the only thing this city has going for it. We didn't spend much time together outside of work. His schedule was pretty full taking care of his sister and her family, but we worked well together and he laughed at my jokes. I set the empty coffee can I had prepped the night before out in front of the register. It was covered with brown paper with a hand-drawn message that read "Fighting Cancer is Tiring Work, Help Us Buy Her Coffee." I couldn't think of anything more inspirational, but it had a little picture of Declan's sister that I had asked him for. She wouldn't approve of us crowdfunding her treatment, but maybe this would help her get some real food while she was dealing with the garbage they served in the hospital. With a nod to Declan, who clapped me on the shoulder, we unlocked the door for our earliest regulars.

I existed in a bizarre duality where I hated my job but loved what I did. When I dropped out of college I didn't have a lot of options. I had intended to become a bartender because I thought mixology was an amazing combination of art and science. You could make good money if you found the right venue, too. There were some issues with that, though. Problem one, being a bartender in a college town is a combat sport and I wasn't that interested in the chance of getting my teeth knocked in by some frat boys. Second, any opening expected you to have years of experience. I could have become a barback but that sounded like a different kind of hell, and there was no guarantee I'd ever move up to being a bartender. If I wanted an in, I'd have to take a certification course which cost money that I didn't have. I was enjoying a cappuccino at a coffee house I used to frequent when I realized that, watching the barista behind the counter, I could apply my love for mixology to a different medium. Getting a job making coffee was a lot easier, and after I had put in some time getting good at it, I landed the job at The Fix. Turned out that I loved coffee, the science behind it, and the art of making it even more than the idea of being a bartender.

The day flew by in a caffeinated blur of espresso shots, designer lattes, and a substantial amount of internal screaming to get me through the day. I finally hit the end of my shift and dropped my apron into its cubby, grabbed my bag, high-fived Declan, and ran like hell for the door. Just because I loved making coffee didn't mean that I liked the customers. On balance, they're not terrible, but one or two bad ones each day made the whole thing hard to bear sometimes. I hated my job. My job hated me right back. At least I got paid. Hey, a haiku. I felt a little better because I was supposed to hang out with some friends that night, to escape thinking about the caffeinated capitalist hellscape I was going to have to return to tomorrow.

CHAPTER 2

The friends I was hanging out with that night were self-proclaimed Satanists. As far as I knew, they didn't worship Satan, or even follow the New Age book section ramblings of Anton LaVey. They dressed however they wanted, usually without regard to popular taste or fashion sense, and claimed to harness the power of their *Dark Lord*. This also meant they were a blast to hang out with as long as I didn't take them too seriously. I also couldn't *tell them* that I didn't take them too seriously. They were going to do something that night in a graveyard and had invited me along earlier in the week. I didn't have anything planned, and I was inebriated enough when they asked that I said, "Yes." Did I mention they have absinthe? They brought it everywhere, and they liked to share.

Have you ever had absinthe? It used to be illegal in the United States because the original formula contained wormwood, otherwise known as poison. Let's gloss over the fact that alcohol itself is poison and get back to the lovely green stuff. If you've been to the French Quarter in New Orleans, or read your share of vampire novels, you may have heard of chartreuse, which is a similar green alcoholic beverage. It's got nothing on absinthe. Absinthe is green like a neon sign and smells so strongly of anise that you can just tell what it's going to taste like. Yes, that's right: Green. Licorice. Death. I learned about it when I was considering getting into the liquor trade, and the method for making it more palatable was fascinating. The traditional way of enjoying absinthe is to dilute it with water that is poured over a sugar cube, which rests on a special slotted spoon, into a short glass. They weren't bougie enough for that so usually just drank it straight from the bottle, but that night they wanted to include it in their ceremony. I had picked up a battered antique absinthe spoon on the cheap a while back and offered to pour for them if I could lurk around the graveyard with them. The leader of the group, Rob, was quick to agree and that's how I had secured my spot. I may have also teased him about not being a properly dark poetic soul without an absinthe spoon of his very own.

All the merits of questionable alcoholic beverages aside, I planned on spending a starlit night surrounded by the graves of someone else's ancestors. It sounded depressing, exactly the kind of mood I was ready to wallow in. When you sling coffee for eight hours a day, you might not mind some time when nobody was yelling at you for giving them Equal when they asked for Splenda. A graveyard seemed like the perfect place to find some peace and quiet. If my friends brought along a little offering to the dead and shared it with the living? Well, so much the better.

Some people found it offensive that anyone would want to spend time among *other* people's dead relatives. I didn't see a reason for all the negativity. They were dead, we were not. If there was an afterlife, they probably didn't even know that I hung out where they left their bodies. If there was truth to spirits wandering the earth, maybe they'd like some company. Plenty of other cultures celebrated and venerated their dead, visiting their graves with picnics and telling stories, but America never adopted similar practices. Everyone seemed to agree that cemeteries were best left alone after dark, but that's mostly to discourage crime. I was neither a vandal nor a graverobber, so what's the worst that could happen? I'd get a stern talking-to from the police about visiting hours and an order to march myself home. New Haven was a college town, so they were used to this kind of thing anyway. I'd been through my share of cemeteries at night when I was a kid. My friends dared me to do stupid things like going into a graveyard and spending a whole minute in a mausoleum, that kind of thing.

I was always the first to volunteer for stuff like that, and you might wonder why. Well, I have a secret, but please keep it to yourself because if word got around, I'd lose half of my street cred. Deal? Good.

I'm not afraid of things that go bump in the night because there's so much more to worry about in the real world without having to worry about black cats and zombies rising from freshly dug graves. I'm not claiming to be an atheist, though I respect anyone willing to thumb their noses at religious establishments for the right reasons. I'm more what you would call a hesitant believer. I believe in a higher power for no particular reason other than it makes sense to me and I'd never turn down some proof if said higher power decided to show itself. God? The Devil? No reason they shouldn't exist, but since I'd never seen a miracle, or shaken either of their hands, I'd considered myself a skeptic.

The end result? I liked walking in graveyards at night because the only thing to fear was my fellow man, and few of them liked to hang around places like that. In addition, I wouldn't be walking around alone, which helped to improve my survivability rating when wandering around at night. It wasn't an unsafe city unless you didn't know where you were going, and even then there were only a few areas that held any real risk. People are people, and most people just want to be left alone at night. The cemetery they wanted to go to was off Fitch Street, right near SCSU. That's Southern Connecticut State University, for all of you in South Carolina. It was a decent school with a moderately sized campus and one of the best parts about it, as far as I was concerned, was that it wasn't Yale. I had nothing against Yalies on an intellectual level.

It's an Ivy League school for a reason, but half of the ones I had met had been stuck-up brats. That's not exactly a ringing endorsement. "Get your degree from Yale: If you're here on scholarship, you'll fit in just fine with the help." No thank you. I would take the honest kid who wanted an education from a state school any day. SCSU had its own crime issues, but in general, the neighborhood was safe enough to walk around, especially if I wasn't by myself.

I went home after my shift to change out of work clothes and into something comfortable and suited to midnight strolls. A grilled cheese sandwich and a bowl of tomato soup would fortify me against an evening in the cold. It was December, just before the holidays, I didn't think it was going to be bitterly cold. We'd been having an unseasonably warm winter, but comfort food was always nice before going out in any sort of chill. My heart had said artisanal bread and fresh tomatoes, my bank account said processed American cheese food and generic canned goodness.

The phone rang while the food was cooking and I managed to pick it up before it went to voicemail.

"Hello?" I tucked the phone against my shoulder.

"Hey, Nick, it's Amy."

"Oh, hey, Amy. What's up?"

"Just wanted to make sure you weren't chickening out. Still on for tonight?"

"Of course! Just having a little something to eat before I head over to Rob's place." I managed to not drop my phone into the soup. "We're meeting there, right?"

"You got it. Okay, see you there."

"Later." Click.

Amy was a nice girl. She wore a lot of black and a dizzying assortment of silver jewelry but she had that pixie thing going for her. I'd never mistake her for one of those all-out nihilistic goths; she smiled too much.

Sandwich and soup were devoured, video games played, and emails checked, I hopped into my car and drove over to Rob's place. I didn't need to get there until around eleven o'clock; they were planning on making it a midnight run. Something about the witching hour, but I hadn't paid much attention. Rob lived in an apartment on Willard Ave, a decent neighborhood if you don't walk too many blocks in any direction. Luckily there were visitor spots left, so I parked and strolled up to his door. The buzzer went off and a muffled voice chimed, "You rang?" through the speaker like Lurch, from the *Addams Family*.

"Ha ha, Rob, lemme in." A familiar buzz led me through the entryway, down the stairs, and past the mushrooms to his door. It was a basement apartment with carpet in the entryway; he didn't ask much of his landlord because the rent was cheap. I didn't live there, so I just didn't step on the mushrooms, or walk around the hallways without footwear. Inside the apartment were hardwood floors and linoleum, so I guess it was hard to complain when the fungus stayed outside your door.

The door was open when I got down the stairs, so I walked in and dropped my bag by the coat rack. I strolled into the living room and spotted Amy sitting on the sofa, and Derek at Rob's computer, tapping away.

"Hey, guys," I said as I plunked down on the L-shaped couch, opposite Amy. She was dressed simply in a tight, long-sleeved, top and peasant skirt (black of course) which fitted nicely over her frame. She didn't fit the "goth waif" stereotype and had curves in what I considered to be the right places. I glanced at her, catching a glint in her green eyes framed by her strawberry blonde hair that was cut in a cute bob. Her slightly cherubic face held a warm smile, and I let myself take in her appearance for a moment before shifting my attention back to the rest of the room.

I got a chorus of "Hey, Nick!" with Rob's voice coming from inside the kitchen. "Nick, how do you take your coffee?"

"Black, like my soul," I replied with a grin. Drinking Rob's mediocre black coffee was probably worth the joke, I hoped.

"Perfectly appropriate for tonight's endeavors," the voice replied, chuckling, from the kitchen. "I'm making up a thermos to take with us and that's less sugar packets I have to carry around. No cream either, and no whining from the two of you. You should learn to drink coffee like me and Nick. Like real men, it puts hair on your chest."

"I'm a girl, Rob," Amy protested loudly, from the living room.

"Sure you are, Amy," said the disembodied voice of Rob.

"Jerk!" she yelled toward the kitchen.

"Exactly."

"That's enough out of the two of you," I said, pushing up from the couch. I walked into the kitchen to see Rob. "Anything I can do to help?"

"Nah, we're almost ready to go." Rob lowered his voice to a baritone pitch. He tended toward the dramatic, and it was reflected in most of what he did. Rob was dressed to impress (if your target audience was a heavy metal concert) in black jeans and a ripped t-shirt sporting his latest band obsession layered with a denim jacket. His sense of style matched the dorm-room chic of his apartment. Rob was tall, lean, and lightly muscled, his brown hair falling to his shoulders. "It's getting to be about that time, kiddies. Everyone got their gear?" he yelled toward the living room.

Gear? Did a spoon count as gear? No one said anything about gear. What kind of gear did you bring to a cemetery? Waitaminute.

"Uh, hey, Rob." I tried not to sound too concerned, realizing I hadn't asked the purpose of the trip. "What exactly are we doing tonight?"

"Don't worry your pretty little head. *You* aren't doing anything besides pouring the libation. Otherwise, you're a bystander, potential alibi, and possible human sacrifice. Just calling up Satan, you know, the usual." Rob smiled with a wicked gleam in his eye.

"Why must you taunt me like this?" I didn't like him when he smiled like that. All the charisma of a comedian, but evil.

"Smile, Nick. We're not going to do anything to you." Rob's smile didn't go away. "We just need to bring some stuff. Incense, candles, and the like. Blood of the virgin optional. Why do you think we invited you?"

I tried not to blush. "I'm not a virgin, Rob."

"Sure you're not." His smile turned into a leer. "Amy says you are."

"Shut UP, Rob!" squealed Amy from the living room.

"Anyway, I said we're not going to do anything to you, and we're not... much." He winked.

I looked around the apartment while they were getting their "gear" together and didn't notice any knives, so I decided that I could let my teeny tiny bit of paranoia go. They were my friends, and they weren't *real* Satanists. Just dark hippies bonding over candles and booze in a cemetery. Right?

"So, whose car are we taking?" I asked. I drove a little Dodge coupe, which seated four when all of my junk wasn't piled up in the backseat, so I wasn't going to offer to drive.

"I borrowed my mom's minivan." Derek looked up from tapping at his keyboard, his shoulder-length black hair falling over one of his brown eyes. He wore his usual black cargo pants and long-sleeved t-shirt sporting either a heavy metal band or Satanic iconography. Or both, it was hard to tell these days. He stood up, throwing a dark hoodie over his shoulders. "It'll fit everyone. I took out the car seat while I was at her house."

We were going to a cemetery, in the middle of the night, in a blue minivan. Something seemed vaguely wrong with a self-proclaimed worshiper of Satan carpooling to a dark summoning in a minivan, but at least I wouldn't have to drive.

CHAPTER 3

I learned something about suburban camouflage that night. If you park a blue minivan on the curb near any house in a college town, people will assume that it belongs there. It works even better if the van has seen better days as this one had. I suppose college kids have better things to do than wonder whether or not their roommate has some friends over that he doesn't feel like meeting, so the vehicle goes unnoticed and, more importantly, unreported to the authorities.

We parked a few blocks away from the cemetery and then hoofed it over to the back gate. Luckily, this wasn't one of those cemeteries that they locked up tight at night, so we just walked in and headed for the shadowy side of a mausoleum.

"Okay, Nick, we're going to need a few minutes to set up," Rob whispered as he unpacked a small bag. "You can stick around with us, or take a stroll around. Just try not to let anyone see you. We'll call you back when we need you to do your thing."

"Fair enough," I replied, then moved away from the trio. I didn't like to interrupt people when they worked, especially since I'd be annoyed if someone stood around me asking, "What's that candle for?" or "Why do you have to tie that chicken up like that?" I assumed for this case it was all delicate work, and I didn't want to intrude on anyone's spirituality even if I didn't believe in it myself. I was a skeptic, not a jerk. So I did the next best thing, I found a patch of ivy and laid down in it. The sky was clear, and I was looking for Orion's belt while simultaneously trying to not fall asleep. It was midnight if you recall, and I had been up since five in the morning.

"Psst."

I jerked my head up from my ivy pillow. Must have fallen asleep for a few minutes.

"Nick?" I heard someone whispering my name. I guess I hid myself a little too well. "Where are you? We're all set."

I levered myself up into a crouch, brushed off my pants, and crept back over to the others. I thought I managed to sneak up on Rob.

"Boo," I whispered directly into his ear.

"Nice try." Rob was unphased. "We're ready to go, you ready?"

"You were scared, I know it. Yeah, I'm ready to watch whatever this is going to be." I looked at what they had done, and I had to admit, it looked pretty cool. A cloth with a hand-drawn pentagram was set with black candles, incense, the whole nine yards. In the center of the star was a short wine glass, for my part. I didn't know a lot about that sort of thing, but I had been hanging around with them long enough to get some of the basic terminology down. Rob nodded to me, very seriously, and that was all the cue I was going to get.

I tried to match the solemnity of the group, even if I didn't feel it myself. I had volunteered, so I wasn't going to make a mockery of it. Matching energy was the least I could do. I flourished the bottle that I had kept with me, the cork already half-out for easy pouring. I pulled it the rest of the way with a satisfying pop and slowly poured a generous portion of green malice into the glass. I carefully set the slotted spoon over the glass with a small clink, placing the sugar cube with steady hands. The flask I had brought with purified water came last, pouring drop by drop over the sugar until it dissolved into the liquid below. Pleased with my performance, I turned to Rob and bowed slightly. He rolled his eyes a little but smiled at me. I waited for a moment, looking at each of the other participants. "Uh, now what?"

"Just stand outside the circle, however close you want. You'll know if something happens, and you'll know when it's over. Good?"

"Fantastic. I'll just sit over there and contemplate my poor life choices." I pointed to a small spot of grass a few feet away.

I wasn't entirely sure what to expect, so I just took a seat and focused on listening to what they said. Sadly, at least in the beginning, they weren't saying much, so I took the time to gingerly pour some absinthe into the now much less full flask. No one could blame me for having a tipple of my own, after all. After lighting the candles and incense, there was a bunch of meditating and looking spooky, then they got down to the speaking parts. It sounded like a B-grade horror movie, all "Oh great one, we beseech thee..." blah, blah, blah. It looked like they each pricked their fingers and then squeezed a drop of their blood into the glass of absinthe. They passed it around the circle and each drank from the glass. It struck the practical part of my brain that remarked on how unsanitary that was. I had been sipping from my flask and was thankful that my portion, at least, was as nature intended. Finally, Rob took the rest of it and poured it into the center of the pentagram. This was getting a little too intense for my, uh, blood.

Suddenly, my ears felt clogged with pressure and then popped when I moved my jaw, like when you change altitude. Rob didn't seem to notice and they kept going with their little ritual. I shook my head and then started paying attention to what they were saying again.

"Nice night, isn't it?"

I froze. I think I stayed that way for a solid minute until I had enough of a handle on my heart rate to turn my head to the left, without screaming like a child, toward the shadow of the mausoleum where the voice had come from. I'm no coward, but I normally hear people when they sneak up on me and there was no sneaking going on. Color me creeped right the hell out.

Sitting to my left, and slightly behind me, was a man in a black suit, black shirt, and red tie. His eyes were so deep brown to be almost black. His sable hair was choppy and short but perfect in its slight disarray. He had a small, tightly trimmed, van-dyke beard and slim features. The suit was well-tailored and slim fit, accentuating a lithe build. He sat with a performer or dancer's poise, looking at me. I remembered that one of the local clubs had a goth night on Thursdays... probably just another peaceful cemetery walker like myself.

He repeated himself as if I hadn't heard him, "Nice night, isn't it?"

"Uh, yeah, nice night." I hoped there was no quaver in my voice.

"I love cemeteries at night," continued the man with the red tie. "So peaceful, don't you think?"

I glanced over to the circle. Amy sat across from Rob, facing my direction. I tried to make little motions with my hand and catch her eye. She looked up, smiled at me but motioned to their little altar with her head, and then went back to staring at the center of the circle. Thanks, Amy.

"Quiet as the grave," I quipped quietly and immediately cursed myself mentally for needing to be clever. "Just what I was thinking. I hate to ask, but do you know these guys? They don't seem to mind the fact that you just showed up, so I don't want to assume that you mean trouble."

"No, sorry, I don't know those three. And trouble?" He feigned shock, then smiled. "I mean no trouble at all. Actually, Nick, I popped by to see *you.*"

"Well, that's very friendly of..." I stopped talking as my mouth closed on the last syllable and I realized he had addressed me by name. My name. That he didn't know. Because I'd never met him, and he claimed not to know my friends. Top it all off with the fact that I had remembered to take off my name tag, and I felt decidedly uncertain about my situation. I decided to fake it, "...you. I can't say that we've met before, I don't usually forget such friendly faces."

"We haven't met, but I'm more than willing to make introductions." He reached a hand toward me. There's something instinctive in the human condition to return an offered handshake, so I shook it. "Call me Lu."

"You don't look like a Lou," I said, eyeing his outfit.

"You were expecting Cypher or something, I take it?"

I cleared my throat, realizing I had probably insulted him. "No, uh, sure thing. Lou."

"No no, not Lou. Lu."

I tried to hear the difference, but couldn't. "I'm guessing you don't mean Lu like 'Lulu,' do you?" I asked as nonchalantly as possible. This was getting decidedly weird.

"In pronunciation, yes. In meaning? Entirely different." He grinned and I, if I wasn't already imagining things, might have said his eyes flickered. But I was still thoroughly convinced that I was imagining things, so maybe I made that up.

I smiled, because I couldn't think of anything else to do, and went on like a blithering idiot, "So, Lu, what brings you to a graveyard in the middle of a dark mass to see little old me?" Why did I say that? Why, God, why?

"You're wondering why my sudden appearance doesn't bother your friends, aren't you?" Lu seemed to like to state the obvious.

"I was thinking something along those lines, yes." I looked at the flask I had been drinking from, wondering suddenly if I hadn't managed to get my hands on the good stuff after all.

"I'll tell you a secret. You'll have to come closer, I need to whisper it." Lu wore a sly grin that would make the Cheshire Cat whimper.

What choice did I have? If you've ever been punched in the gut by the brass knuckles of freakish circumstances, then you know I didn't have a choice. I was already sitting, so I sidled closer to this strange man who called himself Lu.

He leaned over and put his mouth right by my ear, and then with the slightest of breath, he whispered, "*They can't see me.*"

I laughed aloud, covered my mouth, and looked guiltily over at the circle. The three of them had paused and looked over at me like I had grown a second head, and then they shook their heads in unison and went back to chanting. They didn't even look at Lu. I turned to him again and said, "You're serious, aren't you?" Lu nodded sagely, then put his index finger to his mouth and shushed me.

"They're going to think you're insane, talking to yourself like that." He stood up and started walking over toward my prior patch of ivy. "Why don't you walk with me? We can have a chat."

I looked at Lu, and then over to the circle. No one was looking at me, so I had to clear my throat to get Amy's attention. She was the only one facing my direction, and no one seemed happy with me for laughing before. I caught Amy's eye again and made walking motions with my fingers. Either she understood or was just happy to assume that I was going to leave them alone, then smiled and nodded to me. I stood up and followed Lu, who started us on a slow stroll through the cemetery.

"You think I'm crazy, don't you." Lu made this a statement rather than a question.

"Not exactly," I replied. "I think *I* might be the crazy one. Schizophrenia, or paranoid delusions, or whatever is going on doesn't run in the family, but I wouldn't put it past me to drive myself crazy somehow."

"Let me put your mind at ease. Well, as much ease as this statement will give you. You're not crazy, Nick. You're perfectly sane, or at least as sane as any human being can expect to be in this era."

"How can I be sure that you're not just Crazy Me," I reasoned, "a little piece of my psyche trying to convince myself that I'm perfectly sane? I'm pretty sure I'd do that too."

Lu frowned slightly. "Look, Nick, this is all going to be much easier if you realize that I am not a figment of your imagination, and just accept that you're in a slightly peculiar situation. Slightly peculiar is much easier to deal with than entirely insane, wouldn't you agree?"

The thing was, I didn't *feel* crazy. I felt pretty normal, honestly. On top of it, the weirdness of having some guy in a suit appear behind me, knowing who I was, and wanting me to take a walk with him, was wearing off. Sure, this guy was weird, but I'd met weirder. They just didn't know my name without being introduced first and weren't invisible to people around me.

"Fine by me. I'd rather not be insane, to be perfectly honest with you. Okay, so let's get down to the nitty-gritty here. You said that my friends couldn't see you, right?"

"Right."

"Well, maybe you can start by explaining to me why that seems to be true."

"All right, I will, but first I'm going to ask you a question. Do you believe in God?"

"Yes, I believe in some sort of God," I replied, unable to tell if he was beating around the bush or getting to the point.

"What, no equivocation? No qualification or rationalization?" Lu seemed genuinely surprised.

"No, not really."

"Fair enough," Lu continued, "you believe in a god, how about his counterpart?"

"You mean the Devil?" I barked a short laugh.

"So to speak, yes."

"Well, give me a second to think about this rationally." I sat down on a bench. "I believe in a god, and there's enough suffering in the world that I'll have to admit that some sort of counterpart probably exists. I'll also say that I've got no proof for either case."

Lu smiled and then clapped his hands together quietly. "And that, dear boy, is why you can see me. You *believe* in me. Or at least you believe enough in *something* that I've chosen to reveal myself to you."

"I'm sorry, what?"

"You believe in me, and I chose you. It hasn't sunk in yet. Give it a minute." He smiled and started walking away.

I was probably being dense. Maybe it would come to me if I put all the facts together. Sudden appearance. Check. Well-tailored black suit accented with red. Check. Knowing who I was. Check. Fiery eyes and sly, but friendly, demeanor. Check. Asking if I believed in ultimate good and evil. Che... hold that check.

I whispered, almost under my breath, "Lu... cifer."

Lu stopped walking down the path and turned about as if he heard me. Hell, he probably had heard me. He strode up with a bright smile on his face, looking not enough like the devilish conclusion that I had drawn. He stopped in front of me, put his hand flat to his stomach, took a small bow, and said, "At your service."

"You. Lucifer." I was not very intelligent at that moment in time.

"Yes, that's correct. I do like that moniker much better than the others. It has a certain amount of class to it. Much better than Satan, I'm no one's enemy. That and the kabbalists are using that name again. Beelzebub? Sticks in the throat, no ring at all. Lucifer," he breathed in and out dramatically. "It just rolls off the tongue like honey liquor, no?"

"Uh," the densest part of me tried to come up with a reply, "it's a good name."

"Yes, I thought so. People don't usually get the reference at first when I introduce myself as Lu, but that's what I get for being progressive. No, it doesn't hold the fire it used to, but it helps to blend in at parties."

"So, you're the Devil." It was my turn to state the obvious, or the not so obvious in this case.

"I thought we covered that. Maybe it's time to move on?"

"Right. So... wait a second. You said that I could see you because I believe in you. Rob's, like, some big Satanist. That's what they're doing over there, calling you up with some sort of devil mojo." I was grasping at straws at that point.

"Funny you should mention that," Lu chuckled dryly, "I can explain it for you if you're interested."

"My middle name is Interested." I couldn't turn off the jokes.

"No it's not. It's Michael, which is a slight disappointment for very personal reasons, but that's not important." He should warn people before trotting out personal information like that. I opened my mouth to interject but he just kept going. "They're doing some sort of modern interpretation of a summoning ritual, meant to appease me and ask for my presence. So boring nowadays, not like the old times. Oh, the virgin sacrifices, the burnt offerings." Lu sighed wistfully. "*Those* were the good old days. No, they couldn't see me for two reasons. Number one, I didn't want them to. Number two, they don't believe in much, let alone me. I lied when I said I didn't know your friends, I do know them very well. I may know them better than they know themselves, just like I know you, Nick. Not socially, we've never been introduced, but I know their deepest fears and darkest secrets. I know yours too, Nick. Every. Single. One."

I swallowed the anxious lump stuck in my throat with a gulp. I must have looked like a panic-stricken deer. Luckily, Lu noticed before I had a heart attack.

"Too much with the creepy? I'm sorry. I'm not here to scare you, just to talk to you." Lu sat down at another convenient bench and patted the spot beside him. "In fact, I'm here to make you an offer."

I couldn't remember if there was an old axiom about what to do if the Devil made you an offer. I didn't think there was, but I could have been wrong. In either case, I was at an impasse. What was that old saying? Better the Devil, you know? I didn't know this Devil very well, but I sat down nonetheless. I asked the first thing that came to mind, "Why?"

"I admire your honesty. The first thing so many people do when a powerful man like myself tells them he has an offer for them is to say yes immediately. It makes my job easier, frankly, but less interesting." Lu paused before continuing. "Your question makes it more difficult, but I've got answers. Why you? Why not? If the stories tell it truly, I'm out to get every last soul on Earth under my sway, but you don't look like a guy who believes everything he reads. If I told you I was going for quantity over quality, where do you think I would start first?"

I thought about it for a minute and then answered without hesitation, "Rob."

"Bingo!" Lu exclaimed as he snapped his fingers. "But what would that get me? I told you they don't believe in me. They don't believe in anything, not even God. They make nice noises about it, but if I showed up in the middle of that circle, they'd run like rabbits back down into their burrows. Do you know why? It's because they don't expect it to work. They expect their faces to get warm but that's from the breathing. They expect their hands to get cold and that's just because it's December. They convince themselves that they've had a nice séance and then get back to the world they believe in. Brick, mortar, and steel, nothing more. Could I convince them? With a snap of my little fingers, I could do nearly *anything* I needed to convince them. But what would that get me? They didn't believe in me until I showed them who I was. *You*, Nick, you believed in me before we even met. I'll wait until the day before judgment itself to convert non-believers like that to my cause because then all I'll have to do is show myself to them. But you, I need a little head start with."

"I must be missing something." I recalled something he said earlier. "I believe in you, I believe in a god, so why don't I just ignore you and stay on his side? Or is it her side? I mean, you've met, right?"

"Him, her, makes very little difference, kind of an Everyman that way," Lu replied, waving his hands. "It doesn't matter. Why not just ignore me? Well, I'm very persuasive. Not to mention persistent. But I'm not going to bore you with threats about unending pain and hellfire, that sort of thing. That would just drive you right to Him. I've got something better. Remember when I said that I knew everyone's fears and secrets? Well, I also want to know your hopes and dreams, your most base and lofty desires. They don't make my name synonymous with temptation for nothing, you know."

"I don't think I'm going to give up my soul for a nifty gadget, woman, or anything like that if it's what you have in mind." Living below the poverty line enforced a kind of minimalism that I'd grown accustomed to, and I hoped one day to genuinely fall in love but the idea of selling my soul for a girlfriend didn't appeal to me in the least.

Lu laughed. It was a nice laugh, like one you would hear in a crowd somewhere and say, "That sounds like a cool guy," but then I remembered that he was the Devil. "No, definitely not." Lu chuckled again. "No women or gizmos for you, Nick. I've got something better in mind for you. You see, I know something that you don't even realize yet. Though you will, of course, once I tell you. Let me tell you something special. You desperately, underneath all of your pessimistic bluster and sarcastic wit, want to do good in this world. You hate your job, but you love taking care of people. You're a bleeding heart trapped in a barista's apron. Tell me that's not true."

"It's not true," I lied. How could I not lie? It *was* true. But I couldn't tell the Devil that he was right. It just seemed, well, wrong. So I lied, which gave me time to think of a suitably pessimistic response. Damn. Who didn't want to be a good person? What kind of jerk would I have to be if I said that I didn't want to do something good for the world, for society? Everyone I knew had something going on that could use a little bit of help, even me. Amy was going to school, but having a hard time with tuition. Her parents made too much money for her to get good student loans, but they weren't helping her pay for school. My parents were hounded by creditors for bills that they couldn't pay because my dad got laid off and couldn't find another job with the same salary as his old one. People got shot every day for doing nothing but breathing. Children were starving in all corners of the globe. War made for daily suffering for any number of countries.

I lived in a dinky apartment in a questionable neighborhood in New Haven and worked as a coffee cretin. I did want to take care of people, to help them, but how could I help anyone else if I couldn't even help myself? Of course, I wanted to do something important with my life. Everyone wanted that, didn't they? Something that would make people's lives better, more than dropping a few dollars into homeless people's cups. What the hell could *I* do? Nothing, really.

"You're overwhelmed," Lu said with what appeared to be real concern in his voice, "and who wouldn't be? Tell you what, why don't you meet back up with Rob and company and we'll get together tomorrow night for dinner? Just the two of us."

"Why not lunch?"

"You've got a full shift tomorrow, and you only get half an hour for lunch." Lu grinned. "I'm assuming our conversation will take longer than that. You've got a lot to think about; I'm more than happy to give you some time to rally your thoughts and continue tomorrow. I'll pick you up at seven? Great. Nice to meet you, Nick.

You're good people. Have a great day at work tomorrow, the little moments matter a lot to people." He shook my hand and walked off toward the main gate of the cemetery.

"Hey, Nick!" I heard Rob's voice calling me from where I had left them. Lu and I had made a nearly full circle of the cemetery but hadn't gotten back to my original spot. He was whispering loudly, trying to find me.

"Coming!" I replied in my own loud whisper and went back to where the circle had been. I say 'had been' because everything was already broken down into the few bags that they had brought with them in the first place. They looked satisfied, and I followed them back to the van with a sheepish look on my face.

"It's okay, Nick. This kind of thing isn't for everyone," Amy said to me as we were getting into the van. She must have thought I felt bad about interrupting them and then going off on my own. I just smiled back and didn't say anything else until we got back to Rob's. I didn't stick around. It was almost three o'clock in the morning, and I still needed to get up for work.

CHAPTER 4

The alarm clock didn't have a chance to make more than two beeps before I turned it off. I didn't sleep. Would you have slept? I doubt it.

I got up and showered, then wrapped myself in a towel and looked in the mirror. Despite my bloodshot eyes, I wondered if I was seeing myself clearly for the first time in a while. My face was thin without being gaunt, covered with a day and a half of scruff. My shoulders were already slumped, and when I realized that I rolled them backward, getting a satisfying pop from my mid spine. How long had it been since I stood up straight on purpose? I rubbed my hand over my rough cheeks, sighed, and made the conscious choice to shave. It was early enough, so I actually ironed a shirt for once and found a decent pair of slacks before I dressed and left the apartment. I was walking into the coffee shop twenty minutes before Mark even showed up. I had gotten the store ready to open, made myself a triple espresso, drank that, made myself a double latte for sipping, and had two pots of coffee brewing before he walked through the door.

"Mrognan." I tried to say "Morning" but the word mashed itself together as it tried to leave my mouth. I decided that my first attempt was an absolute failure, and I should try again. "Morning, Mark."

"Uh. Morning, Nick. You're early. Um. Good to see you're trying to improve your work ethic." Mark looked me in the eyes once, saw nothing good, picked the newspaper up from the counter, and went into his office. I had already read it front to back. Twice.

I had, long ago, broken my caffeine-ometer to the point where enough of it will keep me awake but no amount of it will give me the usual lift that the average person looked for. I was able to keep myself upright that shift, but I was only partially conscious. Customers came and went, the coffee flowed like brown rivers, and the conversation I had the night before with a snappily dressed man wearing a red tie ran through my head like a train wreck. I just couldn't look away, I couldn't think about anything else. I was so nonchalant last night when it was all happening, but my nerves were jangling messes now. So my body was on autopilot, serving drinks and making change, but slowly I started noticing the little moments that Lu had talked about. Maybe it was the way a customer smiled gratefully when I handed them a freshly brewed coffee, just the way they liked it. There were the regulars that I joked with, teasing them about their drink choices for the day. The way a patron's eyes lit up if I complimented them on their outfits or accent pieces, a nice tie, or a piece of jewelry. The angry people would always be there, and they peppered my morning, but their tiny tirades fell away as I tried to be present despite being dead on my feet. For once, I was feeling pretty good about myself.

I kept this up until my lunch break, then fell asleep in the back stock room for a full thirty minutes— I woke up to Mark standing over me as I was slumped back in a rolling chair. He shook his head. "You can't sleep on the job, Nick."

"It's my lunch break, I've been kicking ass all morning, Mark," I shot back.

His face darkened, and I could see conflicting emotions warring behind his eyes. "You can't sleep in the shop. It would look bad if a customer saw you."

I looked around at the back room, incredulous. "You mean customers that aren't allowed and never come back here?"

"You need to care about our image," Mark replied.

"I pressed this shirt today, *Mark*." I couldn't keep the sharp tone out of my voice.

"Just sleep somewhere else next time, got it?" he said, walking back to his office.

I sighed heavily. Apparently, I couldn't even catch a break on my best days. Four more blurry hours and fifteen shots of espresso later I was about to tag out (Declan arrived for the evening shift) when Lu walked in the door. He waited in the short line and gave me an approving look when he reached the front. I looked over at Declan, a little stupidly, but he motioned back to my customer. Alright, everyone else could see him this time. I had hoped that I was dreaming the night before, or having a psychotic break, but I guessed not.

"What can I get you?" I asked, in my best customer service voice.

"I'll have a doppio and a flat white to go," he said, cheerfully. It wasn't a bad order to go out on, just some pulled shots and steamed milk. Flat whites were one of my favorite drinks, so I made that my last brew of the day. He paid in cash and dropped a twenty into the can for Declan's sister, for which Declan gave him a fist bump. I handed him the takeout cups when they were ready, and he walked outside. I didn't see where he went, but I was too busy putting away my aprons and getting ready to leave to notice. I walked outside and someone cleared their throat loudly before I got more than two steps out the door. My head swiveled and there was Lu, leaning casually against the wall of the shop sipping at his espresso. He waggled the flat white at me as he moved it in my direction.

"For me?" I asked.

"Don't want you falling asleep during dessert," Lu said, grinning. "I realize I didn't tell you where we were going to dinner, so you didn't know what to wear. But it looks like you're already in good shape."

"Thanks," I replied with a genuine smile. Mark had noticed but not commented on my look of the day, so it was nice to get a compliment. Despite popular opinion, I clean up fairly well. I didn't own a suit. I didn't need one to serve coffee, and I didn't expect any high-powered job interviews any time in the near future. I didn't qualify for any of those jobs. Remember me being in one of those hard to escape situations? Yeah.

He walked me over to the curb and gestured toward a 1967 Impala, all black, parked there. When I say all black, I mean all black. Black rims, grill, accents, tinted windows, the kind of car you wonder how it's street legal. "Hop in," he said, peeling out of the parking space before I had even put my seatbelt on.

"Nothing like a classic car," Lu said on the way to the restaurant, "especially this one. A muscle car like this just screams for attention."

"Yeah, I can imagine you get a lot of that driving this around."

"Well, this isn't my only car, it's just my favorite. It's impressive in a particular way, without being too pretentious." He smiled smugly. "What do you drive?"

I cocked an eyebrow. "You mean you don't know?"

"Oh, I know. I just wanted to hear you say it aloud."

"Really?" I sighed. "I have a 1987 Dodge Shadow. Are you happy now?"

Lu chuckled. The Devil made fun of my car, how messed up was that? "Well, if you decide to take me up on my offer, I'd recommend you change that fact as soon as reasonably possible."

"Hey, it's not that bad of a car." I felt the need to defend my car's honor. "At least it's the turbo."

"With a mismatched door."

"That wasn't my fault."

"Yeah, I know, but you replaced the door with one of the wrong color. What does that say about you?"

"Mostly that I'm poor, but also that I don't care about style."

"Fair enough, I just have hope that you'll appreciate the finer things in life. Driving in style has its perks."

"I thought you were supposed to be converting me to your cause." I became a little indignant. I had always wanted a nice car, even if muscle cars weren't my thing, and being teased about my inability to afford one stung. I went on, "Being a jerk about my car isn't winning you points."

"Oh, right. Sorry, I just get carried away with cars. They've been the status symbol of man for some time. I've gotten into it a bit. Sorry." He sounded contrite, but I doubted he was sincere. What else would I expect?

"Where are we going, anyway?"

"Oh, just a little place I like to visit when I'm in the area. You'll see." With another devilish grin, he stepped on the gas and thundered down Chapel Street. We drove past the Green and then parked on the street. He didn't put any money in the meter. I gave him a look, and he shrugged as if to say, "Devil." I looked around and realized exactly where we were going for dinner.

"Café 126?" I asked incredulously.

I'd never eaten at the Café. I'd heard about it, and smelled it while walking by on the street, but had never even been inside. It was supposedly one of those great waiting jobs to have, where you could make great money working in a swanky establishment. It was also one of those places where if you worked there, and then had a good meal there, you would spend an entire paycheck. The Devil wanted to take me there for dinner. Maybe the Devil wasn't such a bad guy, he just got a bad rap back in the day. I was such a sucker for a good meal.

"You'll love it, trust me." Lu smiled and walked across the street. He didn't look both ways either. I did. No reason to trust the Devil to have my best interests at heart, right?

We went inside and met the maitre'd who, after greeting Lu warmly by name, promptly escorted us to a table in the back. Menus were set quickly on the table before they returned to their station. I picked up the menu and started glancing through it. I had never even been to a restaurant with some of this food before. *No, Nick,* I tried to tell myself, *don't give in to the Devil for haute cuisine. You're better than that. Probably.* A waitress came by nearly immediately to inform us of the specials and ask our preferences for cocktails. Lu ordered a bottle of wine for the table, red, which he didn't ask if I wanted. He already knew I liked red wine, so I just went along with it.

"Oh, make sure you order the Jerusalem artichoke soup with apple-wood smoked bacon. It is to die for, believe me, and that much cream? People have."

"Can't say that I've ever been here, so I'll take your recommendations." I picked out the most expensive things on the menu that I thought I would actually eat. The waitress hadn't come over since taking our drink orders, so I thought it was time for some small talk. "So, does this mean Christians are right?" Way to go, Mr. Conversationalist. Biggish small talk.

Lu smiled while settling his napkin onto his lap and said, "I will agree to answer all of your questions tonight, on one condition." He held up a finger and paused to see if I would respond. I didn't. "That condition being that you will go home tonight with a full belly, an open mind, and consider my offer fully."

It didn't take me long to consider, as far as conditions go this one had no obvious strings attached. "Done," I agreed.

"Excellent." There might have been a little sibilance in that word, but I couldn't tell. "So that's where you want to start? Are

Christians right? Very well, though I do hope you'll have something more interesting to ask me once we get to the main course."

Our waitress chose that moment to come by and take our orders. I did order the soup, it sounded delicious even though I had no idea what an artichoke from Jerusalem tasted like. We had a few awkward moments post-order to see who would pick up the conversation first, and I charged right ahead.

"Well, it *is* a fairly obvious question to ask."

"Too right, and I can't say I haven't answered it a few million times already. Let's make this fun."

I shrugged, and suddenly I was sitting across from a gorgeous redhead in a black evening gown, scarlet-accented evening gloves, and immaculate makeup. She flashed me an incandescent smile and waved the fingers of one hand in greeting.

I sighed, trying to downplay my surprise at the change. "Well, that's a little cliché, isn't it?"

"If I thought a woman would have a better chance of winning you over, I'd have introduced myself as Lucinda. Tricks of the trade, my boy, but that's not the point." The woman in front of me donned the same devilish grin that I had become familiar with and then Lucinda was Lu again, black suit and all. "Pay attention, because this is something I won't answer more than once. A deity has to have his pride, after all. I can appear as anything I want, but what I will choose all depends on you. Well, not you, but whoever I want to perceive me. If I were speaking with a Hindu, I would appear as one of their darker gods, depending on their religious affiliation. If I was speaking with a Jew, I might decide to be the serpent. Conversing with a Catholic, I would be a *much* darker depiction of my current form. Does that clear it up for you?"

"I suppose it does... but that makes you more than just the Devil, if you could be an evil god from any religion. You also might just be lying."

"What if I was? Would it make that much of a difference? Either they're right, I'm the Devil, and I'm trying to get you into my clutches, or there's not just one answer, and I'm the personification of something. I wouldn't call it evil, but I'm certainly no goody two shoes. The only reason I made myself look the way I do, and gave myself the names I have, is because it's a framework you'll understand."

"Or, you could be lying." I tried to make a point.

Lu disappeared, and in his place was something that looked like a squat caveman with a sloping brow, bulging muscles, pointed teeth, and luminous red eyes. Almost as soon as I saw it, Lu was back.

"What the hell was that?" My chair screeched as I pushed back involuntarily from the table about to run like a scared primate.

"Just proving my point." Lu smiled broadly and showed his decidedly non-pointy teeth. "Nothing to get overly concerned about. That was a demon god from prehistory, no one you'd have ever heard of. I don't get to trot that one out very often, but you were being very difficult. That's my last show and tell and *don't* ask me to do my impression of a Mormon waiting room, it's terrifyingly boring even for me."

"Mormon waiting room... no, never mind. I don't want to know." I paused, taking a few deep breaths, letting my monkey brain calm down a little bit more. "Okay, Lu, I'll take you at your word on this one. No more questions about who's right or wrong."

"Thank you, I've had enough of those wardrobe changes for one night. Oh good, the soup is here."

I was no country bumpkin, but I only knew enough about "fine dining" to get through a meal without creating an international incident. Eating utensils: starting on the outside and working my way in. Don't put my elbows on the table. No slurping, burping, or expelling. The basics. Watching Lu eat soup was like watching an artist brush paint on a canvas, elegant and dignified. I suppose you had to give the Devil his due. Oh, that was horrible. Why did I even think that?

The soup was a transformative experience. When I saw it, it looked as though the chef had painted a scene in cream on top of the golden soup. When I smelled it, the smokey scent of the bacon invaded my nostrils. When I took a sip, my taste buds exploded in a symphony of spices and flavors. Lu knew what he was talking about, it was to die for. I'd seen artichokes before, but never had them, and nothing in this soup reminded me of a spiny alien plant. I must have looked blissfully confused.

"A Jerusalem artichoke is a root vegetable, not a plant from California. Your gustatory experience is sadly lacking. I was hoping this would be a good experience for you. Tasty, yes?"

I smiled stupidly, not knowing what gustatory meant, and managed to get more soup into my mouth without looking like a child having applesauce for the first time. I enjoyed myself in silence for a few minutes and then, after savoring the last bite of soup and bacon, I decided I had recovered enough from my foodgasm to talk.

I couldn't help but ask, "Why me?"

"Well, we covered why not other people, but that gets to the crux of the matter." Lu cracked his knuckles and then pointed at me. "You, my friend, have a great lot of potential sitting around inside that brain of yours, combined with the good intentions in your heart. It's not entirely your fault that it's gone underutilized for this long, though you're somewhat to blame. No college, no real training, but you're incredibly well-read and well-spoken for someone your age without any sort of credentials."

I was twenty-eight, and I never went to college beyond an aborted first semester. I couldn't afford it by myself and realized I didn't want to take out a whole mess of student loans just to land an office job and literally pay them back for the rest of my life. It was something I always planned on doing once I set myself up enough to handle it. I got a gig right out of school, then went through a series of dead-end jobs until I switched to coffee mixology and landed at the coffee shop. Being a barista didn't pay too badly if I was in a good location, and I had enough money to pay my rent, bills, and enough left over to buy myself the occasional toy. It wasn't a bad life, but I was getting to the point where I needed to make a decision to do something else. I had a few college coursebooks back at the apartment, and some half-completed applications on the kitchen table. Inertia was hard to fight, you know?

"Hey," I said, "just because I didn't go to college doesn't mean I'm stupid."

"*Nick.* Nick." Lu motioned for me to calm down. "I'm not calling you stupid. Far from it. The fact that the world hasn't entirely beaten your desire to help others out of you is something I recognized. I'm trying to tell you that I see what you could become, regardless of whose side you chose, with some real resources at your fingertips."

Ah, the pitch. "Resources?"

"I hear the doubt in your voice. 'This is where the Devil gets me to sign on the dotted line,' he thinks. Look, here comes the food. You eat, and I'll give you the details of my offer."

The waitress cleared away the soup bowls and started laying out the main course. I didn't even remember ordering half of what was on the table, I guess Lu ordered more to share when I wasn't paying attention. I made a mean stir-fry, but my lean cooking skills had nothing on what was served. I won't go through all the gory details, but there could have been four other people at that table and no one would have gone hungry.

"I am prepared to offer you a very reasonable package that will give you the opportunity to stretch your potential and develop your skills to the point where you will be able to make changes in the world. I'm a gambling man, how could I not be, and I am betting that once you get some experience under your belt and have a chance to see things my way, you'll join the team."

I stopped eating long enough to say, "Don't I have to sign first? Isn't that the way it works?"

"Ah, you've got me. I *could* get you to sign first. The experience would be just as enjoyable for you, but I do like an element of chance in my business endeavors. What do you think hell would be like?"

I almost choked on a bite of spicy lamb. "What?"

"Hell. What do you think it's like?"

"Aren't you supposed to tell me?" I asked, still trying to swallow my last mouthful.

"Oh, I will, but I want to know what you think you're getting yourself into."

"Uh. Hell. Well... I suppose it's unpleasant?" I realized I was understating it. "Some would even go so far as to use words like 'unending torment' and 'everlasting pain.' Things like that."

"How quaint." He smiled for a minute or so and had a few bites to eat. "I do hope you're enjoying your meal, they're quite good here."

"Yeah, I am. Thanks. What do you mean quaint?"

"Quaint, provincial, silly, incorrect—take your pick."

"Well, I only know what I've been told, and since this is the first time we're talking about it, perhaps you should enlighten me."

"Enlightenment, such a lofty goal. Of course I'll tell you, the last thing I want you to think is that by accepting my offer, you're committing yourself to never-ending torment. That's just untrue. Continuing with the Socratic method: what does man supposedly have that angels do not? We'll continue with the Christian framework for easy reference, no point in theology hopping at this point."

I'd never had a sauce this good on *anything*. "Give me a minute." I was stalling, this much thinking put my brain at war with my stomach. Stomach wanted to finish eating and then find a warm rock to sleep on. Brain wanted to get its hands dirty in the big conversation that Stomach wasn't entirely aware of. "I remember reading something somewhere." I had no idea where. "About man's greatest gift from his creator being free will."

"Ding. Good job. Takes some others long to ponder that one, if you haven't read the right books or seen the right movies. That's also, of course, assuming that they even got this far. So you've got this nifty thing called free will. What do you do with it?"

"Anything I want?"

"Smart-ass answer, but accurate enough. The other part of the answer is nothing. So many people have all this freedom to act and do absolutely nothing about it. Why don't you put down your fork for a minute?"

I put my fork down.

"Now, pick it up again," Lu said.

I didn't. "Why?"

"You see? I told you to do something, and you didn't have to do it. Imagine that you didn't have that pesky little thing called free will. What would you do?"

"I guess I don't know."

"Good answer, because it's definitely not 'whatever I want' anymore. Hell, explained in very simple terms, is the absence of free will. None of this 'removed from God's grace' silly business, you just don't have free will. Now does that sound so bad?"

I thought about it. Do I control my own actions? What about destiny? Well, if destiny had me working in retail for the rest of my life, I could use a little less of it. It sounded like he was talking about control, or the lack thereof. I wasn't a control freak. I was fine when other people led the way. Maybe it was more about choice and having free will meant you got one. I thought about it some more, and I realized that it was the most frightening thing I had ever heard.

"I don't think I like it," I said to Lu, picking up my fork again with a slightly shaky hand. We finished the meal quickly in silence. The waitress came by to pick up our dishes.

"Oh, don't go all introspective on me, Nick." Lu pouted slightly and topped off my wine. "It's not as bad as all that. And the best part? Me. All kidding aside, I should finish explaining the deal before you think too poorly of me. As I said, I'm a gambling man, so let me give you the details." He started ticking off his points on his fingers, "First, we prepare you for a job in our organization. Second, you will work in a role, as yet undetermined, where you have an opportunity to get a feel for our work, as well as pursue personal humanitarian desires as time permits. Third, once you have been given sufficient time to get your feet under you I will offer you a choice. You'll get to choose between the life that we've created together and the life that you left behind after agreeing to my little proposal."

"Organization?"

"No can do, you'd need to agree before I could disclose that information. I have to protect our public face, you know. Let's just have some dessert, maybe a nightcap, and then I'll take you home. I'm afraid I've given you a lot to think about again. Only this time there's no more question and answer period."

I'd like to say that the dessert tasted like ashes in my mouth, with all the heavy implications of the evening's conversation, but the chocolate torte we were served made that impossible. Lu was definitely trying his best to continue making a good impression. We had dessert, after-dinner drinks, and then we left. I could at least clear up one possible misconception about the Devil, he tipped heavily. He drove me home without incident— it was late and he probably had special Devil powers to avoid traffic.

"I hope you enjoyed yourself, Nick." Lu shook my hand. "I look forward to hearing from you. I'd make this all dramatic and say you have until sunrise, but that's a little too old school for this kind of thing. I'd appreciate it if you got back to me within a week, just so I can have everything done for the new year. Here's my card so you can reach me."

It read:

Lu

Public Relations

*666

I closed the door behind me, and the impala thundered away. I was alone. That seemed like a good thing for once. I had no expectations about what hanging with a deity would be like, but it was nerve-wracking. I was dead on my feet, and waiting to fall over. In the morning I would barely recall walking up to my apartment, laying down on the bed, and passing out before my head hit the pillow.

CHAPTER 5

R ule number one hundred and fifty-two: Don't sleep in your dress clothes. I felt wretched, and there was nothing like stumbling into the bathroom wearing dress shoes on swollen feet at eight o'clock in the morning to make you feel like you were probably not going to make it through the day. I stripped down to boxers and a t-shirt before making it into the kitchen and sitting down at the table. My grandfather wore T-shirts under his dress shirts, so I wore T-shirts under my dress shirts. I didn't question it, I just did it. I poured myself a bowl of cereal and then banged my head against the table a few times to get the blood flowing. The only good thing about this morning was that I didn't have to work until the evening shift. I needed to talk to someone but who?

Me: So I've got this sweet offer from the Devil. I just have to decide if I want to be someone's eternal bitch.

Perfect stranger: Dude, what the hell is wrong with you? Get away from me before I call the cops.

No, that wasn't going to work. I needed to talk to someone who would believe me. Someone who had some experience with wacky stuff like this and wouldn't want to commit me to a mental hospital as soon as they could pick up a phone. Rob? No... not Rob. Amy. I wasn't your typical guy and would freely admit to the other sex that women were often smarter than men. It didn't usually help me get girls, but it didn't hurt my chances either.

Regardless, Amy would probably be a better sounding board than Rob. Rob would probably just try and get himself an interview. I called Amy, told her that I was having a bit of a crisis, and asked if maybe she could help me out. She was fine with it but was planning on taking a walk, did I want to come with her?

So I drove myself over to Westville, near-ish to Rob's house, and parked on a side street. There was a park with a large paved path near a public skatepark that Amy liked to walk at, so I was going to meet her there. I found a nice vacant bench to sit on; no one else was at the park, so I had the place to myself. Winter tended to do that— the only people who were outdoors were the ones that either wanted to be or those that had to be. Casual nature-goers were put off by the chilly temperatures and often unfriendly skies. I loved the winter, for the most part. I could have done without shoveling out my car and the freezing wind, but it fit a lonely character like myself.

I suddenly felt arms wrap around my neck, "Hey, Nick!" Amy cheered right next to my ear. Luckily I managed to keep still, despite my lazy-cat-hit-with-a-hot-poker reflexes kicking in, so I didn't back my head into Amy's nose. She would have appreciated the effort, had she known, but I felt no reason to do anything except let out a small whimper. Amy smiled at me, her disposition at odds with her decidedly all-black ensemble.

"Hi, Amy." I turned around and returned the hug. She wore a military-style parka over a full black peasant skirt. "You look goth-tastic today. New skirt?"

"You like it?" She twirled, letting the skirt fly out.

"Looks great." I couldn't say that I wouldn't be interested in seeing Amy in more romantic circumstances, but she had never been anything more serious than a flirt with me. I made it a personal policy to assume that I'm just friends with a woman unless she tells me otherwise; it makes for good boundaries. It was easier to not screw up when I didn't make assumptions about people's interest.

That, and it was pompous to assume every cute girl I met wanted to have anything to do with me. It took all kinds, and I didn't like to assume I was everyone's type. But she did look good in that skirt.

"Are we going to walk, or are you going to sit there staring off into space all day?"

I stood up from the bench and dusted myself off. "Walking now."

We headed down the path, across a walking bridge over a rivulet, and strolled along. It was a nice day. Blue sky, puffy clouds, just a pleasant winter afternoon. The kind of day where you could forget that you had a crisis like a guillotine hanging over your head.

"So yeah," I rambled, "I've got this weird situation. I was hoping you wouldn't mind listening to the story and then telling me if I'm crazy or not."

"Sure!" she answered, grinning. Way too perky for my serious train of thought, but I appreciated the energy.

"What if I told you that your ritual went better than you thought?"

"What do you mean? It went fine. We did the chanting and everything, and the candles stayed lit the whole time, nothing went wrong." She looked a little confused. I felt a little confused.

"No, it went fine. I'm not talking logistics. I'm talking about your intentions, you know, to call up something. What if it worked?"

"But nothing happened–" she started to say.

"Something happened." I interrupted her, and she went white, but I pushed on. "Something weird."

We took a turn and went across another bridge into a less traveled section of the park. I told her the whole tale, from meeting Lu in the graveyard to our dinner conversation.

"What did he mean, we didn't believe in him?" she asked. "I don't understand, shouldn't it have been us that saw him?"

"It's complicated," I began, chewing on my lip and trying to not sound insulting, "but it had more to do with your intentions than your belief, if I followed what he said."

"But we were intending to summon him," she replied.

"Right. Think of it like making a phone call but the person you're calling lets it go straight to voicemail..." I trailed off, as Amy's glare caught me.

"We were *trying too hard*?" she asked, voice going up an octave.

"Maybe? It sounded more about your motivations than anything, but I was a little too distracted to dig into it more, and when we went to Café 126–"

"You ate at 126?" Amy exclaimed as she punched me in the arm. "I've *always* wanted to go there, and you not only get to go, the Devil himself takes you out to dinner. You lucky jerk."

"C'mon, Amy. I'm being serious here."

"So am I!" She pouted at me. "You couldn't ask if you could bring a friend?"

"Amy, I've been propositioned by the Devil, and you're mad at me for not inviting you to dinner. Let's take a step back and look at this for a second." I rubbed my arm, she hit harder than I expected.

"Oh, I'm sorry, Nick." She put her hand on my arm. "I didn't mean to hit you so hard. It's not a big deal, it's not like you could have... Oh, holy crap! It worked! I gotta call Rob!" She excitedly pulled her cell phone out of her purse.

"No!" I yelled a little too loud. "Please don't call Rob. *Please* don't call. I don't want him to know. This is freaking me out and I wanted to keep it to as few people as possible. Namely me and you."

Amy looked at me a little strangely but put her phone back into her purse. "Okay, Nick. I'm still not super happy about getting the brush off from Satan, but okay. What are you going to do?"

"You believe me?" I asked.

"Of course I believe you." She cocked her head to one side. "You're one of the most honest people I know. Either you're telling me the truth, or you've gone absolutely insane. Either way, I'm in."

I still had some time to kill before I needed to go to work, so we did what every twenty-something did when they needed to puzzle something out. We went for coffee. Amy went to SCSU, so we hopped over to the student center and grabbed cheap cups of coffee to nurse in a quiet corner. Colleges were great settings for weird conversations, anyone who managed to listen in would probably assume you were either a freak or a drama major and move along. I was a coffee gourmet, not a coffee snob. I'd drink good coffee when it was available, but I'd settle for something black and caffeinated when it was not.

"So," she asked again, "what are you going to do?"

"I have no idea. Can I take the offer seriously? I'm dead-ending right now. No higher education, no vocational training, just a crappy job at a coffee shop and rent that I can manage. Maybe I should at least take him up on the offer to get me started; then I could quit and go do something useful."

"You're talking about trying to take *advantage* of *the Devil*. You realize that, right?"

"Yeah..." I sounded a little sheepish.

"You're clever, but didn't he invent clever? I just think you might get in over your head if you agree to any of it."

I hid in my coffee for a minute. It was bad coffee, so I quickly surfaced again. "I suppose assuming the offer is entirely on the up and up is a bit naive. Wait, you sound like you're against the whole thing. Don't you want to serve His Darkness?"

"Well..." She paused and took a sip of coffee. "Now that you mention it, I'm not sure how cool I am with this business any-more."

"You mean since I told you it was real?"

"That didn't hurt, but I've been wondering about it for a long time now. I've read so many books on witchcraft, paganism, spirituality, and stuff that I've been thinking about changing the way I practice." She paused and rolled her cup between her hands before continuing. "I'm just not into the whole 'evil' thing. The rituals are all cool, but I don't like what they're trying to do. Doing, in your case. I think I'm going to start having my own rituals, maybe get involved with some of the local pagan community."

Well, if my dance with the Devil could help steer her where she wanted to go, then one good thing came out of the mess so far. Maybe she wasn't cut out for all the heavy stuff Rob was trying to get them all into. "I can't say that I'm surprised. I never understood why you hung around with Rob and Derek. You're way too positive a person to get sucked into all that dark, depressing stuff."

"Aw, that's sweet of you Nick." She gave me a broad smile. "But let's get back to what we were talking about. None of my personal junk helps you right now. How can you say yes?"

"He wasn't like the fire and brimstone that you might expect. Well, he kind of is, in the way that he's the embodiment of every negative deity in the world. But he was a nice guy... Devil... whatever. The question becomes, what if he's telling the truth? Maybe giving up free will, whatever that is, isn't such a bad thing."

"Or he's lying," she countered.

"Or I'm crazy." I twirled my finger around my ear. "But I don't think I am. It's hard not to at least consider his offer. If it's a gamble, then I might be able to win."

"That's probably what he wants you to think, but I trust you to make the right choice. Want more coffee?"

"No, that's okay." I looked at my watch. "Yikes. I've got to go, Amy. Work's in an hour and I have to stop at home and change. Look, I'll talk to you later, yeah? Just promise me you won't tell Rob."

"I promise, Nick. Cross my heart. Don't worry, you'll make the right choice. Just don't make up your mind too quickly, okay? You said he gave you a week, so take your time. Gambling man or not, I'm guessing he plays for keeps."

The best thing to come out of that conversation was the fact that someone believed me. It was the validation I needed right then. Amy wasn't phased by it either. It was all just part of some big drama that would "work out in the end" once I decided what to do. I hadn't come away with a decision, but I went to her for support, not answers. I realized then that the only person who could make that decision was me, and I needed to get to work. There would be plenty of time to think about it during my shift.

I was early again. Mark had already left for the day so I handed off with Declan before he headed to the hospital to see his sister. The evening shift closed up the store, usually one person by themselves, two if it was a busy time of year. I was by myself for once. I usually worked the day shift, since I didn't have any classes to get in the way. Like I needed a reminder that I wasn't doing anything with my life. Alone in a coffee shop on the Saturday before Christmas, a metaphor for my life. I sat at the counter with my chin propped up in my hands and stared off into space. I must have had the blank stare of a psychopath as I was contemplating my choices, because a couple of people came in, saw me, and then left immediately. I didn't mind, I wasn't much in a people mood.

I only had a week, almost until New Year's, to decide. That hardly seemed like enough time, so what was I going to do? Research? Either I believed he was telling me the truth and accepted the offer, or I assumed he was reeling me in like a fish and turned him down. One decision would possibly lead to a new life, and the other would leave me right where I was. I felt ill, thinking too much about heavy subjects was like trying to give myself an ulcer. Eventually I went home feeling no more certain than at the start of my shift. I had been working for Mark long enough that, even with my episodes of tardiness, he tried to give me the days off I requested, and I had requested Sunday and Monday off. I liked to avoid the Christmas rush whenever possible, even if the tips can be substantial. I didn't need to set the alarm before going to bed, though I might not have even if I did have to work the next day. It was that kind of night. I wanted to sleep until I felt better. I just hoped I wouldn't have any weird dreams.

CHAPTER 6

There was sleep, in one form or another, that night. It wasn't good sleep, that nice, unconscious, heavy sleep. It was the light "almost awake" sleep where you drift from one dream to another in a flurry of lucid moments and roll around in bed like a rotisserie chicken. There were nuns and monsters, Rob and Amy made guest appearances, and Lu was a prominent character most of the night. I didn't want to remember those dreams, let alone talk about them. Let's just say they were both unpleasant and bizarre. I woke in a sweat, early the next morning, more tired than I was the night before.

That Christmas went out with a quiet whimper. I didn't leave my apartment for two days. I barely ate and didn't sleep more than two hours total. I didn't call anyone, and I didn't take any calls. The messages piled up wishing me a "Merry Christmas!" and I ignored every one of them. I was never particularly religious, but my recent experience put Christmas in a whole new light that I didn't have the brainpower to unpack yet. I spent all of my time sitting in front of my computer, on the internet, going from website to website. Never before had I attacked the search engines like I did, inputting crazy keywords like "deal with the Devil," "talk with God," and "free will religion." By the end of my research phase, I had found so many different web pages about the varied forms of evil gods that I was a closet expert on the subject. I was desperate to find some sort of clue to telling the truth from lies, to help me decide. Charlie Daniels' *The Devil Went Down to Georgia* became my anthem, I had it on repeat for more than twenty-four hours. Honestly? I think I went a little insane. Hunger and sleep deprivation will do that to a person, and I was a whirlwind of thought sitting in a cheap swivel chair.

By the time Tuesday morning rolled around, I had come to a few conclusions: First, we don't know anything about the nature of gods or devils beyond absolute conjecture based on ancient scribblings on scraps of papyrus. Second, I was now a leading authority on the subject, having had a conversation with a deity naming himself "Lucifer," without even trying. Provided that I wasn't just insane, but I had to assume my own sanity at this point. Third, no earthly fountain of knowledge was going to make this any easier for me.

Let's look at these in order, shall we?

Conclusion number one. There was absolutely no consensus about the nature of higher powers. I've never been a good Christian, in the strictest "going to church and following all the trappings" sense, but I did try to lead a good life. This was the only common ground I could find in most of the world religions. They all had different ways of going about it, but the end result was an effort to inspire, manipulate, or outright threaten their followers into leading good, moral, and ethical lives. The morals were whatever was passed down by their specific holy doctrine, granted, but even that didn't differ too much when sticking to the basics. Murder. Theft. Mimes. Those were the kind of things that most of the religions agreed on. Maybe the mimes thing was just me, but I thought we all hated mimes. It was a good revelation to give myself, but it only helped support Lu's short explanation of religion. I still didn't know if I was working to prove Lu right or wrong, but I was trying like hell to do something. So conclusion number one stood; we know next to nothing.

Conclusion number two and this one is a doozy. I was trying to find people who had similar experiences to me, which led me down the rabbit hole of the "god-touched." Have you ever read anything written by someone who claims to have been touched by the divine? A good percentage of them were probably insane. Really insane. Like wrapping the entire house in aluminum foil to repel the alien brain ray type of crazy. What did that mean to me? It meant that I probably couldn't take them seriously, even if I wanted to. Every claim of divine intervention from a crazed housewife or toothless hillbilly became a likely lesson in what the divine was *not* like. The rational accounts of conversations with any sort of god were usually from people proselytizing their faith. That meant it was likely they made it up so they could attract people to their flavor of worship. The worst part? Other than contacting these people directly, and the ones that provided their contact information were few and far between, there was no way I could see if their experience was anything like mine. I risked reaching out to a few of the people I could find, whose experience was even remotely similar, and was either ghosted entirely or invited to subscribe to their YouTube channel and schedule a one-on-one coaching session for a modest fee. On top of that, most of the information I found was about people reporting their relationships with the *good* gods. If more people had conversations with an "evil" god, they weren't sharing their information online. Conclusion number two stood, no expert was going to pop out of the woodwork to be my spiritual guide.

Conclusion number three? I was on my own. The reality of my situation began to sink in at three o'clock in the morning on Tuesday. No amount of information, regardless of how accurate, was going to make my decision for me. In fact, the more I read about world religion, and other people's experiences with the divine, the more it felt to me like I was getting a handle on myself. Grateful for the clarity, after diving through the chaos, I was grounded again.

I felt calmer than I had in months, and in the back of my mind, a decision formed. I didn't know what it was, even then, but I knew that I had hit the wall and come away with some real insight into myself, and what I wanted for my future. It was five o'clock in the morning on Tuesday, and I was back to myself.

Clarity didn't mean I had the day off from work, but I didn't need an alarm. I was still awake and would need to get up at six, so I decided an hour of sleep was worthless. I showered, dressed, and headed in to work early. I opened up the store by myself and was tossing back my fifth shot of espresso when Mark walked through the door. I threw myself into a frenzy of activity that week, and no one worked harder than I did at the shop. Mark wondered if I was bucking for a management position, but when he approached me about it I laughed uncontrollably until he walked away looking very confused. I even cleaned my apartment from top to bottom one night after getting home. I was looking desperately for some purpose in my life, and I found that I could put my thoughts in order more easily when I was doing something. So I did things, quite literally looking for meaning under the couch cushions. Not necessarily important things, but things that felt like they needed to be done. I even went so far as to go to the pound and get a cat, which was a big decision for me. I worried that I wasn't connecting with living things enough, you know, to get some sense of belonging and fulfillment. That, and I always wanted a cat. I didn't have a pet clause in my lease but, at that point, I didn't care. Odin was a black long-haired Maine Coon with one eye, the look of a brute with a sweet disposition, and massive biscuit-making paws. It was a good experiment, but I immediately learned from Odin that you got the kind of fulfillment that a parent must get from a college student. He was mostly independent but came and bothered me when he was hungry or needed some laundry done. Not his fault though so I let him stay when he promised to kick in a little rent now and then.

Friday rolled around quicker than I wanted it to. I was startled awake when the alarm went off, Odin managed to leave my face unharmed when he jumped at the noise and commotion. Note to self, discourage the giant cat from sleeping on your face. I peered blearily around my bedroom and propped against the telephone on my nightstand was the card from Lu. Why put it off any longer? I dialed *666 and his friendly voice filled my ear.

"You've reached the voicemail of Lu, public relations. Please leave a message after the tone and I'll get back to you sooner than you imagined possible." Beep.

"Lu, it's Nick..." I took a deep breath and sighed. "I'm in."

Chapter 7

I didn't even get to say anything else before Lu interrupted my train of thought. "Hey, Nick. Good to hear from you."

"I thought I was leaving a message."

"You were, but like the message said I'd get back to you faster than you thought possible. That's right now."

"Oh. Right."

"So you're on board?" I could almost hear his grin.

"Yeah, I am. What happens now?"

"That's great, Nick, really great. Don't worry about a single thing, I'll take care of everything. Your rent is paid up for the next six months, and I'll have someone in to look after your cat. Just sit tight and I'll call you back in a few with more details." Click.

Wow, that was fast. I looked at Odin, and he stared back at me with a look that said, "You're one mighty stupid human. I like you." I got up and filled his dish, and then sat down in the kitchen. The phone rang. "Hello?"

"Hey, Nick, it's Mark." Mark's voice had a note of concern in it that I'd never heard before.

"Hi, Mark," I replied, "what's up?"

"Hey, I'm sorry to hear about your grandfather. Your dad called and told me you'd need to take some time off. Things have been kinda slow, so if you want, take as much time as you need. He said that you'd need about six months, and I can just hire you back at the end of that. Traveling to the backcountry of eastern Europe, man that's gotta be a pain. So, uh, just take it easy, and give me a call when you're ready to come back to work."

"What?" I couldn't keep the surprise out of my voice. What the hell was going on?

"No, it's alright," Mark reassured me, "don't worry about anything. Your dad apologized for contacting me directly instead of waiting to hear from you, but he said you were having a rough time with his passing. I can keep your spot open for a while, it's no problem. Take care, okay?" He hung up, clearly uncomfortable with the level of emotions he was expecting from me.

I repeat, what the hell was going on? That was one of the dumbest things I had ever heard. The phone rang again. "Hello?"

"Your job is all set, Nick. Ready for you if you should decide to return." The confident voice of the Devil was on the other side of the phone line this time.

"You're kidding me."

"Not at all."

"My grandfather? One passed away when I was like twelve, and the other is still alive. He *is* alive, isn't he?"

"Of course he is, I didn't kill your grandfather just to get you out of work for a few months. That would be excessive."

"And the backcountry of eastern Europe?"

"Oh, that. That was just a little piece of brilliance I cooked up. Mark thinks that you have to be in quarantine for a month before you're allowed to travel for an extended stay," Lu replied, chuckling to himself, "and then again when you 'get back.' It's all very simple, he doesn't know *anything* about international travel."

"But it's all ridiculous lies." I was gobsmacked.

"And? One thing you're going to learn very quickly is that the bigger and more outrageous the lie, the more willing people are to accept it without question. I'm also very persuasive, some might even say I invented persuasion. They'd be right."

"So you impersonated my dad, got me out of work for six months, and paid my rent."

"And I'm having someone watch your cat if we need you to be away from home for extended periods." Lu sounded positively smug.

"Right..."

"Oh, and don't forget the per diem, car insurance, and gas allowance, since you won't be working for a little while."

"Per diem?" I asked. I'd never worked for a corporation, so I was only loosely familiar with the concept.

"Think of it as a daily allowance," Lu replied, "I'll have an advance deposited directly into your bank account today that should see you through your expenses until you get your first check."

"Ah. Uh." I couldn't get more than a few syllables out.

"Not getting cold feet, are we?" His smugness faltered for a moment replaced with genuine concern.

"No," I paused to consider, then continued, "I don't think so, but you have to admit this is all a little overwhelming."

"Too true. That's why we have orientation. Have a pen handy?" I did, and he gave me the address for my orientation classes, which would apparently make all of this just a little easier to swallow. Right. "So take the rest of the day off," he continued, "relax, enjoy yourself, and tomorrow you'll come in and we'll get some paperwork out of the way. See you soon, Nick. Glad you made the right decision."

I hung up the phone, went back into the bedroom, and laid down again. The Devil just told me that I had made the right decision, which instantly made me question it.

Maybe it was going to be one of those days where it would be better if I just stuck my head under the pillow until it was tomorrow. I must have fallen asleep because the next thing I knew the clock said it was ten o'clock in the morning and a giant ball of fur was curled up on my stomach. That explained the dream where

I was drowning. Stupid, heavy cat. I finally decided that I would treat it like any other day off and make the most of it. I pet Odin until his biscuit factory threatened blood loss, got up, showered, shaved, and dressed. Maybe Amy wanted to go for another walk. I probably owed her an update after dragging her into my tornado of decision-making. I was sure there was some rationalization going on too, reaching out to her again. I was only human, and a guy at that. I liked girls, especially ones that were adorable and wore flouncy skirts and would actually talk to me. That last bit is a little self-indulgent criticism but my self-esteem wasn't great these days. There was also some altruistic intent: I didn't want to get Amy wrapped up in my downward spiral of corruption, and I still owed her an explanation. I called and got her voicemail, left a message, and sat around for a little while to see if she was going to get back to me. I had a staring contest with Odin. He won, as usual.

No callback, so I decided to go out and waste some time. Amy was probably at work or in class. Wasn't it the way of things? Whenever I had a day off, I assumed that the rest of the world had the day off with me. So I would call my buddy on his cell and he would say, "Dude, I'm at work." And then I would remember that it was a weekday and I was the only one who got the day off. People didn't like when they were at work and you weren't. It was your average envy except they would have to work in retail to have the same days off. But you know what they say about misery. I decided to pay a visit to a mecca of consumerism and drove out to the mall in Milford. It wasn't that far, but it gave me a chance to drive faster than twenty miles an hour and zip down a few back roads that I knew on the way. City living was great, but sometimes I just wanted to speed down a winding road. Rush hour in New Haven meant crawling along at fifteen miles per hour, waiting for people to jump out in front of my car. It wasn't fun, I assure you.

Shuffling around a mall by myself sounded like a good idea until I was standing there. I had walked two slow laps around the whole place, bought a soda, drank it, and contemplated lunch when I realized exactly how bored I was. I decided to do some people-watching to pass the time; I didn't have anything else to do. I thought it was sad that I wasn't getting any sort of special powers from my deal with the Devil, it sounded like standard business fare, when I noticed one of the people I was watching was watching me right back. He was a middle-aged man dressed in a button-down shirt and jeans, looking like a pretty average guy. A bit balding, and he wore glasses, but not an abnormal specimen of the human race. But he was staring at me, with concentration on his face. I waved, feeling a little stupid for calling him out, and he waved back. He got up and walked over to where I was sitting.

"Having a bad day, son?"

I was confused, confusion seemed to be a regular state of mind for me lately. "Huh?" I replied eloquently.

"You've got something weighing your soul down, I can see that."

"Uh, no, I'm fine. Thanks."

"Well," he went on, "If you ever find yourself in need of a friend to help you through dark times, give me a call." He produced a business card from his pocket that identified him as Walter Prospect, youth outreach minister. Youth? Me?

"Um. Thanks." I put the card in my pocket, not wanting to appear rude. What was with all these weird conversations I was getting into?

Walter walked away after that, shaking his head slightly. I decided that lunch wasn't appetizing anymore and made my way back to my car, taking the card out of my pocket so I could get a better look at it.

"Religious zealots," I complained, tossing the card away. It flew a few feet and landed under a bush. I didn't look twice as I walked out to my car. My phone rang as I latched the door. It was Amy.

"Hey, Amy!" I greeted her excitedly.

"Hey, Nick! What's going on? I got your message."

"Oh, nothing much," I replied, "I just figured you'd want an update on the 'Devil Went Down to Georgia' situation."

"Right, that was today, wasn't it? How'd it go?"

"Well–" I started to say.

"You said no, right?" I could hear the expectation in her voice. I hoped that she wouldn't hang up on me.

"Um... no." I paused, listening for the faint sound of a disconnecting line.

"Oh." She sounded disappointed more than anything, "Well, I, um..."

"Amy, let me explain. It's probably going to make more sense in person. Want to have dinner?" I cringed, not expecting that invitation to come out of my mouth.

There was a pause before she replied. "A dinner date for describing a deal with the Devil?" she asked alliteratively. "Are you asking me out?"

"What?" My voice cracked with nerves. "No, no date, just food and conversation. I owe you an explanation, and the least I can do is cook you dinner. You can meet Odin too."

"You have a roommate? That's an interesting name, is he from Norway? And since when did you cook?" I had her distracted from my potentially bad choices. This was going better than I expected.

"No, Odin's my cat," I replied and started to get a little defensive, "and I can cook a few things well but we may be having omelets for dinner. What do you say?"

She sighed. "Okay, Nick, you win. I'll eat an omelet and give you a chance to explain why you did whatever it is you did."

"Great, see you around six-ish?"

"Fine by me. See you." Click.

That conversation was both harder and easier than I thought it was going to be, but the tough part was still ahead of me. First things first, I had to go to the store and get ingredients for dinner. The "cook her dinner" idea sprang fully formed out of my mouth without consulting my brain. I didn't have more than a frozen burrito and some cereal in the apartment at the moment. If there was one immediate benefit from the whole thing, it was the extra money I suddenly had in my pocket. I checked my bank balance and my eyes widened when I saw that I had enough to pay my rent and expenses for two months. Lu was not messing around when he said I'd get an advance. Did I feel guilty overspending on dinner because the Devil was paying for my apartment? A little, but it meant I could eat well, and that was almost never a bad thing. So a quick trip to the grocery store meant a small feast to celebrate my newfound prospects. Sounds cheery when I said it like that, didn't it?

I went a little more upscale than omelets. I wasn't trying to impress her, but I wasn't *not* trying, and my ecstatic experience with my soup the other night made me want to make something special. I thought about it and decided to try to recreate the bisque from the other night, along with a dish of chicken breast with sauteed broccolini. Plus a salad, you needed a salad for a fancy dinner. I figured surprising Amy with a good meal would lighten the evening. I hoped, anyway.

Jerusalem artichokes were harder to find than I expected, and I had to go to a specialty organic market to get them. I realized I didn't have a blender either, so it was a shopping spree on top of groceries. I was killing time after getting most of the dinner prep out of the way, and unpacking my new immersion blender, before realizing I was a bachelor. Well, no, I knew that I was a bachelor, but the state of my domestic existence escaped me until that moment. I looked around the apartment and realized that, despite my cleaning spree last week, the apartment had devolved into the lair of a poor bachelor again. It wasn't terrible, but I still didn't have time for anything fancy, so I just picked everything up from the living room and shoved it onto the bed in the bedroom. I know what you're thinking, but I didn't think of this as a real date, so I felt safe putting the clothes and junk on the bed. Otherwise, it would have all ended up in the closet or something, in case of possible bedroom activity. Yeah, that didn't come out right. Amy was one of the guys, and she wasn't interested in me, so I didn't think of it as a date, exactly. Just a little. Because she was cute. And smart. Not to mention that she was coming to my house for a home-cooked meal that I totally didn't jazz up to impress her. Shut up, brain, you told her it wasn't a date.

I was saved from this overly cerebral exercise in futility by the door buzzing. I ran down the stairs to let Amy in, because my building's remote door unlocking thingamajig had been broken since before I moved in and the management company, if there even was one, wasn't inclined to fix the problem anytime soon. I bolted downstairs and then remembered the "not a date" status of the evening and slowed myself before I came into view from the door. I tried to put a relaxed smile on my face and strolled over to the door, opening it with a flourish.

"Welcome to the casa, Amy," I said, trying to sound laid back.

"Thanks, Nick." She wrapped her arms around me for a quick hug. "I've never seen your place. It's, um, nice so far."

My apartment building was a study in the kind of property you didn't want to buy if you were looking to become a respectable landlord. My building was the kind you wanted to look at only if "local slum lord" was on your list of acceptable titles. I exaggerate, it wasn't that bad, but the paint had seen better decades, both inside and out, and there were bars on all of the first-story windows giving some insight into what the owners thought about the safety of the neighborhood. As I said before, the remote entry door wasn't so remote and that's only looking at the place very superficially. I tried not to blush, embarrassed by the state of the building as if it were a statement about my own appearance, and led Amy up the stairs.

"It's not that bad, it's just seen a few too many years without some care. I promise, my apartment doesn't have any cracked walls or peeling paper. Cross my heart." I was so happy that my landlord gave me a break on the first month's rent if I painted the apartment before I moved in. Yes, he was just that cheap, but I was even poorer back when I moved in, so I took advantage of his laziness for my own gain. Now it was paying off, at least I didn't have to be embarrassed by my own apartment. We got back to my floor without encountering any of the other denizens of my building, which was for the best. The good news was that I hadn't locked myself out of the apartment, that would have turned it into an entirely different sort of evening. The kind that started with an accident and then ended up with me and my friends either in jail or bailing someone out of it. No, I opened the door and let us both in, taking her coat and tossing it quickly into the bedroom on top of everything else, shutting the door before she could see the pile.

Amy walked into the living room, the only decently sized room in the apartment, and surveyed the decor as she dropped her purse on the couch.

"Nice place, Nick," Amy said with a smile, ducking her head into the little kitchenette and then coming back to stand in the middle of the living room. "I would've expected more posters or something, like Rob's place."

"Rob doesn't exactly scream 'interior design' when I look at him."

Amy was peering at some of my knickknacks when a loud thud, followed by a louder meow, sounded from the corner of the room. Odin had been sleeping off his late night of keeping me awake and chose that moment to grace us with his presence.

"*Who*," Amy began, "is this perfect gentleman?"

I pointed accusingly at the furball. "This is my cat, Odin." My massive feline took the opportunity to saunter up to Amy and rub against her ankles, then proceeded to sit and lean against her foot. "He clearly hates you," I deadpanned.

Amy crouched down and scritched him between the ears, he rewarded her with the not-so-subtle revving of his purr engine. "He's so adorable," Amy gushed, "but why did you suddenly decide to adopt a cat?"

I blanched, considering the longer tale awaiting us during dinner, and rushed to find a different topic. "He's a unit, isn't he?" I picked Odin up and tossed him onto my shoulder, before encouraging him to go back to his window perch. "Spends enough time sleeping on my chest that I've gained muscle just from breathing through the night. Care to join me while I cook?"

I led Amy into the kitchen and sat her down at the table so we could talk while I finished making dinner.

Amy grinned and looked around. "What's for dinner?" she asked. "It smells amazing in here"

"You'll just have to wait and see," I teased, earning a tongue stuck in my direction, "or at least wait until I start cooking. The people above me can smell what I'm cooking, and I can hear them listening to music with the volume set on 'one,' so I'll give you pretty fair odds that you'll be able to figure it out." That earned me a full raspberry, complete with spittle. I got to work preparing the rest of dinner, hoping that witty banter would ensue to give me a little more time to think about how I was going to tell her what I'd done. I felt like I needed to stall so I blitzed the soup with my new toy which bought me another minute.

"Wine?" I asked, moving from the soup to pick up a bottle of white wine from the counter. It was sauvignon blanc, if you care. I had learned at some point how to pair wine and food though I couldn't recall how, probably movies combined with trial and error. It was cheap wine, though not as cheap as I usually bought.

"Sure!" Amy had a particular smile that she wore when she was obviously happy about something. Her cheeks got high and round, showing a lot of teeth, and her eyes closed almost all the way. It was very cat-like, super adorable, and it appeared right after I mentioned the wine. Hey, I always tried to entertain people that came to my apartment. If there was dinner, there would be wine. I got out two glasses and unscrewed the bottle with a flourish. They made a lot of good, cheap wine nowadays, and screw tops were just scientific evolution for storage in bottles. The only problem was that you didn't get the satisfying "pop" that you got with a cork, so you had to improvise. The guy at the liquor store that I go to showed me a trick with a screw-top. Loosen the top just slightly, so it moves back and forth with a tiny bit of effort. Crack it once, fully, put the side of the screw top against your bicep, and then roll the bottle down your forearm. If done right, the top ends up in your palm and the wine is ready to pour. If done wrong, well, I might need a towel. Possibly another shirt. I had enough dexterity to get it right the second time and used the trick whenever I opened a screw top, just to keep in practice.

Amy had never seen that trick, so I received a kind round of applause while I poured two glasses of wine. I had an additional audience member as Odin materialized in the kitchen, eyeing the cap in my hand. I looked from the cap to the cat and tossed the screw top out into the living room, Odin pelting after it. Maybe it would keep him busy, so he didn't beg for scraps.

"So, how did your meeting with the Devil go?" she asked, and as I turned back to her, I nearly knocked over both glasses. So much for stalling. I carefully put the bottle on the counter and hoped that my hands wouldn't shake as I put them in my pockets, turned around, and leaned against the counter.

I thought more evasion might work. "It went fine," I said and turned to the stove to check on the breasts in the oven and finish sautéing the broccolini. I hadn't taken a lot of time to reflect on my recent choice, and the reality of explaining it to a friend made it a little more real than it was in the morning when I had made the call.

"Fine?" she asked with a quirk of her eyebrow.

"Yeah, fine." I carried her glass of wine to the table and set it in front of her. "It wasn't a big deal."

She left the glass on the table, untouched. The chicken wasn't done yet, so I turned off the stovetop and started to assemble a small salad. I was chopping up a pepper when she said, "What?" The knife slipped, and a deep gash suddenly appeared in my thumb. I looked at it dumbly for a minute, watching the blood slowly well up from the cut.

"What do you mean no big deal?" Amy asked. "Nick?"

"Um," I said stupidly, "I'm bleeding." I blinked and shook my head to clear it, then shuffled over to the sink to run my thumb under cold water. Amy jumped out of her chair with a squeak and ran, figuratively, the two feet to the kitchen counter and grabbed a paper towel. I was applying pressure to the cut with the towel when I smelled something burning. "Oh, hell," I muttered, "Amy, can you grab the chicken out of the oven?"

"Sure!" She grabbed the pan out of the oven and put it on a cold burner. I prayed that the chicken was salvageable and the soup edible since the only other food in the house was the afore-mentioned frozen burrito and, if luck had it, a packet of Ramen noodles leftover from the last case that I bought.

I ran into the bathroom, found the Band-Aids and antiseptic, and patched myself up, trying to get back into the kitchen as soon as possible. Despite the immortal terror of being asked questions I didn't want to answer, I wasn't going to leave Amy in the kitchen while I cowered in the bathroom trying to avoid the inevitable.

"Be right out!" I yelled through the bathroom door. What was I going to say to her? She deserved the truth and the whole truth at that. She didn't think I was crazy when I told her that the Devil had found me in a graveyard and wanted to take me out to dinner for an offer that he thought I couldn't refuse. That kind of trust needed to be rewarded, but how could I explain choosing what so many people would consider the "wrong" side? Sure, she had spent a lot of time claiming to chase after dark powers, but that didn't make her a bad person. Maybe she would understand. Maybe. I opened the door and walked back into the kitchen, Amy sat at the table drinking the wine that I had poured her.

"Everything all right?" she asked. "I saved the chicken. It looks fine. A little closer to Cajun than you probably planned, but it still smells delicious."

"Thanks," I said, with a pained smile, "I'm pretty sure I avoided bleeding on the salad too." I picked up my glass of wine, took a large mouthful, and almost choked on it. First, I cut myself and nearly bled to death, and then I almost drowned in a glass of cheap wine. It was shaping up to be a bad night after all. "Yeah, it wasn't a big deal." I grabbed some dishes out of the cupboard and laid things out for dinner.

"I'd ask what you meant by 'no big deal' again," Amy said, looking at me wryly, "but then I'd just be repeating myself. Don't be a jerk. Tell me what happened!"

At that point, I realized that my careful facade of nonchalance wasn't working. At all. When dealing with difficult topics, I had long since realized that if I couldn't get away with the offhanded comments and humor, it was probably best to move straight to brutal honesty, bypassing misdirection and flattery entirely.

"I decided to give him a chance." It came out of my mouth quicker than I wanted, but at least I had managed volume above a whisper and no stuttering.

"You *what*?" Amy asked, voice rising slightly.

"Well, uh," I stammered. Mayday, mayday, we were going down fast. "I took him up on his offer."

"You WHAT?" Amy asked, louder this time. A lot louder. "You took him up on his offer? How could you?"

"Well," I took a deep breath, "I told you what he was offering, right?"

"Yeah," she said, sounding suspicious.

"Remember the part where they would train me to do something better than waiting on the caffeine-addicted masses? How could I turn that down?" I'd like to think that I was above trying to win a conversation but when backed into a corner I chose to bring out the bigger guns. I wasn't trying to guilt her, but I definitely felt like I was on the defensive.

"How? By remembering that you have to give up your soul? You know, your soul? That little piece of you that gives you all of that important free will that the Devil wants to take away from you. That soul."

Amy one, Nick zero.

"But I don't have to give up anything yet. Lu said that I could try them out, get some training, and then decide whether or not to give up my soul in exchange for more of the same. I mean, how could I pass that up?" I ladled soup into bowls and delivered them to our place settings, then went to work slicing and plating the chicken and vegetables. "What's my soul worth to me right now? I've got nothing! I'm in a dead-end job, living in a crappy apartment, with no real life to speak of, and no prospects ahead of me other than becoming an evening manager at the damn coffee shop." I didn't slam the knife down on the counter but definitely placed it more forcefully than I intended. I grabbed the plates and dropped them with a heavy clink on the kitchen table, sitting down at the table and lowering my head into my hands. "I'm sorry. I didn't mean to blow up at you. I invited you here to tell you what happened and explain it all to you. Not to yell at you. You said you trusted me to make the right choice. Well, in this instant, this is the right choice for me."

Amy sat next to me. It wasn't a big table, she would have been sitting next to me even if she sat across from me. "It's okay, Nick. I shouldn't have freaked out when you said that you took the Dev-, uh, Lu up on his offer."

I couldn't help but smile, I needed a little reassurance that she was still on my side. "We should probably eat. The food's getting cold, and I went through all this trouble to burn it to perfection. If you find any blood in it, I'll order a pizza."

"I'm sure it's fine," Amy said, taking a sip of the soup. Her eyes widened, and she looked at me appraisingly. "I didn't know you could cook like this. You really undersold your skills when you invited me over for dinner."

I blushed, taking a moment to compose myself by having my own taste of the soup. It wasn't the same as the other night, but I had done a pretty damn good job. "When you said you'd never been to 126, I figured I'd try and give you some of the experience I had the other night. It was..." I trailed off, having a hard time finding the words. "To say it had an impact on me would be an understatement."

Amy searched my eyes for something and seemed to find it. "I think I'm starting to see that," she said, slicing into the chicken. We ate in silence for a few minutes and, at some point, I got up and poured us more wine. I knew that I needed a drink, and hoped that a little more alcohol might make the rest of the explanation a little easier on the both of us. I was gnawing on a particularly blackened bit of chicken when Amy steered us back to the matter at hand.

"So, what happens now?" she asked, sipping her wine.

I swallowed the chicken, painfully I'll add, in an effort to answer quickly and satisfy her curiosity before she could take the subject and worry it in her teeth like a pit bull. "Now?" I mused. "Now I attend orientation and find out what's going on."

"What're you going to do for work? I mean, you still need to pay rent, right?"

"Not really," I said, a bit too low for her to hear me.

"Come again?" she asked.

"Not really," I repeated. I aim to please, especially when a lady asks nicely. "They're paying my rent and car insurance. All of my expenses, actually."

Amy's eyes widened and her mouth became a little O of surprise. "You're serious?"

"Very," I said, with a little smile of my own. "I get a per-diem too."

She leaned back in her chair with a sly look on her face. "You think they have room for one more at orientation?"

I laughed. "Oh, shut up." Amy joined in with a giggle of her own.

"Hey, I'm just saying," Amy continued, "if they'll pay my rent and insurance, I might not want my soul either. I could just lay around all day not having to do anything important. I like that idea."

"What happened to all that important free will and stuff? You know, *that* soul." I tried to mimic her voice from earlier in the conversation.

"Now you're just being a jerk. My soul's not good enough to give up, is that it?" she asked, staring at me with a mock scowl.

"No, that's not what I'm saying."

"We'll have no devilish double standard here!" she said, jabbing her finger at the table to make the point.

"Okay fine. Your soul is *too* good to give up for something as cheap as rent and car insurance. Are you happy now?"

Luckily Amy had the good taste to blush at that very moment and said, "Aw, you say the nicest things, Nick." Unfortunately, that made us stare at each other for an uncomfortably long pause in the conversation, looking away or into our laps as the case may have been. I started clearing the dishes away. Amy offered to dry if I washed. It was a cheap apartment, but I still had a dishwasher. Me.

We quickly fell into a relaxed rhythm, me scrubbing the dishes into submission while she dried them before placing them gently back into the cupboards. It lasted all of ten minutes; cooking for two people on the cheap didn't exactly cover a lot of ground in the kitchen, but it helped smooth out the awkward silence that had fallen at the end of dinner. I poured us a little more wine, drained the bottle, and brought the glasses into the living room. We both sat down on the futon, not close enough to touch. Amy sat with her legs tucked underneath her skirt, tracing wine around the lip of her glass until it hummed a clear tone. Her hair had fallen forward a little so that, when she looked over at me, her eyes were slightly obscured by stray strands. Overall the effect was a lot more alluring than she intended it to be. I put down my wine glass deliberately. I didn't need to think those thoughts at the moment, and the wine had relaxed me a little too much. I had drunk a lot more of the bottle than Amy, soothing my nerves. Have I mentioned that Amy is pretty? Yeah.

"So," she said quietly, echoing her question from earlier, "what happens now?"

My breath caught in my throat before I realized that she was asking me about my predicament, not whether or not I was going to invite her to spend the night. Shame, that. I breathed out as evenly as I could. Stupid brain. "Honestly? I don't know."

"Do you think you'll be able to take advantage of the Devil, Nick?" She spoke with that quiet kind of voice that let me know exactly how serious the conversation was, and how seriously she was taking it all. "I mean, I'm no good Christian or anything, but isn't that what he does? Taking advantage of people?"

"I guess," I replied.

"You're trying to outfox a fox."

"Might be true," I admitted, "but if what he's offering me is real, I should be able to get out of it if things don't turn out to be what I want. I just need to make sure that I keep a hold on myself, and not get caught up in all the glitz that I'm sure is going to be on display."

"Couldn't you just work hard, and get the same kind of thing that he's offering you another way? Like going to school, or something." She wasn't pleading, not quite, but there was a certain edge of hopefulness to her voice.

"Not like this," I sighed, "I don't know if I explained it well enough. It's not just about job training, or money, even though it sounds like a big part of it. He's giving me the opportunity to do something important, to help people."

"Isn't that very un-devil-like?" Amy asked.

"Well, I guess that's where the temptation comes in. They're going to train me up and give me time to myself to work on whatever kind of humanitarian effort I like, and that's where the choice comes in. I'm going to have to decide if it's more important to keep going like I was before I ever met Lu, taking things as they come and trying to do the best that I can with them. Or, I can do something important with my life, whether or not I have a soul at the end of it."

Amy slid closer to me on the couch and put her hand over mine, which was resting on the back of the futon cushion. I could smell her perfume; it was sweet and subtle. "You're a good guy, Nick," Amy said, looking into my eyes. "That's why all of this is tempting you. If you were a bad person, the Devil wouldn't need to come and collect. He'd know that you were going to be standing on his doorstep someday. If you were a religious man, he'd know that there was no way he could tempt you to walk another path. But you're just Nick: a good guy, who wants to do good things. I get that." She stood up slowly and held her hands out to me, to rescue me from my carnivorous couch, and helped me to my feet. We stood closely, to the point where I could feel the warmth coming from her. She turned away to recover her purse, and I forced myself into motion to get her coat out of the bedroom.

I was so grateful for the heavy presence of a bed full of random apartment sweepings, grounding me back into my body at that moment, that I almost tried to hug the pile of junk before bringing the coat back out to Amy. She gave Odin one last scratch behind the ears and promised him that she'd come to visit again before turning to me.

"Thanks for dinner," Amy said, flashing her closed-eyes smile. "It was wonderful."

"I'm glad you liked it," I said lamely, leading her out the front door of the apartment. "You're welcome here anytime." *Oh great, be obvious, Nick.*

"I might have to take you up on that," she said. "You'll need a friend who'll believe you when you tell them about your day at the office. And I am your friend, Nick. Believe me." She put her arms around my waist, and laid her head against my chest, giving me a hug worth a woman twice her size. Then she pushed herself back a bit, and kissed me on the cheek, light as a landing butterfly. "You need your friends now, more than ever," she said, and then walked away while I still stood dumbfounded in my entryway.

I took a very long, and very cold, shower before shoving everything off the bed to go to sleep. Odin curled up on my feet, rumbling like a truck. My mind was very full, though thankfully not racing. My guess was that the wine took care of that. I listened to Odin shifting gears as I stared up at the dark ceiling. I was thinking about what Amy had said, what Lu had said, pretty much everything everyone had said since this whole thing started. I was thinking about all of it when my eyelids became too heavy to lift, and all of my thoughts melted together into nothingness.

CHAPTER 8

I'm sure some of you were wondering where my parents were in all this. I wasn't so young that I still lived at home, but I wasn't so old that I couldn't lean on my folks if I needed some help, right? How would *you* explain it to your parents? No, you didn't have a better job or a nice girlfriend but, yes, the Devil had stopped by and given you a great deal on some job training. No, you didn't need any help. The Devil, who likes to be called "Lu" by the way, was taking care of everything. Yes, you'd probably keep a hold of your soul, but not to worry because you hadn't signed anything yet and were just calling to let them know what was going on in case they didn't hear from you for a while.

You thought it would go better than that? Just imagine the knock on the door signaling the arrival of nice men who just happened to bring a stylish white coat for you to try on, step right this way, sir. Sirens? No, they didn't use them because they wouldn't want to spook you. They just showed up because your parents tipped them off that something could possibly be rotten in the Denmark of your brain, and they probably asked if the van could be sent soon. Just to make sure that you didn't show up at their house. What *would* the neighbors think of that Devil nonsense?

Let's just leave it at the fact that I didn't feel any reason to worry my parents, or ask for their advice on the matter. They had their own problems, and the one thing I always promised myself that

I would never do was to heap my troubles on them when I could deal with things myself. As far as I was concerned? I had everything under control. Or, at least, as under control as it was likely to get.

So where did that leave us now? Orientation.

I could bore you to tears telling you about the typing tests and the administrative training, the endless seminars on business and management, and the general weirdness of doing it all on the Devil's dime. I *could* do that, but it would be a tiny fraction of the fascinating time I spent at what I affectionately called "Devil U." It was the most fast-paced two months I had ever lived in my life. I wasn't the only person going through the program, though I was the only New Haven resident, the rest were temporary transplants staying at the local swanky hotel. I almost asked to be put up there just for the experience, I don't know that I'd ever stayed in a hotel with more than two stars before. I didn't want to push my luck, and I still had a cat to take care of, so I just day-tripped it from my apartment.

My job was going to be acting as an "agent" which probably sounds as vague to you as it did to me, but that turned out to be part of the point. An agent was a Swiss army knife that seemed to range from administrative assistant, I really did have to do those typing tests, to foreign diplomat. In between those two fascinatingly different goalposts were private investigator, accountant, and paralegal to mention a few.

The curriculum was split into two segments: the first month being theory and background, the second being fieldwork and practical application. One day I was reviewing old files and they expected me to come away with a summary of where I thought the prior agent had made a mistake, and on another I was watching surveillance videos where the instructor would pause random-ly and ask questions about the subjects, testing our situational awareness. It would be a while before I stopped paying attention to the color of people's socks. There were seminars on contract law, which I found interesting, and workshops on negotiation and haggling which I found *fascinating* partially because it was taught by an older man from India who took us to a local bazaar and demonstrated in real-time.

In the practical portion of the training I observed contract negotiations and back-room review of the same. I did ride-alongs with private eyes that usually involved a lot of watching and waiting, and drinking thermoses of coffee, but had very little action beyond taking pictures or making notes. Some of it was clearly intended to give the students the understanding that it wasn't all going to be a fast-paced romp, despite what the various legal and police procedural shows we watched and had to critique had to say. I even took some basic self-defense training, which made me wonder exactly how "hands-on" this job was going to be. But I loved it. Except for the brief internship at a telemarketing call center (he *is* the Devil after all), but even that was a master class in learning how to be calm in the face of adversity. I was rarely short with customer service people, but I would *never* be anything other than angelic with them in the future.

I'll skip the interpersonal anecdotes though. Sure there could be all sorts of neat stories about the people I met in the classes, the fellow possibly damned, but let me tell you something. They were just people, like you and me. Well, mostly like you and me. Average would be a good way to describe most of them, and weird would be a way to describe the rest of them. Ultimately they were the same as me, stuck in a situation they didn't like and they were given an opportunity to get out of it. I couldn't blame them, they couldn't blame me. We all made the same choice for any number of different reasons. No one talked about how they got there, and no one asked. It was a bit like Vegas; there was an unspoken expectation of confidentiality.

One was a priest though. That was a little creepy.

Anyway, that's pretty much how it happened. I was given a fast-track education to become an agent for Devil-corp, and surprising no one more than me, I passed all my classes with flying colors. Well, mostly flying colors. I didn't do as well in the economics seminars. They were held early in the morning in a room on an upper floor where the heat was set on stun, and I had a hard time staying awake through the lectures. That, or economics just made me want to hibernate. Or both. Either way, the next step was going to be placement, where I found out what I would be doing in the "organization." I was effectively on sabbatical at home, waiting for my assignment to come through. What was I hoping for? I wasn't sure, honestly. I didn't expect to work with Lu directly, I figured I'd get stuck with one of his subordinates or something.

It was the second of May and I had just gotten back from a final meeting with one of my advisors from the program, to talk about my placement and what some of my duties were going to be, when the phone rang. Odin sat on the end table by the futon, part of his furry bulk hanging over the receiver. I pushed him off the table, though it was more like I nudged him, and he decided to move on his own. You couldn't force a twenty-pound cat to do anything, you could only strongly suggest that they move and hope that they took the hint and got out of the way. Luckily, he decided it was better to move than to engage in a contest of wills that I would most assuredly have lost. It would have been a waste of time on his part, but he was gracious about it and let me off the hook.

I picked up the phone, expecting to hear some sort of recorded message telling me what I was going to do with the next phase of my work-study, and listened.

"Hey, Nick," said the decidedly non-recorded voice.

"Hello?" I said.

"It's me," said the man, "Lu."

Oh. Right. The Devil. It was amazing, the power of the human mind. I hadn't heard from Lu during my entire training program, so I'd already forgotten the sound of his voice. Well, I hadn't forgotten, but my brain did that magic bit of processing that put something I hadn't experienced in a while to the bottom of the memory pile.

"Oh," I croaked, "Hey, Lu. What can I do for you?"

"I was just thinking about your placement and wanted to get your thoughts on the matter."

"I didn't think I had a say," I replied.

"Well, you don't. Not per se. But sometimes if I like a prospect I'll give them a ring before the final decision, to see where they think they should end up. No one knows you better than yourself; sometimes you know better than us where you should be placed." Lu chuckled to himself, a deep rumble. "Okay, that's not true. I know you a lot better than you know yourself. It's part of the job. I do, however, like to give people the impression that they know more than me and enjoy listening to people's aspirations. It keeps up appearances. So, where do you think you should end up?"

"I hadn't thought about it that much." I had, actually. Despite thinking about it whenever I had a minute of downtime, I never assumed where I would end up. Honestly, I had no idea what to expect. What kind of boss would you expect to get, when you were training for a corporation that's a front for the Devil himself?

"Well, think about it now for a second, you've got lots of possibilities. What field do you think you'd be best suited for? We gave you a lot of groundwork, but from here on out, you're going to have to think about specializing. We've got footholds in politics, law, academics, media, all sorts of stuff. Even the church, but I don't peg you as a religious type." Lu stopped talking, obviously giving me a minute, listening for my response.

I couldn't think of a reason why I should have been surprised by this, but I was. I always heard stories about how evil was everywhere and had its hands in everything, but until I was offered a choice of profession based on where the Devil had connections, it didn't hit home. The moment of silence went on for a little too long, I had to say something.

"I'm not picky, Lu," I replied. "I'll go anywhere."

"Team player, eh?" Lu said with a chuckle. "All right, here's what we'll do. Do you think you can handle being an assistant to a high muckety-muck? Real important guy, dabbles in a little bit of everything, one of my most important assets."

"I don't see why not. It's what I was trained for, right?"

"Too right, and don't I know it. Well, we'll give you a chance and see how you do. If you can't hack it, we'll just have to find you another placement."

"That sounds fine to me." My brain worked overtime, trying to imagine who I was going to be working for. A financial mogul? Diplomatic attaché? The president? "So, who will I be working for?"

"Me," Lu said.

"Ha ha, very funny Lu. No, really, who's it going to be?"

"That would be me."

"Seriously?" I asked.

"Would I kid you?"

"Yes."

"Fine," he conceded, "maybe I would. But I'm not. Cross my heart and hope to... whatever."

"Work for you?"

"I think there's an echo on your phone line, you should have that checked out. Yes, for me. That was the whole point of this exercise, wasn't it? You would get a chance to see what it was all like, working as one of my personal assistants. Most people end up working for some other dam—handpicked candidate, but I like you, Nick. I want you to see what it's like from the top. I told you that you've got a lot of potential, and where's the best place for you to stretch those newly trained legs of yours? With me."

"I don't know what to say, Lu," I finally managed to stammer.

"Don't thank me yet. I'll work you like a dog."

"But what about—"

"Yes, yes, you'll still be given time to work on your pet projects, all that goodness and light stuff that you want to try out. Good luck with it, just make sure you don't let that get in the way of the work you're doing for me. Right?"

"Of course, Lu. I mean sir."

"Cut the sir stuff. You only need to trot that out when we're in public situations. When it's just you and me? It's Lu, I told you I prefer that name."

"Okay, Lu, if that's the way you want it."

"You're catching on. Just keep thinking along those lines and you'll do fine by me. I'll see you in the office at eight sharp. Oh, hey, speaking of sharp, what do you have for business attire?"

My mouth dropped open far enough that I could have swallowed the phone. "Uh, well, I..." I definitely *sounded* like the receiver was stuck in my throat, "I hadn't thought about that. Sharp dress, you say?"

"You don't own more than one tie." This was not a question.

"Um." I thought about lying. "No." Lying to the Devil was probably bad form, or maybe it was expected, but I figured discretion was still the better part of valor.

"We can't have you looking like a second-rate accountant," Lu chided. "It wouldn't uphold the image we try so very hard to present to the clientele. Tell you what, you know that tailor downtown?"

There was only one real tailor downtown anymore, every other specialty shop had gone the way of the dodo. "You mean the place that looks like my grandfather would shop there?"

"Cute, Nick, real cute. Yes, that's the place. Go, ask for Dominic. He'll make you look like a million bucks. Nothing like a man from the old country to make a suit that fits."

I didn't have the money to cover new suits. Sure, the "company" was covering my expenses while I was being trained, but I doubt their generosity went as far as clothing me. "Lu, I don't know how to say this—" I began.

"But you can't afford new threads right now?" Lu was smiling, I could feel it. "No worries, kid. I've got it covered, he'll put it on my tab. If your new boss can't give you a little 'welcome aboard' gift, then who can? No, don't try and stop me. It's already done. You get yourself down there this afternoon for a fitting, and I'll see you in the morning."

"Great. Thanks, I appreciate it."

"My pleasure, Nick. You deserve it. You're going places." The line went dead and I hung up the receiver.

I looked over at Odin, who had chosen to sprawl across the coffee table in retribution for moving him from his earlier perch. He yawned, obviously not at all interested in the recent developments, and rolled over to have his belly scratched. Not wanting to upset the once again delicate balance of peace with my furry roommate, I obliged him. "Must be nice to have your priorities straight, fluff butt. Me? I've got an appointment with destiny, and destiny is a tailor named Dominic."

One last rub to the belly put Odin into a cat coma. Then I took the opportunity to fix myself a quick lunch before heading downtown. I had never owned a suit, just borrowed one from a friend once to go to a funeral. The idea of donning a monkey suit didn't appeal to me, but if I was going to jump into the deep end, I should probably be wearing the right clothes. Finishing lunch quickly, because you shouldn't keep friends of the Devil waiting, I headed downtown. The building was an old brick-and-mortar, the kind that New Haven was famous for. Sure, a lot of them were chain fast food joints, but some of them had managed to retain the charm they held back in the fifties. Fabrizzio's was one of those places. It just oozed old world as soon as I walked in the door and heard the bell chime above my head.

"You must be Nick! Please, come in, come in! Lu phoned ahead and told me you'd be coming. Business has been a little slow lately, so I thought it was a fair assumption that you are the one I was waiting for," said Dominic as he reached out a steady hand to greet me.

Okay, since we were making assumptions, I only assumed it was Dominic. He was a short, wrinkled gentleman, probably in his seventies, with a soft measuring tape draped across his shoulders like a stole. His eyes were bright and he had the quick smile of a successful salesman. I did not possess that smile.

"And you must be Dominic," I replied. "Nice to meet you." I shook his hand firmly, he was still pretty strong for a man his age, and smiled. "I don't know what I'm doing here other than following orders. I've never owned a suit in my life and only seen tailors in movies, so I'm not sure what you need from me."

His smile didn't falter but in the blink of an eye I could tell, by the set of his jaw, he had already made several judgments about me. First was, as I later found out, I had a thirty-eight inch chest with a sixteen-inch neck and thirty-four-inch sleeves. Oh, and a thirty-two-inch inseam. I'd never been measured for anything, and that continued to be true. Dominic just *knew* in that surgically mathematical way someone with an eye for shapes and sizes knew. Second was that I deserved a nice suit, and he was the one who was going to make this first suit-buying experience special, like a kindly grandfather. It was a happy bustle from the floor to the displays to the fitting rooms and back again. We looked at three-button suits, three-piece suits, and walked quickly past zoot suits. He didn't think they were professional enough based on my benefactor and tutted at me when I was captivated by a wide pin-stripe number.

During my fittings, I decided to ask about the elephant in the room. "So how do you know Lu?" I asked as nonchalantly as possible.

"Me?" replied Dominic. "My story is fairly boring, if you must know, I'm not sure a young man with an exciting future would be very interested in it." This was spoken with the conviction of someone dying to tell a story but wanting to confirm my interest first. Like a statement spoken through smiling teeth, almost proud.

Never one to leave the bait, I told him that I was interested and didn't have a lot of people I could talk to about my newly found associate.

"Well," he began, "I was a young man in Milan. My family, not so rich but not too poor, owned a small vineyard in the countryside and made Lombardia. Eh, excuse me, Lombardy wine. I liked the wine, red and delicious, but not so much the making of it. I had other brothers and sisters who were more than happy to take up the family business, so I wasn't pressured too much into anything. I missed the war so didn't feel the need to enlist and, more importantly, there was a girl I was quite fond of who moved to Milan with her family," he said this last bit with a particular glint of amusement in his eyes. "You are not surprised, I see. Amoré, yes? No one is surprised when a story starts this way. Well, my young friend, let me tell you that I lost the girl. I was naive and she was engaged to be married to a young politician, hence the move to the city. I ended up, what is the phrase, sticking to my guns and making a living in the city. It brought me to the attention of the local shopkeepers, and I worked odd jobs for them until I found myself working for one of the local tailors. I was fascinated by the skill of his eyes and hands, taking something as complicated as a person's body with all of its lumps and bumps, and turning it into something else. The ugliest man, he could turn him into a king when putting him in a suit. I worked for him for many years, learning what I could, until one day a young man came in looking for a suit. The owner? He was with another customer, so he told me to see to the man. I had a knack for sizing, as you may have noticed, and within minutes, had the man testing jackets to see what was to his liking. He was impressed, and when everything was said and done, I had sold Mr. Lu a suit and had an invitation to a small gathering he was having that night. To make a long story much shorter, I met some people and heard some incredible things, and by the end of the night, had an offer to make something special out of myself. Designer, creator, and clothier of kings and queens. I told him I would think about it and I did, for years. Priorities change as one gets older, no? I married, had a child, the world moved on, and I kept fitting suits. It was what I was good at so why stop? And one day I decided to take Mr. Lu up on his offer."

"Why?" I couldn't help but ask.

"Maybe one day you will see this for yourself, but I did not need much. My family, my career, and a comfortable life. I decided I wanted to keep doing these things for much longer than this old body would allow for."

I missed something, and it wasn't coming to me quickly enough. Dominic saw it in my face, took pity on me, and finished his story.

"I am an old man, Mr. Nick, but I am in good health and good spirits. My wife is the same. This shop is doing well enough, and I practice my craft with a deft hand. I will continue to do so for quite some time."

A light went on upstairs, and I realized what Dominic was trying to tell me. "What about your daughter?" I asked.

"Well," said Dominic, "she has a choice to make, but it is not for me to make for her. She is about my age now. Well, how old I look I should say. I've aged well, yes? If I had made my decision earlier, things may have been different but that's water under the bridge."

"Y-yes..." I stuttered.

"It is a simple pleasure, knowing what you have now, and what you will have later. It was worth the price for me and for my wife. Do we have regrets? It is a sad thing to watch those you love grow old and pass on. I would like to have avoided that, it does weigh the soul down. My daughter, if she does not make the same choice? Or, worse, she gets no offer at all? Then I suppose that would weigh the heaviest." He sighed, his eyes sad and distant for a moment. Dominic must have realized he was standing on the precipice of melancholy because he seemed to shake it off and continue, "But we enjoy our life together. I make Lu's suits, and he leaves with a wink each time." He continued checking the break in my pants hem.

"Thank you for telling me your story." I couldn't think of anything else to say, I felt like I had intruded on someone in the privacy of their home, but it was a story freely given.

"Many people have many different opinions. About that, I would not make your decision for you. But suits? Trust me," he said with his eyes mostly closed and a wry smile. So I trusted him. What did I know about this stuff? By the time we were done, it was almost dinner time. A few other customers had come in but Dominic apparently had an assistant so talented that I didn't even know they were there. In the end, I walked out of the shop with a garment bag containing two suits, suitable for wearing interchangeably, and even more information to chew on than before.

When I arrived back at my apartment, the first thing I noticed was that the buzzer panel, which had been broken since before I moved in, looked entirely functional. It was shiny brass and bright black buttons with all the names engraved on removable plates. I pressed mine just for the fun of it and heard a satisfying *bzzz*. I thought that maybe the building supervisor was having a productive day when I got to my apartment door and my jaw dropped to the hallway floor. My front door, previously a functional but otherwise boring metal entry door, had been replaced with a gorgeous multi-panel frosted glass number. Walking into the apartment itself I saw that the color palette had shifted from industrial gray to a combination of blues, greens, and gold, some of my favorite colors. My furniture had been swapped for a similar, but upgraded, style, and when I walked into the bedroom to hang up my suits I was greeted by a king-size memory foam bed that nearly brought me to tears. I wandered around the apartment, Odin seemingly already used to the new luxury, touching the new commercial-grade appliances in the kitchen and marveling at the fridge fully stocked with gourmet ingredients. There was a note on the new kitchen table that read, "Welcome aboard."

This was either done with magic, given the afternoon that Lu had to complete it in, or by a renovation team that would make twenty-four-hour home makeover crews throw in their tool belts. I thought about my life, and how I had gotten to this point. "You sneaky bastard," I said out loud to no one in particular. "I'm absolutely screwed."

CHAPTER 9

The first day is the most nerve-wracking for anyone at a new job, right? I bet their anxiety had nothing on mine. I stood in front of the mirror for about thirty minutes, staring at a version of myself I had never seen before. Dominic had done his magic, and I was looking at an upscale version of my former self. Before you wonder if I was a throwback from the grunge era, I splurged on a haircut the day before, after my fitting, and I managed to not cut myself with the razor that morning. We've all seen those movies, where someone gets a semi-professional makeover and the person walks into the room and everyone is knocked over by how amazing the transformation is. The good news: I looked pretty good. The better news: No one was in my bedroom to see the terrified look on my face as I witnessed this step toward my first big-boy job. The fact that it was working for the actual Devil was almost lost in that moment of surprise. Almost.

The training center wasn't anywhere near the office building I was supposed to report to. Downtown New Haven was a strange amalgamation of modern glass and steel, and old stone academic buildings. I drove downtown, to a parking garage near Yale New Haven Hospital, where I had been given a parking pass. Amy told me that it was almost worth selling her soul just for the parking pass, given how expensive it was to hold a monthly there.

Speaking of Amy, I hadn't seen very much of her in the past few months. We got together occasionally for coffee, just not at The Fix since I was supposed to be in travel quarantine and dealing with the "death" of my grandfather. It all felt a little too weird for her so we pretty much stopped doing that. That was okay, I was so busy finishing up my coursework that other than a philosophical objection to her absence, I didn't mind.

I walked over to a tall glass high rise, number 127 dispelling any expectations of stereotypical 666 addresses, and took the elevator to the fifteenth, not the thirteenth, floor. I met the office administrator, a nice young man named Lester, and sat down in the reception area to wait. I didn't need to wait long, as soon as my posterior hit the padding, Lu walked around the corner talking to someone about something I didn't quite catch. I stood up as he walked in my direction.

"Nick! Good to see you." Lu put his hand out, to shake mine. "Hope I didn't keep you waiting long. Of course, I didn't." He shook my hand firmly. "Looking good, I see. Dominic earns his money, doesn't he? Comes from years of experience. Great talent there. Well let's not waste too much time out here, you need the nickel tour." The office wasn't as large as I might have expected, given that it didn't occupy the whole building, just one of the floors.

Lu took me around the office and showed me the water cooler, the lunch room, conference rooms, cubicle farms, and offices. My desk was right outside of his office. Well, one of his offices. During the tour, I asked about the situation and how he could stick around in New Haven so much when he was, you know, lord of the underworld and responsible for the entire globe. I won't get too deeply into it, because he used small words to make sure I understood it, but he basically said he co-locates. That meant he essentially could be in more than one place at once. I didn't ask for more information, because he answered my question easily enough and it would have been weird to ask how when every answer was "because I'm the Devil."

"And here's your setup," Lu finally said with a flourish at the cubicle outside the office. "Nice new everything. Laptop for working remotely, your company-issued cell phone next to it, all synced up. Nothing but the best for the team."

"It's almost like you're trying to impress me," I said, smiling.

"I hope it's working," he replied.

"Yes." I couldn't help but be impressed, I certainly had never gotten the kind of royal treatment that this test run with Lu had been like so far. If this was what selling my soul felt like, I was surprised the entire world hadn't already flown the Lucifer flag high.

I did notice one thing, mounted above my cubicle. It was a small flat display, like a marquee I'd expect to see a scrolling message going across. Now that I noticed, the same thing had been in some of the other areas of the office we passed on the tour, only they were active and moving. I decided to sate my curiosity. "What's that?" I asked, pointing at the display.

"Those?" Lu replied. "Those are tickers. Like the stock market, but they track the only commodity I'm interested in."

"Gold?" I volunteered, jokingly. Did I mention that I make bad jokes when I get nervous? The fancy dress didn't help, and I was definitely feeling off my game.

"Ha, no," Lu said. "Souls, my boy, sweet tasty souls." He must have seen the slightly horrified look on my face. "Too much with the creepy again? Sorry, Nick. I don't eat them, that would be counterproductive. The first part was true, this office helps monitor the market and how much of it we've cornered. My agents, like the position you've trained for, work day and night to make sure that everything is running smoothly in this engine we've got here. The New Haven office is a good example of a tight ship. Good numbers month over month, with a good set of teams. Most of what we do is a ground game, which is why the office is the size it is. We've got one in pretty much every metropolitan area and regional offices serving the more rural parts. Mix a little community outreach with some instant gratification, or more long-term happiness for those playing the game. Add a little bit of evangelism, some good old-fashioned sales work, and you've got our operation here."

I asked the obvious question that he didn't answer, "But why is there one above my desk?"

"Oh, that." Lu chuckled. "Well, we need a way to track your progress. Ultimately, the decision is going to be yours, but we like to keep an eye on how your activities influence your shares."

"I'm stock?" I asked, a little worried.

"Not exactly, but it's a good analogy. Look, let's start the clock running and I'll show you what I'm talking about." He pointed at the marquee with his fingers like a gun, brought down his thumb like the hammer, and the display activated. It showed "Nicky index: 0."

"I hope you don't mind the little joke," Lu said. "We thought it was cute. Like the Nikkei index in Japan. Oh well, I liked it anyway. So zero is where you start, all unaffiliated, and as you continue working for me and performing acts in my name, you'll see the accumulation there. Hit a thousand points and you might as well sign on the dotted line, but you may have already at that point anyway."

"But I can always say no," I argued, "you said that."

"Why yes, my boy." Lu grinned. "I did. I meant every word, and yes, you can. I'm just giving you my perspective based on previous endeavors. I don't make up the numbers, but I suppose people have been blaming statistics on the Devil for years. What's the saying? Lies, damn lies, and statistics? Every person who has ever hit a thousand points in their introductory period has decided to stay on as permanent staff." He walked over to the chair by my desk and patted the top of it with both hands. "Look, just get settled in and we'll talk more about this later. Oh, and while most of this is sunshine and roses, we can't keep a small element of hell out of this whole thing. You'll need to make sure you complete your new-hire training. Boss's orders."

Another pat on the chair and he turned and entered his own office, closing the door.

If I wasn't clear enough before, I had never worked in an office. The good news was all of the training I was put through actually prepared me for this moment. I sat down, reviewed all of the perfunctory "how do I work this computer thing" information, and started on my first day at "work." Enough quotations? It was hard at that point to accept what was happening as anything other than a surreal dream, so I just buckled down and pretended that this was all normal.

We can probably skip ahead a few days unless you want your eyes to bleed from all of those slideshow presentations too. I was finding my rhythm, getting to work in the morning, making the first pot of coffee for myself and the office, checking my emails, which mostly talked about projects I had nothing to do with other than update my boss, the Devil, and keep some mental tabs on. I did find out that there was a whole new evil called "computer-based training" but I didn't even want to get into that. It was Thursday before I heard anything about going anywhere outside the office.

"Let's go meet a client," Lu said, walking out of his office and leaning over my cubicle walls. "I want to get you started on a project, something I think you'll enjoy." I was honestly not even sure he ever entered the office this morning, he kept the door closed so everyone just assumed he was in there whether he was or not. Given that he could pop in whenever he liked, it was mostly for appearances and to not startle the office staff.

"Sounds good to me." I rubbed my eyes and stretched a little as I rose from my chair. "I could use the fresh air."

"That's the spirit! Casual acceptance," Lu winked, "I like it. Come on, I'll drive."

A quick drive, which probably should have taken a little longer given normal traffic law, and we were in one of the less affluent neighborhoods in the city. We arrived at a chain coffee shop and parked on the street. No parking meters, as if that mattered in Lu's case. We walked into the coffee shop and took a table at the back. Lu sent me back up to the counter with an order for the table. When I returned holding a tray of cups, a middle-aged man whom I did not recognize sat across from Lu.

"Ah," the man said, "and this must be the altruistic young man you said would be working with me on all of the nitty-gritty details." He picked the third cup out of the tray and sipped his coffee, which was apparently made exactly the way he liked it, his salt and pepper beard split into a toothy smile afterward.

"Nick, this is Samuel." Lu gestured at the man, now identified, sipping his coffee. "Samuel, this is one of my newest and brightest, Nick." I had the good decency to blush at this. "Samuel is a new client of mine. I happened to hear him walking down the street muttering to himself the other day."

I took a good look at Samuel. He was perhaps in his forties, middling height from what I could tell seated, with the stocky build of someone who might have been a tradesman of some kind. His eyes were bright and kind, with a smile making a large gap in his full beard. He had a slight accent, I placed it as Slavic or Russian.

"Muttering?" asked Samuel. "That is perhaps the kindest way of saying that I was swearing up a storm to myself. It was not one of my best days, Nick. I will tell you that truthfully." He held his hand out to me, and I shook it with a smile. I liked this guy so far.

"What's the situation?" I asked.

"Samuel, let's bring Nick up to speed on the concept," Lu said, gesturing at Samuel to start the conversation.

"Well," Samuel began, "I have lived in this city for many years. It has been through its own fair share of problems. You might not remember, though if you lived in the city I apologize for telling you things you already know. The nineties were not a decade kind to New Haven. Drugs, crime, everything ran pretty rampant. I have been raising my family here for years, and luckily, the bad elements have not made an impact on us, but it has been very trying for the community. It has been getting much better, of course, but the pace that basic infrastructure, such as schools and the like, has been recovering is too slow. Too many children are hungry, both in the belly and in the brain, and need more help than the government is giving them. The city has become a bit of a shining star, but people aren't paying attention to the tarnish still underneath." He paused to sip his coffee. Mine was going cold, but I was too intent on his story to touch it. "My son, he is a teacher at Amistad. That is a good school, but he hears from the children about friends and family who are suffering elsewhere. One child, specifically, has a friend who is in a terrible situation. Might be an abusive home environment, might just be a troubled neighborhood, might be the boy has bad luck in friends, but regardless the sight of a child as young as he with as many black eyes as he sports infuriates me." He paused, hands curled tightly around his cup.

"So we're going to do something about it," Lu said, smiling mischievously.

"Like," I swallowed, "what?"

Samuel chuckled. "You look a little squeamish. I don't know the extent of what is going on, but I think you should not worry so much. Well maybe a little, depending on where your mind has wandered, but probably not. There are two parts to my plan."

"He wants to build a school." The words burst out of Lu's mouth. "Exciting, isn't it? Sorry, Samuel. I couldn't wait for you to get to the good parts."

Samuel heaved an exaggerated sigh. "Of course, Lu. I am no storyteller, however you need the tale to continue." Samuel smiled again, showing even more teeth hidden under that beard. "The first part is the school. I am not an overly sentimental man, but the thought of a legacy of this kind is appealing. My children will remember me when I am gone, and hopefully theirs after, but a free school providing what the neediest of children in this city requires? Whatever we end up calling it, it sounds like a nice piece of stone to leave behind with my name on it."

"That sounds amazing," I said, sipping a now cold latte, "but I'm not exactly an architect. Or an engineer. Or a construction worker." I smiled but looked a little puzzled. "I'm not entirely sure what my job is on this one."

Lu put his hands up in mock surrender. "Nick, you jumped too far ahead. Samuel?"

Samuel cleared his throat, looking a little sheepish. "I have never been a violent man," he said softly, "but I cannot let something as heinous as a child being abused continue. There are many organizations and services that attempt to correct injustices such as this, but this particular boy seems to have fallen through all of the cracks. I want something done to correct this."

"I'm not sure what this has to do with the school..." I trailed off.

"Ah," said Samuel, "you are correct. The school is the 'cake' and this is, I suppose, what you would call the 'icing.' If I am going to sell my soul," and at this, Samuel winked at Lu, "I'm going to get what I want plus a little extra to keep me grinning smugly well into the afterlife."

I pushed my chair back a little bit and placed my hands on the table. I wasn't sure if I was going to stand up, knock my chair over, or just sit frozen. No, wait, definitely the third one. "I don't think you've got the right guy for this one," I said, a few ugly as-seen-on-TV scenarios passing through my mind.

Lu sputtered a laugh into his coffee, I didn't realize I had interrupted his drink with something funny. "Do you think we're asking you to break some kneecaps? Go a little Mafioso? Hired hitman? *Nick*," Lu said, stretching my name out, "what do you take me for? No, don't answer that. You're making the wrong assumption here. Think of it as an investigative assignment with decision-making power. I want you to look into the situation, determine what's going on, and decide what you think the best course of action is."

My hands found their way back to some semblance of a normal position, and I shifted a little more easily in my chair. "That sounds like something I could do."

"Of course it is!" exclaimed Lu. "I wouldn't have told Samuel here you're the man for the job if you weren't. He's got every confidence, right Samuel?"

Samuel turned slightly toward me and looked me straight in the eyes with his own. They were sky blue, unflinching. "Do you have family, Nick?" he asked me.

"Just my folks," I replied.

"Imagine," he started, "that you had a younger brother, for which you cared a great deal. Perhaps more than anything."

"Okay," I said.

"Now," continued Samuel, "imagine that one day you came home from school and found your brother crying in his room. His face was bruised in a way no child should be. He tells you that his own father, your father, did that to him. In his innocence, he only wants to know what it was he did so wrong to make his father hit him."

I was stunned, my mouth partially open with no sound coming out other than shallow breathing.

Samuel's eyes narrowed, and he continued staring into mine as he asked, "Does this thought upset you?"

"Yes," I finally managed to breathe out.

"Does this thought make you angry?" he asked.

"Yes," I said firmly, with no hesitation.

Samuel continued staring at me, making a silent judgment, then turned to Lu and nodded. "This is the right man," he said and turned back to me. "I could be wrong about this, Nick, about this child and who is responsible. I could be wrong, but I am afraid that I am not. You will find this out for me, and make it right."

"Why?" I couldn't help but ask.

"Why? Or maybe you mean to ask me 'Why this way?'" Samuel smiled. "They say God helps those who help themselves. I see before me a powerful force. I am not a man to hold a grudge but, as the figure across from me proves that something like God must exist, this God lets many things happen that I would not condone. On top of that, he has not come to shake my hand and offer me a solution to my problems. If you ask some people, it would be the work of God that led me to Lu, or him to me. Who would say to me that this is wrong, when the results will speak for themselves."

Samuel stood up, and Lu followed suit. Samuel clapped me on the shoulder as he left, I continued to sit at the table trying to digest the task ahead of me. Lu motioned for me to head toward the door and I joined him in the car. We rode back to the office, not chatting about anything more important than the weather.

CHAPTER 10

The ride wasn't very long, so we got back in short order. We were in the elevator before Lu said something that snapped me back to reality.

"The file is on your desk," he said.

"Hm?" I mumbled.

"The file, about the boy and his family, it'll be on your desk. Make sure you keep me updated when you've got something to go on. If you need advice, I'm here, but I'd like to see how you approach this yourself."

"Oh, thanks. I'll get started on that right away."

We hit our floor and walked back to Lu's office, parking me in my cubicle. He stopped on his way through the door and turned back to me. "You'll do fine. And don't worry so much, this is your chance to do something good."

"I don't get it, Lu."

"What don't you get? The lack of brimstone? The surplus of good deeds? The world's a little topsy-turvy, isn't it." That last was more of a statement than a question.

"Yeah," I stammered, "it's all just a little much. I mean, I didn't expect to be prodded with pitchforks but the first job you throw at me is public service for a guy who's selling his soul to build a tuition-free school."

"Too goody-goody, eh?" Lu said through a brief smile.

"Let's say I wasn't expecting what I'm seeing, even after all of the generosity."

Lu walked back toward my cubicle and waved for me to follow him. "Let me show you something, Nick."

We wandered toward the back of the office, near where our IT department was located. Together, we entered the office of a woman named Sonia, it was on her nameplate, who greeted Lu and myself warmly. "What can I do for you gentlemen?"

"Sonia, I need you to bring up a video feed on some activity happening downtown, nothing too explicit. Oh, and bring up the monitoring software too. I need to show Nick something."

"Sure thing, boss." She had a bank of monitors next to her desk, which had been showing various scenes around the city. All of them went blank and then came back to life displaying a large image, spanning all of the monitors, of an alleyway somewhere downtown. There was a young man leaning up against one of the walls smoking a cigarette. Superimposed on the bottom right corner was what looked like a progress bar, it showed around ten percent full. Suddenly, someone in a black hooded sweatshirt walked into frame with their hood drawn up. It was cool outside, which didn't put his outfit out of place, but I had a sinking feeling that something was wrong. Just as quickly as the person came into frame he jumped toward the kid and, in a blur, the young man was on the ground, bleeding from the head wound he had just received courtesy of a pipe held in the hooded person's hand. There was no audio, but by the frantic gesturing and the man on the ground pulling out his wallet and holding it in a shaking hand to be snatched by the assailant, the story unfolded. The mugging was quick and efficient, and soon the only person on-screen was the victim, shakily standing and staggering toward the end of the alleyway.

I turned to Lu, horrified. "If you knew that was going to happen, why didn't you stop it?"

"We already covered this, Nick. Free will. You have it, all of mankind."

"But he'll probably get away with it!"

"Not as far as I'm concerned," Lu said, gesturing at the bottom corner of the monitors, "take a look." The bar, which was previously at ten percent, now showed twelve percent.

We walked back to Lu's office, and I followed him inside. The office of the Devil should be impressive, but the first thing I noticed was how sparse it was. I guess when you had an infinite number of offices, you stopped caring about how fancy they were. Lu sat behind his desk as I collapsed into one of his guest chairs.

"Why all the philanthropy and caring?" Lu leaned forward, steepling his fingers under his chin for a moment. "Let me explain something to you. It will sound obvious once I do; you'll probably kick yourself. I don't need to cater to the lowest common denominator. I'm not evil, Nick, never said I was. All of the stereotypes, well, they're not all lies, but most of them aren't based in reality. Criminals and the like, evil-doers if you must, they punch their own ticket. I don't need to convince them that their souls are best kept in my care, they're doing it themselves." Lu cleared his throat. "It's not the same scale, so don't worry that you're in the same boat as murderers and thieves. Bad people fall down a path of corruption, and that's how I refer to that progress. The more bad things people do, the more corrupt their souls. Once they're entirely corrupt, I become their shepherd and the man upstairs wants nothing to do with them. Free will be damned, they're mine to handle."

I must have looked a little confused, though I was following along with most of the explanation.

"It was a deal made long ago," Lu continued, "and I'm not going into it because you're already having a rough enough week for surreal conversations as it is. Suffice it to say that I get to spend my time and energy convincing the rest of humanity that their souls are safer with me, and I get to do that in fun and interesting ways. The bad apples sort themselves out."

"But if we all end up in the same place, what's the difference between me and the murderer?"

"That's not what I said." Lu shook his finger at me, "I said that I have to convince you all that your souls are best kept in my care. I never said they were in the same place."

I took a breath.

"And before you ask," Lu preempted my next question, "I think that's enough explanation for now. It's your first week, Nick. I've given you an assignment and want you to make some progress on that before we discuss more philosophical points. You may be my assistant, but until you're a company man, there are things I'm going to have to keep to myself." He turned to his laptop, clearly dismissing me.

I walked out of the office, past my desk, into the men's room, and rested my forehead against the cool tile of the wall. A few deep breaths, some cold water splashed on my face at the sink, and one long stare into the mirror later and I was ready. Ready for what? Not much, but ready to leave the restroom I had marched into so purposefully. I decided that the lump in my throat needed to be drowned, so I headed for the breakroom to grab myself a coffee before slinking back to my desk and digging into my first project.

"You had 'the talk,' didn't you?" said a voice behind me that I did not recognize.

I turned from the counter, swallowing the scalding sip of coffee I had taken before it cooled properly. I failed, squeezing my eyes shut with the sudden burning sensation. "Excuse me?"

"Sorry for startling you." Lester the admin, who was the owner of the voice I didn't remember, stood in the doorway. At least he had the good decency to look contrite.

"Do you always sneak up on the new people and scare them into an early workman's comp claim?" I filled a cup with cold water, nursing it to cool my sizzling tongue.

Lester smiled, blushing slightly, "No, but I already apologized, so I hope you'll forgive me. I noticed you charging into the restroom and heard some thumping on the wall. I assumed you were having a moment after getting the 'we're in the same boat as the murderers and thieves' talk."

"Yeah, I think I'm still processing."

"You're still doing better than a lot of the other new people. Some of them walk straight into the elevator," Lester gestured down the hall with an expansive wave, "and we never see them again."

"Well," I sighed, "I may not have always been the most motivated but I've never been a quitter. I've got some more work to do before I make that call."

Lester nodded, with an appraising look on his face. "Good for you. It's not what most people think it is, this whole place. I won't try to influence you, though I've got my own take on it, but I'm glad you're giving it a shot. Let me know if you need anything, okay?" Lester gave a low wave and left the breakroom. I was about to take my coffee to go when he poked his head back in. "Unless you want to go for a drink sometime," he said, blushing, "then I'm a talker." Then he was gone, as quickly as he had returned.

I shook my head, added more sugar to the coffee, and headed back to my desk. The file was waiting for me, as promised, front and center. Sitting down, I put both hands on the folder, taking a deep breath. How sinister could an innocent manila folder be? It was plain, with the name Samuel penciled onto the tab. Inside was a very professional-looking report on the situation, though I had nothing to compare it to beyond movies I'd seen where private investigators kept dossiers.

Samuel's son, David, had been teaching at Amistad Elementary for three years. He was a good teacher, by all accounts in the report. The student in question was a young boy named Eric Digger who was, despite the unfortunate last name, a good kid also by all accounts. His grades were good, no disciplinary problems, just the fact that he came in at least once each week with a fresh bruise. It all sounded like a stereotype when you were talking about signs of abuse, but not all stereotypes were false. The report sent my stomach spiraling, my coffee went cold and untouched. Black eye [door knob], bruised shins [fell while playing], sprained wrist [rough-housing], the list just kept going. Every single incident had some perfectly mundane excuse. Separately, one would never wonder about them, but his teacher, David, saw the pattern. David reported his suspicions to the school, but nothing happened. There was even an investigation but, according to details in this report, there were never any charges and the pattern of "accidental" bruising continued. If I thought my parents were a little absentee they had nothing on Eric's. The father was a general contractor, and the mother stayed at home but worked odd jobs in the community. Most days, the mom was gone for the majority of the day on errands or short-term work, and the dad was doing shift work maintaining equipment for housing developments and apartments in and around the city.

None of these details explained why Eric showed up with unexpected body art all the time. Samuel was right. I was getting angry.

I nearly fell out of my chair when there was a tapping at my cubicle entryway.

"You look focused, Nick. I see you found the file." Lu leaned against the cube wall. "Nasty bit of work, isn't it? The investigator didn't get a lot of details, and couldn't get in too close, so we're not sure what the full picture is. I thought this would be a good experience for you, start from a bit of a distance and then work your way in. But it's quitting time, so you should probably get some rest."

I didn't realize how long I had been studying the file. Glancing at the clock, it had already been three hours.

"Why do you need me to investigate this?" I asked Lu, gesturing with disgust at the folder. "Can't Sonia just bring it all up on the monitors?"

Lu shook his head, "It's not as simple as that. I've got a lot of surveillance in public spaces but I'm not omniscient. Modern technology has made this easier for me, but it's all still fueled by human beings doing the work. How do you think it worked in the old days? We've traded traveling salesmen for 1080p camera resolution, but I still need eyes to see what's going on. Easier to have you step in and oversee the project, than get all 'big brother' with the family. Too many variables, too messy. That's what I need you for Nick."

I nodded, thinking it through. All the time that I would need to spend, while this child was still probably being beaten at home. "Couldn't you just make it stop?" I looked up at Lu from my chair. "Couldn't you just stop all this with Eric?"

Lu's eyebrows tilted upward and he had a sad look on his face that said I was missing something.

"Could I?" Lu asked quietly and walked away.

CHAPTER 11

S takeouts started with coffee, right? Step one was going to be my own eyes on the situation, but I'd only had about half my intake of caffeinated beverages that day. I hadn't seen Amy for a while, and when I started thinking about the file I had read, it made me want to see a friend.

A few texts later and we were meeting at The Fix. It had been three months and Mark, my old boss, wasn't there. The staff had turned over since I left. Declan had even sent me a message that his sister had gone into remission, so he was able to return home to Boston. He also told me that his sister appreciated the donations keeping her well-fed while she was in the hospital, which warmed my heart to hear. It was unlikely that anyone would recognize me there. Hell, I barely recognized myself. I took a tall table in the corner and sat with my back to the wall, feet hooked around the long chair legs. I waited for a while, people-watching until she walked through the door. Her eyes scanned the tables and passed right over me at the back. Amy started walking through the shop and didn't stop until I waved my hands above my head like a muppet, trying to call her over to the table.

"Hello? Over here!" I said loudly from my perch.

Her eyes got wide, and it took me a second before I realized she was giving me a full visual once-over.

"What?" I chirped as she took the seat opposite me. I had already ordered for us, the paper cups sitting like two large chess pieces on the table.

"I didn't even think you owned a suit," she said, "but you clean up pretty well."

I forgot that I had come straight from work. My jacket was slung over the back of the stool but I was still wearing the rest of it, including the tie. I had always seen the way men unbuttoned their collars and loosened their ties in movies, that artfully messy look. I always thought it looked pretty slick, so I had been doing that on my way home after work every night that week so far. Give a guy a break, I was getting used to wearing the clothes, might as well have some fun with it.

"Thanks, Amy. You, uh, look great yourself." She wasn't dressed any different than usual, just retail casual, but I should always return a compliment if possible. Especially if it's true. Especially if it's from someone I may or may not be quietly interested in. Or not quietly. My brain was doing some extra loops on that one. I didn't manage to impress girls of any kind very often, let alone ones that I knew or liked. I hoped my attempt at flattery wasn't too lame.

"It's been a while, hasn't it?" Amy picked up her cup. "Cheers!"

"Cheers." We toasted, and drank, and then looked at each other awkwardly for a minute before I broke the silence. "So..."

"So... how's the new job?" Amy sounded genuinely curious rather than it just being small talk. That was a good sign. *I hoped.*

"It's not what I was expecting," I began, "granted I have no idea what I was expecting, but it wasn't this."

"That sounds... bad?" Amy said, scrunching her nose slightly.

"No, no," I held up my hands, "not bad-unexpected. Like, you know how when you're going to take a test in school and you're dreading it? And then you get there, take it, and it wasn't as bad as you expected?"

"Okay."

"And not only was it not as bad as you expected," I continued, "you're almost disappointed at how not-bad it was?"

"You're saying," Amy paused for effect, "that there's nothing bad about working for the Devil."

"I'm not saying that, it's only my first week, but it's more surreal than anything else." I hid my lack of something to say with my cup.

"What do they have you doing? Repossessing souls? Kicking puppies? Making people read the phone book?" she gave a pondering look, "I can't think of anything sinister that you might actually do."

"I don't think you'll believe me." I grimaced, slightly.

"Look, stupid," she pointed a finger at me, "I'm sitting here, believing that you've started a new job working for Lucifer, and you think I won't believe you?" She stood up in a mock huff. "I should leave right now. That's exactly what I'm going to do."

"Funny," I laughed. "You're right. I'm wrong. You've got nothing but faith in my ability to tell the truth. In fact, we're talking here because you're the only person I can talk to about this who will believe me. So sit down, and let me tell you about my week."

I told Amy about the office, the people, and what Lu had put me up to with Samuel. I told her about the school, but when it came to the part about Eric and the possible abuse? I kept most of those details to myself.

"You went to work for the Devil, and he's having you investigate and stop a potential child abuser, while also building a free school for needy children?" She gaped at me, summing up what I had told her.

"Yeah," I said, a little sheepishly.

"That tricky bastard," she whispered almost to herself. "That sounds good enough that I want to work for him now. Serious sales pitch, huh?"

"I guess you could call it that." I tilted my head slightly. "I'm not sure. It all seems legit, even the admin is happy I'm giving the place a fair shake. I think he also might have been hitting on me, but the other part was genuine too."

Amy giggled at me.

"I said might." I sounded a little defensive. "He could just be friendly. Either way, it's totally surreal, because the reason I joined up was to try doing something good. I expected to have to do something horrendous before getting a shot at something that helped other people. But this thing with Samuel... it's just... good."

We spent about an hour after that, catching up and talking. She had gotten a new job downtown at a bookstore and had plenty of gossip to catch me up on. It wasn't just Amy, I hadn't seen *anyone* for the past few months. Come to think of it, I hadn't even talked to my parents, that was going to be a doozy of a conversation when I finally got around to it. My first week was winding to a close, and I realized that I needed to reconnect. Luckily, I had Amy to talk openly with, and I felt a little bit more normal being able to do that.

"I think I need to tell you something," Amy said before we were getting up to head our separate ways, "and I don't want you to be mad at me."

"Why would I be mad at you?"

"Well, you shouldn't," Amy rushed on, "because I didn't say anything to anyone."

"Amy." I felt like I was about to be made unhappy.

"Nick." She mirrored my tone exactly, and I softened a little bit. "I think Rob suspects something. He hasn't come right out and asked me, or said anything, but he's been a little weird around me especially when you come up in conversation." Her voice stumbled a little. "Uh, not that you come up in conversation much. Just that if you did. It happened. I thought you should know." She blushed slightly.

"Okay, thanks for letting me know. I'll try to make sure I don't do anything hellish around him."

"Oh!" her eyes brightened. "Do you have some sort of super-power now? Being a minion of hell?"

"Ha ha." I dripped as much sarcasm as possible. "No."

"Well, that's a little disappointing."

I sighed, "Tell me about it."

CHAPTER 12

I checked my phone before leaving the coffee shop and had an email from Lu. Paraphrased, it said I didn't need to come into the office in person, so long as I was actively working on the project. The next day was Friday, and never let it be said I looked a gift horse in the mouth. Despite not knowing why that colloquialism even made sense, I wasn't going to go into the office on a Friday if I had the blessing of my boss. I wasn't going to play hooky, mind you. I imagined the surveillance system at work could find me playing video games in my underwear just as easily as it found that mugger in the alley.

I decided to call off the stakeout for the night and get a jump on it in the morning. I had brought the file home with me so it sat on my nightstand while I slept. Odin slept on top of it, just to make sure it didn't escape in the middle of the night.

He must have been satisfied that the folder was afraid of him enough to stay put because I woke up early with a furry scarf across my neck. I managed to sneak out from under the snoring furball and left him sleeping off his night-watch duty while I went through my morning routine. I opened the file to look at while I ate breakfast, looking at the family's schedule. The father worked and drove the boy to school in his company van. The mother stayed at home. School started at... eight a.m. I glanced at the clock in the kitchen; it was only six forty-five. Looked like I had enough time to start a day of personal surveillance. The file didn't have any personal notes in it, just a straightforward professional summary of information. Times, dates, physical observations, birth dates, license plates, and much more. Lu was pretty clear that he expected me to fill in the blanks and come up with a recommendation on this.

Odin was still sleeping by my pillow after I got dressed, so I tucked him in before I left. The school was pretty close to downtown, so it only took a few minutes to get there. I had plenty of time to find a convenient parking spot and lay low before all of the bustle of morning drop-off started. I had pictures of the family in my dossier and studied them for a while to make sure I'd be able to recognize the van as well as the people in it. The van turned onto the street at seven-fifty a.m., getting into the queue of other cars waiting to drop off their children in the dedicated drop-your-kids-here area. The line was moving slowly, so I got to take a pretty long look at the father. Eric, the son, was too short to see much of him through the window from my vantage. Daniel Digger (seriously who named their kids like this) was a nondescript man. Taller than average, from how high he was sitting in the van, with a plain face, clean-shaven, and keeping his eyes on the line of cars ahead of him. He didn't look in my direction, so I didn't get to see much other than his profile, but I tried to pay attention to his behavior. He didn't smile, but he didn't frown either. It was a very stoic look on his face for the entire time he was in line. He turned to his son as he was getting out of the van and I couldn't tell what he said, if anything. Daniel drove off, theoretically toward his worksite of the day. I followed him as best I could. My training didn't include "tailing that suspect," so I lost him a few times on his way across town. He ended up at an apartment building near the highway on the West Haven town line. He unloaded his tools and went into the building. I could only stare at an empty van for so long before I got entirely too bored and started looking through the data that I already had.

The mother, Sarah, often volunteered at the community soup kitchen when they provided food downtown. I decided to leave my post at the apartment building, watching an empty van, and see if I could get some information directly from the source. It was possible the mother was just as responsible, but I was willing to hope for the best. I found Sarah on Broadway, outside of the Episcopal church, finishing a shift serving breakfast for the homeless. She eventually went back inside the church to help with the cleanup. I saw some people moving tables and volunteered to help them. I was dressed incognito, otherwise known as my own ratty clothes, so they were more than happy to have me do some heavy lifting.

First, I took note that I didn't burst into flames upon entering the church. I considered that a small victory, and walked into the main hall to find someone in charge.

"Well, if it isn't that troubled young man." A deep voice boomed from a doorway that led further into the church.

I turned and saw a face that looked only vaguely familiar and couldn't place any of the rest of the man.

"I can see that you don't remember me." The owner of the voice was middle-aged, balding, and bespectacled, and at that moment I remembered where I had met him. "But I remember every troubled young man I meet. Walter Prospect, if you don't recall. Welcome to the house of the Lord!"

"I'm not that troubled..." I started to say.

"Well, be that as it may, you were troubled then. I know it when I see it." Walter wiped beads of sweat from his brow with a white handkerchief. He had been working hard, from what I saw, breaking down the morning's activities. "I'm glad you're well, and that serendipity has put the two of us together again."

"Uh, sure."

"Don't let my grand manner fool you, son." He smiled and his broad teeth made it extra wide, "I'm a teddy bear, and call me Walt. What can I do for you on this fine Friday morning?"

"Well, Walt, I'm a part-time teacher's aide at Amistad, and I've been working closely with a friend of a young man named Eric Digger." I was apparently a big fat liar too. "I heard from Eric that his mother volunteers here, so I thought to come and see the operation. Maybe look into volunteering, and as a bonus, meet her on one of my days off."

"Mrs. Digger?" Walt nodded to himself. "A fine woman, she was here just this morning but you must have missed her. She often leaves quickly after a breakfast service. Definitely a good person to know, if you want to volunteer here. She's been doing it for quite some time and often helps mentor our newer volunteers. Were you interested in signing up?"

"Sure, can I stop by next week?"

"Certainly, son." Walt clapped me on the shoulder. "We're here three days a week. Monday, Wednesday, and Friday. Look, we get plenty of well-intentioned but ultimately invisible volunteers so I won't ask you for any formal sign-up. I'll just hope to see your face one day next week."

"Great. Is there any one day that Mrs. Digger is more likely to be here? I'd still like to kill two birds with one stone and introduce myself while I'm here."

"Yes, yes, she's normally here on Wednesdays and Fridays so you'll stand a good chance if you come back one of those days." Walt walked me out toward the doors.

"Well, thank you for your help." I held out my hand.

Walt shook it with strength. "Any day, son, you just come back and see us next week. If you ever run into more of that trouble I saw hanging off you last time, you come and see me."

CHAPTER 13

I spent the rest of the day in a buffet of boredom from watching Mr. Digger eat lunch and then leave his van empty again, to watching Eric get on the bus at the end of the school day, to watching Mrs. Digger standing at the bus stop and then holding Eric's hand on the walk back to their house, to tailing the work van home again.

I was having a very exciting day.

I spent the weekend being lazy at home, occasionally driving by the Digger's house to satisfy my own curiosity. Eric rode a bike and wore a helmet, and nothing untoward happened on the few times I drove by. It was a very limited sample size, but I took the opportunities I had to observe.

I decided to watch the school drop-off on Monday morning and then go back to the office to make a plan. I could have made a plan from anywhere, but figured I might need to run it by someone since my initial thoughts led me to believe I'd need to be on surveillance longer than a couple of days.

My cupboards were stocked, thanks to my newfound solvency, and Odin forgave me for leaving him alone Monday because of the catnip mousie he was still batting around the apartment from the day before. I started my second week surprisingly at peace with my current lot in life. Strange to say, given the means that it took to get me there.

I woke up early, dressed for the office, purchased a breakfast sandwich and coffee, and swung by the school to watch the dad drop off. I had decided, from my one day of experience, that stakeouts would make me fat. All I wanted to do was sit in the car and eat while I watched. Two days weren't going to kill me, but if it was all sausage, egg, and cheese all the time, I'd need to start doing laps around my car just to keep in shape.

People described something 'turning to ashes in their mouth' and you might think that was just some poetic license. Well, I thought the same thing until I experienced it. I was taking a bite of my sandwich as Eric was being dropped off. Same scene as Friday: stoic father, turn of the head, Eric out on the curb walking toward the entrance. I was too far to get a clear look, but something was different about Eric. The thought of what that "something" could have been made the food tasteless, forgotten in the moment of anxiety. The children weren't being let inside the building yet, so I got out of my car and crossed the street to get a closer look. I wasn't near enough for the teachers to wonder who I was, but enough to confirm my suspicions. Eric had a knot above his left eye, a big goose egg. On such a small body, it looked huge and swollen. Eric was smiling, talking to one of his friends, but my own head hurt just looking at it. I got back in my car and headed straight to the office, going straight past my desk and into Lu's office.

"His head!" I was a little frantic.

"Whose head?" Lu was genuinely confused.

"Eric! Eric's head!"

"I imagine he still has one?"

"Yes, of course." I realized I wasn't being helpful. "But it almost looks like he has two of them. He's got a knot the size of a baseball above one eye. Just from this weekend!"

"Maybe he fell down," Lu suggested, "or was hit with something while playing with his friends. Kids, you know? These things happen."

"You're kidding, right?" I asked. "After what Samuel said?"

"Do you have proof? Evidence? Are you so sure," Lu leaned back, "of someone's guilt that you're ready to prosecute? If you're sure it's this bad, do you at least know if it's the mother or the father? Both?"

"I doubt it's the mother," I said. "She volunteers at a soup kitchen."

"It's the innocent-looking ones you always have to watch out for," Lu tutted. "You never know when the quiet ones will snap."

"Okay, you made your point," I conceded. "I was coming into the office to make a plan of attack. I need to take the week to stake out the dad and meet the mom. So I wanted to clear it with you before disappearing for that long."

"Send me a note in the morning and check in at the office at the end of the day, and you're fine." Lu slapped his desk with one palm. "That's the kind of initiative I like to see."

And so began my week of voyeurism. It was almost interesting, taking that much time out of your life to witness someone else's. I say *almost* interesting because it was supremely dull. But this was important work and, thinking of the already failed social services investigation, I reminded myself that no one else was going to do it. I kept Lu informed, as requested, but other than that I delved into my own spy movie. By the end of Tuesday, I had a detailed map, noting where all of the Diggers went on their daily routines. Eric would be in school every day, check. Mom Digger would be at home except for Wednesday and Friday when she volunteered at the soup kitchen, check. Dad Digger would be at a few different places, as a general contractor he went where the calls were, check. The map looked like a cross between a football playbook and a conspiracy theorist's wall.

Wednesday rolled around and I honestly looked forward to donating some time at the soup kitchen. For being potential monsters, the Diggers were awfully dull so far. Eric hadn't shown up to school with any new bruises that I could see, and it was time for me to try and get some information from the source. I was in-scruff-nito as usual, I had been dressing down for the week. People noticed when a guy in a suit was parked outside their building. They would expect a cop, an evangelist, or worse. A guy with a hoodie and a cup of coffee? Then I'm just some weirdo and no one seems to care that much. The food service at the church started with breakfast at nine a.m., so volunteers had to be there by seven to start putting the meal together.

When I saw Walt again he introduced me to Sarah as one of the newest volunteers.

"He keeps his word, this man," Walt told her, slapping me between the shoulder blades, "said he'd be here Wednesday and look at him!"

"Of course, Walt." Sarah's voice was stronger than I was expecting, like a rich alto. I'm not sure what I was expecting, but it wasn't this. "Welcome to the brigade, Nick." She shook my hand, and then we didn't speak so much as she barked instructions to the volunteers, and we did what she said as quickly as possible.

If you've never helped feed the homeless a meal, you should spend a few of your hours on it. I'd never been without a permanent residence, and the closest to being homeless I ever came was when I kicked myself out of my parent's house for some stupid reason and couch-surfed for a weekend until I realized I was an idiot and went home. Being confronted with the reality of homelessness and poverty was a total brain shift. These folks were all in need in one way or another. Not everyone was homeless, some just needed the hot meal because all their money went to pay for the roof over their heads. Some just brought their children, to make sure they at least got something warm in their bellies. Some came not just for the food, but for the company. Men and women met, chatted, and smiled over their plates of eggs and bacon. There was plenty of room in the basement of the church, where they served today, and people lingered longer than they needed to. It was an opportunity to sit and breathe in a place where they weren't being judged or looked down on.

Samuel said, "God helps those who help themselves," and I understood what he was saying. Helping yourself wasn't always the choice that you would expect. Accepting that you needed help, even just the courage to start, was a big leap for a lot of people. Too many people thought that anyone taking charity wasn't helping themselves, but I got a new perspective when I saw people in that situation. Sure, there was abuse of the system. It was unavoidable, but that wasn't the majority. These were just people who needed help. I saw one man wearing freshly pressed clothes because he was going for a job interview that morning. There was a mother feeding her children while filling out a student loan application. It made me hopeful, just a little bit, and helped me understand even more why Samuel made the choice that he did. Would I sell my soul so that these people could eat? I just might.

We had finished up service, and I hadn't had a chance to speak with Sarah much. I worked my way over to where she was wiping down tables and pitched in.

"Thanks for the help today," I told Sarah, while cleaning a table next to hers, "I've never done anything like this."

"I can tell," she chuckled. "I'm kidding. You did fine, thank you for volunteering. We don't get enough new people, or young people, or breathing people. Any people honestly."

"Well, I'm glad to be here. It's been an eye-opening experience."

"About that," she said, pausing in her efforts. "Try not to make it the only one. Too many people have their epiphany, come help at the soup kitchen for one day, and then decide that they've done their part. It's not a one-time thing, people need to eat every day and when your belly is full you tend to forget about that."

I held up my hands in surrender, "Hey, I get it. I'm not surprised, but I get it."

Sarah stretched her arm to reach the far end of one of the tables, her short-sleeved shirt riding up toward her shoulder. I didn't get much of a look but there was no mistaking the edge of a large bruise on her bicep. She caught me looking and pulled her sleeve to cover it, eyes refusing to find mine.

"So," I tried to cover the awkward moment with awkward questions, "I've been working part-time at Amistad as a one-on-one tutor, that's where I met your son. He had great things to say about your work here. He's very proud of you." I worried about how easily I fabricated this whole backstory.

Sarah smiled when I mentioned her son, and she went back to cleaning her table. "He's a sweet boy, and if it got you here to help, I'm happy for it."

"He doesn't say much about his father, though. What does he do for a living?" I continued wiping, trying to be as nonchalant as possible. This was small talk, right?

"He's a contractor, general work, for one of the property management companies in town." She shrugged. "Not glamorous, but it pays the bills."

"Oh, that's right. Sometimes I see Eric being dropped off by a man in a contractor's van," I improvised. "That must be your husband...?" I trailed off, hoping she would fill in the blank.

"Daniel," she said it heavily, the name held volumes. You could usually learn a few things about how someone felt about a person based on the way they said their name. Just the name. "Daniel, my husband" might have spread the emphasis. "Daniel" was like a brick dropped onto the table.

"Right, thanks, we haven't had the chance to meet yet either."

"He's very busy," she said very quickly.

"No worries. I had just meant to catch him the other day to let him know that I was relieved about Eric recovering well."

"What?" she had frozen, hands gripping her rag tightly.

"The bump," I continued, "the one on his forehead? Eric said he had tripped and fallen or something like that. Kids, right? I just meant to say that I was happy he didn't have a concussion or anything like that."

"Children are very resilient." She had straightened and was still as a statue, looking past me.

"Oh, I know, I remember when I was younger, I could have been hit in the head with a baseball during practice and been laughing about it the next day." These were the good intentions that the road to hell was paved with, I thought to myself. "I had originally thought he should go see the school nurse when he said he hadn't been to see his doctor to make sure—"

"Please," Sarah whispered, but it stopped me mid-sentence.

"Sorry?" I stuttered.

She took a few steps to stand closer to me, so her low-pitched voice wouldn't carry. Her demeanor had changed entirely in those steps. She went from the confident matriarch of the soup kitchen to a timid creature, almost a mouse.

"Please," she said again, speaking so only I could hear her, "don't talk to the nurse. Don't talk to anyone."

"I was just worried about Eric, a lump that size and he certainly could have had a—" I was cut short again.

"No," she spat. "He's fine, it was just an accident. The last time one of his teachers talked to the nurse, they called." She picked up speed, her voice becoming slightly frantic, pleading. "I can't have them call. Please, you don't understand."

"Then help me understand." I tried to adjust my posture, to be as harmless and receptive as possible.

"I can't... it's just..." She was on the verge of either opening up or running away. She took a breath and collected herself, regaining her stature and composure. "I'm a strong woman. I can take care of myself. But Eric is just a boy. My boy. If you tell the nurse, they won't call the house. They'll call *Daniel*." And with the gravity of that name dropped once again, she picked up her rag and quick-marched toward the kitchen as far away from me as she could possibly get.

I finished out the shift and barely remembered to check in with Walt before I left.

"Thank you kindly for your assistance today my friend," Walt said, and as he was a serial shoulder slapper, I was developing a bruise myself. "If your schedule accommodates, maybe we'll see you again next week?"

"I'd like that," I replied, "and thank you for introducing me to Sarah. She's a remarkable woman."

"Yes," he nodded, "I'm glad we can help her here."

I squinted an eye at Walt. "I thought she was helping everyone else?"

"That's true, very true. But sometimes it is in that way everyone else also helps her." Walt put his hand on my back in a fatherly way as he walked me out of the church. "She's more troubled than you are, if you'd believe it. But when she pulls the strings of this kitchen, it sings like a violin. Galatians tells us to 'bear one another's burdens' and so we shall."

CHAPTER 14

Have you ever had the experience of validating your suspicions when all you wanted to do was to be proven wrong? That was me.

I spent the rest of the week, and the entirety of the next, tailing Daniel to keep tabs on where he went and who he talked to. Spending as much time as I did watching someone do the same thing every day, I started noticing little things. Lunch was always out of a small red cooler, eaten outside on the bumper of his van with the back doors open if the weather was good. Some days it was a sandwich, others something out of a plastic container, but every day he had the same thermos. It was still early Spring, so I wasn't surprised to see it. On Thursday, armed with some bias against the man I was watching, and starting to nitpick the scenes in front of me, I realized what had been nagging at me the whole week. It hit me like a bolt of lightning, staring at Daniel's lunchtime beverage.

Steam.

Well, a lack of steam. Every day at lunch he had that thermos, and every day he poured himself cups of something brown to drink out of it. I had assumed it was coffee or tea, but there was never steam rising from his cup, or when he opened the thermos. Unfortunately, that wasn't a slam dunk on "Eric's father is an abusive alcoholic" but I suddenly had something to go on. Necessity was the mother of invention, and I was looking at a difficult problem. Separating a man from what might be his booze was a tricky proposition in even regular situations. I couldn't rightly walk up to him and ask for a sip, no matter how dressed down I was. I didn't think I had the acting experience to pass as homeless. Luckily for me, there was a laundry list of heist movies I had watched ticking through my head, and a plan was quickly formed. This was either going to go off flawlessly, or I was going to need to beat a hasty retreat.

Friday arrived, and I followed Daniel to his building of the day, a brick apartment building on Howe Street. Luck was on my side so far. The weather was good, which meant my target would be outside, and there was a small alley next to the building. Mr. Digger played his part and set himself up with a sandwich and his thermos, poured himself a small cup, and took out his cell phone.

I walked into the alley and called the contracting company that he worked for, asking to speak with Daniel Digger. I made up an excuse that I was calling from his doctor's office and needed to speak with him; they said they would ring him and then patch me through if they could reach him. Watching from the alley, I heard Daniel's phone ring and saw him answer it. I couldn't hear who was on the other end, but I assumed it was the dispatcher. He looked concerned, I assumed it was when they told him it was his doctor's office, but he nodded and walked away from his lunch to get into the driver's seat of his van. I had hoped that he wouldn't want to take a call like that out in public, and my luck continued to hold.

I wasn't going to have much time so I pocketed my phone, pulled my hood up, and strolled as quickly and quietly as I could over to the back of the van. The small cup was empty but I bent over and with one quick sniff, I struck liquid gold. Whiskey.

"Hey!" a man's voice yelled from inside the van. Apparently, a dead line didn't keep his attention for very long once the dispatcher patched him through, and he had turned in his seat to look out the back of the van.

I didn't know what to do, but I sure as hell wasn't going to let him see my face. My brain spun quickly and I grabbed half his sandwich, kept my head down, and bolted away from the van into the alleyway. Halfway down the alley, I heard footsteps beat their way to the entry of the corridor. I was all the way through and turned right, chancing a quick glance through the corner of my hood to see Daniel, back-lit, watching me but not following.

My lungs were on fire and my legs turned to jelly before I let myself stop. I tossed the sandwich into the nearest trashcan and leaned against whatever building I had found myself at. It was five minutes before I got my breath back, and thirty before I walked a circuitous and paranoid route to my car. I was exhausted, I was shaky from the adrenaline, and I had all of the information I needed.

That was overly dramatic, the whole spy thriller mode was getting to me. I had more information, sure, and if I was lucky, Daniel would assume that the hooded sandwich thief was just a hungry homeless person. I went back to the office, assuming I'd be forgiven for coming in casual since it was both Friday and halfway through the day. Lester gave me the hairy eyeball, complete with one raised eyebrow, but didn't say anything. I walked to my part of the office and knocked on Lu's door.

"Come in!" piped a cheerful voice. I had to give it to him, he didn't work very hard to instill fear and despair like the brochure said. I walked in and took a seat opposite Lu at his desk.

"I like the homeless-chic," Lu grinned at me. "No, it's fine, you asked for a week of surveillance, and it's not over yet."

"It's pretty much over," I said. "I've gotten just about everything I need."

"Ready to go over it with me?" He steepled his fingers, resting his elbow on the desk.

"I have decision-making power on this?" I asked.

"Absolutely," Lu replied, "but within reason. Can't have you going off half-cocked on your first assignment."

"I think I'd like to take the weekend and think about it. I'll take this afternoon to put together a report and then sleep on it for a few days."

"Very sensible," Lu nodded. "I like taking a measured approach in these kinds of situations. You bring me your recommendations on Monday morning, and we'll talk about the next steps."

I spent the rest of the afternoon glued to my cubicle, writing up my notes from the week's surveillance. This must be what detective work was like, all this paperwork. It helped with my perspective though, remembering the events of the week, and I felt pretty clear on my conclusion by the time I got to the end of the report. I printed two copies, left one on Lu's desk, and packed one to go with me. He had already gone home, or wherever the Devil went when he left early on a Friday. The whole situation left me feeling a little dirty. I had gotten the information I was fishing for but I had used a few different tactics, none of which were honest. I glanced at the ticker above my desk, I had forgotten all about it until I was mooning over my own confused ethics.

One hundred out of a thousand.

Hell.

Chapter 15

Everyone was a little bit evil, as the saying went, right? I was trying to help someone, someone who was failed by the system so far. I went in assuming I was going to have to improvise, fly by the seat of my pants, and that's what I did. Did I lie? Yes. Did I steal? A sandwich, so I guess yes. But I also helped people at a soup kitchen and confirmed, to a point, that a man was abusing his family and my efforts were going to help stop it.

I didn't feel bad for myself, and on reflection, I was barely surprised that I had accumulated some hellish stock. After I realized I didn't hate myself, I came to the conclusion that I was probably rationalizing all of it and it was a seriously slippery slope downhill from where I was standing, morally.

Forgive the rambling, it was a distinctly confusing time to be me.

I slept for at least twelve hours that night, well into Saturday. A whole lot of nothing (we could call it surveillance), and then a whole lot of something (we could call that running like hell) apparently left my body out of sorts. Luckily, Odin's feeder kept him in kibble for a few days regardless of my intervention, so he wasn't standing on my face, looking at his theoretical wristwatch and complaining about meal time when I finally woke up. He was, however, purring against my chest like a cement mixer, which was what finally woke me up. My dreams had been very strange, which wasn't surprising given my latest escapades. Not only was I buried under a mountain of cat, but I also felt like I had dreamt my way through a few existential crises. If that didn't leave you dazed upon waking, I wasn't sure what would. I spent the day in almost complete inactivity, interspersed with periods of report reading and frantic pacing. I second and third-guessed everything at least twice before declaring to the room, and a very confused cat, that I was absolutely done with the whole business and would spend the rest of the day watching television. They say that the smartest people need to take breaks from their own intelligence every once in a while, otherwise it drives them mad. I wasn't that kind of smart, but I'd take the excuse. I had eaten nothing on the day's rampage of inefficiency so one Chinese delivery later and I was on the couch with Odin, feeding him bits of chicken out of my lo mein. He'd had a rough week, so I figured he deserved it.

I also did something I'd been putting off for months, after the revelations of the week. I called my parents. I wasn't sure how long it had been since I last talked to them. As far as they knew, I was still working at the coffee shop and thinking about what best to do next on the flat rollercoaster that was my life at the time. I won't bore you with the sentimental details but, rest assured, they were as confused as you'd expect. They hadn't heard from their son in forever, and here he called out of the blue to tell them how much he loved them and to thank them for being such good and kind parents. They probably thought I was on drugs or contemplating suicide and asked whether I was okay and should they call some-one. I managed to talk them down from that particular ledge and claimed a stressful week had left me thankful for the good things in my life, which was actually true. They were proud of me for the new job, even though I couldn't give them any real details about it and, when I hung up the phone, I had a warm feeling in my chest that wasn't just heartburn from the take-out.

The day was a complete bust, but I had confirmed one thing in my own mind. I needed to be absolutely, positively, one hundred percent sure that I wanted to give these results to Samuel before finding out what the next step of 'stop the abuse' was going to be. While thinking about this, I poured myself a shot of whiskey from a very small supply I keep handy but just smelling it made me think of the thermos and the day before. I hated alcohol abuse, but I tossed it down the drain and had a cup of tea before bed instead. Resolved to spend one of my days off on surveillance, I set an alarm, picked up Odin, and curled up in bed. Cats make excellent teddy bears when they're almost the size of small bears themselves, and I needed a little human contact. Odin was going to have to do. He put up with me until suddenly he couldn't, like cats do, and then dutifully took up his place at the foot of my bed. Despite my twelve hours of rest the night prior, I fell asleep almost immediately. Sometimes being set on a course of action freed my mind from the worry and let me get some peace.

When I woke up I noticed that Amy had left me a voicemail, it came in some time while I was asleep. She had been working seriously weird hours at the bookstore so she probably didn't even realize it was after ten when she called to check up on me. She wanted to get together for coffee on Sunday— she had been working all day Saturday, otherwise she'd have called sooner. I sent her a quick text that I was probably going to be caught up with work for the day but would let her know if any of that was going to change. I included a note that I would like to see her, even though it took a few re-reads and almost-hitting-sends before I finally sent that part.

I dressed business casual. I didn't want an accidental sighting to put me in the same hoodie I was in the day before. My midnight protector received a whole can of wet food before I left for the day, in thanks for his vigilance, and I found my way back to the Digger house. They lived in one of the neighborhoods west of the hospitals, on Stevens Street. I parked down the street but close enough that I could see the driveway and keep track of the vehicle parked there. I had brought a sandwich and some drinks with me, so there wasn't much danger of me having to go away to miss anything. It was more than halfway through the day when Sarah and Eric left the house on an errand. They had some bags with them, so I assumed they would be out shopping. Daniel, on the other hand, stayed in the house for another hour before getting in his van and heading a few miles away. He parked on College Street on the Green, so I found a space a few cars ahead of him and watched my mirrors until he walked past my car. I hadn't had to do much following on foot but, even on a Sunday, there were enough people walking in the same direction that I wasn't worried about being spotted. He walked south on College for a block, and I followed him until he turned into the Cornerstone, one of the dive bars on that corner. It was a college town, so bars were pretty common, this just happened to be one of the more local dives.

I waited about five minutes before following Daniel into the bar. It was a pretty busy place, for a Sunday. Daniel had found himself a seat at the bar itself. I contented myself with a table by the wall. The place wasn't so large that I couldn't keep a rough eye on the proceedings from where I was. Before deciding if I was going to engage my target, I was going to do some fly-on-the-wall information gathering first.

Observation one: Daniel was a regular. He knew the bartender, Sal, by name, and Sal knew his drink of choice, a double shot of whiskey with a beer chaser.

Observation two: Daniel's choice of bar friends was the grizzled sort. These were long-time tradesmen, mechanics, and laborers. Some people, when the work wore them down, tended to dull the pain and cut loose at the bar. Mostly back slapping and swearing, telling off-color jokes, or making misogynistic comments about the women who were brave enough to even set foot in the bar.

I didn't get to make my third observation for a while. I nursed a beer, reassuring the waitress that I was going to be an easy customer, and watched the evening unfold. Daniel and his barflies drank with a pretty single-minded determination. He was well into his third beer, that was with six accompanying shots of whiskey, for anyone counting, and it was a couple of hours later at that point. It wasn't even time for dinner yet, but I didn't think he was going to spend the whole night there at that pace. I decided to belly up to the bar and took up a seat near Daniel, with one empty stool between us. I nodded in Daniel's direction and then addressed Sal by name and ordered what Daniel had been drinking since he arrived. Sal didn't recognize me, he knew I wasn't a regular, but he'd served so many people he just assumed I must have introduced myself once or twice before and this was a repeat visit.

During my classwork, I learned about the sales technique called mirroring. It was where a salesperson adopted the behaviors of the customer he was trying to sell. It could make the mark more inclined to trust them since they were more like them.

"Now there's a man who knows how to drink." Daniel raised his beer to me, liquid sloshing dangerously toward the lip of his glass. My luck, carrying over from Friday, held.

"Cheers." I raised my whiskey, took a short sip, and then waited to see if he was going to make small talk. He was fairly engaged with his beer so, after a minute or two, I decided to cast some line and see what I could catch. I took another sip of whiskey and blew out the heat of the alcohol with a "Hell of a week, yeah?"

"Huh?" Daniel was working himself toward numb, so it took some effort to focus on me and the conversation I was trying to draw him into. "Oh, yeah, hell of a fuckin' week."

"I think I get a break on the weekend," I continued, "but no, of course not. Wife's nagging me to go shopping, kids want to go see this, do that. I put in a solid week and I want some time to unwind." This, Your Honor, was leading the witness.

"Damn straight." Daniel held his glass out and we clinked, shot to pint. "I had to get the hell out of the house too. Couldn't stand it."

"Amen brother," I said, "wife and kids?"

"Ha," he barked a laugh and sipped his beer, "one good-for-nothing wife that doesn't do a goddamn thing around the house, and one soft pansy of a son. But that's my lot, right?"

"Yeah?" I wanted to sound interested. "That's the standard complaint though, right? No one's wife does enough, and every man's son isn't the John Wayne we all want him to be." I winked at him. "I bet they're okay."

"Wish I was, man," he sighed, "wish I was. Woman's too feisty for her own good, and I get nothing but lip." He used his glass to punctuate his statements, spilling golden drops across the bar. "I'm trying to raise *my* son right. My father did the same, and his father too. We turned out just right. Strong, independent, successful men. Family, house, car, white picket fence. Nothing but arguments from her, 'Oh you can't treat him like that,' she tells me. Don't you tell me what I can or can't do to teach *my* son. I mean, what would *you* do? You've got a boy, right?"

"Well," I improvised again, unwilling to create a family backstory out of whole cloth, "I can't say I had a good example to follow in my dad, doesn't sound like mine was like yours."

"My dad." He leaned against the bar, obviously getting nostalgic. "God bless that man, he was the best there was. Sure, he was hard as hell on me growing up, but look at me!" He posed, and I looked. "You don't need any better. My son? He's only in elementary school. He should want to be a fireman, a policeman, or a construction worker. You know what he wants to be when he grows up?"

"President?" My sarcasm was hard to turn off.

"Pfft. President. He wants to be a goddamned artist. No son of mine is going to waste his life on something like that." Daniel nodded to himself and drank more of his beer.

"Well, he's a kid, what does he know? Your wife is probably just trying to be supportive. Mothers love their sons, right?" I tried to commiserate, but I was having a hard time faking it at this point.

"What does he know?" Daniel's voice rose slightly. "He knows what his father tells him, which should be like gospel, and his father tells him to stop acting like a girl and hit the damn ball when I throw it at him." He was very intense by now, his voice holding an anger that wasn't in any way justified by the words he said. "Now I'm going to go home to a house that isn't clean, have dinner that's barely edible, and listen to my son tell me about all of the sissy things he did with his mother all day."

"Yeah." I didn't have a lot left in me to work this conversation, I'd had enough and was hoping it would burn itself out. Luckily, I didn't have to wait long. Daniel pulled his wallet out and dropped some cash on the bar.

"What was your name again?" He had turned to me, after giving Sal a silent salute.

"Bob," I said and held out my hand to shake.

Daniel shook my hand, in that overly aggressive alpha male kind of way. "Daniel," he said, "good talking with you, but I've been here too long already. You think your wife's nagging about her shopping, well wait till I get home to mine. She doesn't like it when I go out drinking on Sundays. Like that's going to stop me. My house. My money. My rules." He put his finger against my chest and jabbed with each of his points. "Well, Bob, I'll see you around."

Observation three: Daniel was an angry drunk.

Daniel stumbled toward the door. I thought for a minute about calling the cops and reporting his license plate for drunk driving, but then I remembered the conversation I had with Sarah. I'd have felt righteous, but it would have caused her and Eric nothing but trouble. I felt guilty thinking that if he wrapped his car around a tree on the way home, it would make things both more and less complicated for the remaining Diggers. I was just going to have to wait until the next day and talk to Lu about options.

"Hey, Sal." I flagged down the bartender. He stared at me with another look of *Do I know you, pal?* for one second before giving up the search of his mental database.

"What's up, bud?" he asked, propping himself up on the bar with one elbow.

"What's with that guy, Daniel?" I asked, innocently.

"Danny?" he smiled. "What's with him? Nothin', man, he's an okay guy. Sunday regular. Just has a couple drinks before he heads home."

"Seems a little high-strung," I volunteered.

"Eh, he's not the happiest drunk but he's never started a fight here. Talks to some folks, or keeps to himself, but if he gets pissed off, he just takes himself somewhere else. Probably takes it out on his wife or somethin'."

"What?" I looked horrified, I'm sure.

"Hey, bud, I just work here." He took Daniel's empty glasses and walked over to the sink, realizing he had probably been a little too candid, the conversation was definitely over.

I finished my drinks and then took a walk around the Green for a bit to make sure I was sober enough to drive. I couldn't help but worry I had spun Daniel up and it was going to make whatever happened to Sarah and Eric worse.

Maybe I wasn't as good at this as I thought. Either way, I was pretty sure that I was done drinking whiskey.

CHAPTER 16

I tossed and turned that night, waking up at least every hour on the hour. Odin was so annoyed with me that he left the room, sleeping on the couch instead of dealing with me flopping around and throwing the covers over him one more time. You would think that growing up in the Northeast, I'd be pretty immune to guilt. No one, however, was as good at guilting me as my own brain. Nothing would clear my mind of the spiraling thoughts that I had done something to cause Sarah and Eric grief. I thought I understood a bit better what the defense of "I was just doing my job" felt like. It wasn't a very strong one, and it was made less so by the fact that I had gotten caught up in how damn slick I had been.

Sarah opened up enough to me on the first day I met her, and I got Daniel talking within five minutes. I had something to prove! I wasn't just an espresso jockey or a college dropout. I was a problem solver, an out-of-the-box thinker. I was... manipulating people, and I couldn't figure out how I felt about it. Rationalization, and I was getting good at that too, brought certain phrases to my mind like "for your own good," "the ends justify the means," or "it's what they deserve." It was all bullshit, and I rolled around for hours trying to fight my way to some kind of conclusion about what I had gotten myself into, what I had started myself, and what the hell I was doing in this handbasket.

I finally fell asleep around four a.m. but woke with a start at six. I jumped out of bed and hit the shower, getting ready for the office. I was done with my surveillance, I didn't need any more information, but I had to know. Actions had consequences, and if I had been the cause of some, I was damn well going to witness it.

I parked in my usual spot outside the school, ready to watch the drop-off line. I hadn't even caffeinated, I was that anxious to see Eric. I continued the rationalization train and assured myself that last night was probably par for the course for Daniel, and nothing I had done would change anything. Not even I was buying it.

The time dragged on, nothing happened quickly when I waited for it, but finally the van arrived. I got out of my car and moved closer to the school so I could see properly. They had their turn at the curb and Eric got out, walking toward the entrance.

Face: no new bruises, check. Torso: nothing obvious that I could see. Okay, maybe this was just another Monday morning. Except that he was limping. Not enough that any casual observer would make a big deal about it, but I had been watching this kid for a whole week. He had a slight hitch to his right side that said something wasn't right, but he didn't call attention to it by favoring one side or the other. I hated that he must have been used to pretending to be fine.

Guilt filled me, white hot, as I stormed back to my car. Every choice swear I had ever learned was muttered in a litany under my breath as I drove to the office. Lester smiled in my direction and was about to say 'good morning' before he noticed the storm cloud I carried with me and decided it was better to look back to his computer. I dropped my things in my cubicle and sat, trying to compose myself, before knocking on Lu's door. My right leg twitched up and down, and I couldn't force myself to relax. Finally, I stood up, glancing at the ticker above my desk.

200 out of a thousand. Fine, I deserved that.

I knocked on the office door and walked in after hearing a muffled noise that sounded like "come in." Lu leaned back in his chair, reading a newspaper. He folded it as I walked in, and turned to face the front, my report was sitting on his desk. I couldn't tell if he had read it; it was still in the folder I had left on his desk.

"Nick! Come on in." He gestured at the chair across from him. "You look like you've had a hell of a morning. Probably a hell of a night too."

I sat down and took a few breaths. The last time I was in his office, I felt like I had made a fool of myself, sputtering about the situation with Eric.

Lu didn't wait for me to compose myself. "You stole his sandwich?" he said through a toothy smile. His eyes twinkled, full of mischief.

Apparently, he knew exactly how to break through my black mood. I couldn't help it, the fact that he brought up what might be the most inane part of my experience of the past week just broke me. I started laughing, he started laughing, and that continued as a welcome catharsis for the next few minutes.

"What the hell am I doing, Lu?" I finally asked, breathless, wiping tears from my eyes.

"From the look of it," Lu flipped open the folder of my report, "what you needed to."

Even when the boss was the Devil, I felt a little surge of pride when he told me I was doing something right. I didn't let it override the guilt or concern that I had, but it definitely bolstered me for the conversation.

"Look, Nick," he continued, "this isn't going to be the cleanest business. Not the dirtiest either, I wouldn't ask you to do that. I picked you for the way you think, and your mental agility. This?" He stabbed a finger at the report. "This shows me that I made the right choice. Samuel was right to say you were the man for this job, and I'll agree with him there."

I hiccupped slightly, wiping away the last of my tears. "Flattery will get you everywhere."

"Touché," Lu motioned toward me as if awarding a point. "you're sounding like me."

"So what do we do now?"

"Well," Lu stroked his chin, "it's a complicated situation. Our contract is with Samuel, and I agreed to handle two problems for him. First, the building of the school. Speaking of which, you should attend the ground-breaking ceremony tomorrow. Samuel recently came into a large amount of cash, lottery I think, and decided to donate it all to build the school and fund it in perpetuity. Lovely man, really." Lu smiled, smugly. "Second, handling the situation with poor master Eric. He wasn't that specific, just that we make the abuse, if confirmed, stop. Beyond that, we've got a bit of carte blanche. Samuel did confide in me that if Mr. Digger was in a position to disallow future transgressions, regardless of the potential victim, he would rest more easily."

"So we just make it up now?" I wasn't sure how this worked.

"Make it up? You mean like poof," Lu snapped his fingers, "Daniel is on a desert island with an ample food supply, unable to influence the future of the human race?" He chuckled. "I do like the idea of that, but it's not how it works. Remember that whole free will thing I told you about? Troubling business, honestly. I can't just magic him away, he's got his own measure of free will that I can't tamper with directly." Lu paused. "That's what lets him drink heavily and then go home to beat his wife and child." His voice dropped an octave on the last sentence.

"You're not saying we can't do anything, are you?" I was surprised and it showed.

Lu waved his hands. "No, no. I'm just saying it's not going to be as easy as waving a magic wand. Why do you think I have this extensive operation? I'm a busy man, and I'm in a lot of places at once, literally. But there's a limit to the amount of co-location I'm willing to do. I need a trained and diligent staff to work on these problems, with my occasional input. Case in point, you."

"Decision-making power."

"Precisely." Lu pointed at me, hand shaped like a gun, and pulled the trigger. "So here's my suggestion, as your mentor. Go talk with legal and put together a package. We need him to agree to it, they can help you with all of the standard clauses. He's not the brightest bulb, so you can probably hide some language in the appendices."

"You want me to put together a deal that's good enough to get him to sell his soul? Isn't that like rewarding him for bad behavior?"

"Not if you do it right, but I'll leave those details up to you."

I nodded, slowly. "And then what?"

"Then?" Lu's teeth shone in a predatory grin. "You sell it to him."

"You're leaving me a lot of leeway here." I leaned back in my chair, resting my hands on my head, thinking about the scope of what I needed to do.

"That's the idea. I'm not going to lie, everything is a test. That's not just about you; it's about everyone. This isn't your first test. You had to go through a fair amount of training to get here, but it's your biggest so far and the first real independent challenge."

"I'll do my best."

"That's what I expect." Lu picked up his newspaper again, and I was clearly dismissed.

I also had no idea where the legal department was. I decided to ask Lester for help, and he was more than happy to show me to the group and chat my ear off about it on the way there. He explained that, as far as he could tell, each of the sites had their own legal department. There were tons of contracts generated every day, in every location, so the volume was enough to keep at least a small group of lawyers and paralegals employed for eternity. They were situated in their own suite on a separate floor below to discourage random arrivals and help ensure 'intentional' visits. Lester told me that this group was very busy, but mostly polite, and that he'd introduce me to a paralegal that he had drinks with some evenings. It wasn't the lawyers that I needed to keep friendly with, he told me, it was the paralegals. They were the ones who did all the work; the lawyers just reviewed and signed off on it. I wasn't going to argue, but I doubted it was as cut and dry as that. On top of that, it wasn't like any law practice I'd seen before. The Devil didn't need to worry himself too much with legality, it was ninety-nine point nine percent contract law and internal specifications as well.

Jessica was shorter than me and didn't seem nearly as friendly as Lester had indicated but was intensely interested in her job. She had a tendency to peer over her large framed glasses like she was staring at an insect. When she found out that I was new, she wasn't particularly happy with Lester. It seemed he saddled her with a lot of new folk when they came down with legal questions. The good news was I had some idea of what I wanted and asked for some sample contracts given the situation at hand. Jessica sat me in a spare office and gave me a tablet connected to the database. It wasn't open access, I wouldn't even know what to look for if it was, and she fed me samples and templates from her desk.

This scene repeated itself for a few days. I would meet Jessica in the morning, delivering a mocha latte. I wasn't an idiot and needed to keep on her good side. Lester, her club buddy, knew how she took her coffee and was more than happy to help me out. Trading the cup for the tablet, I'd busy myself for hours reading reference material and previous contracts, taking notes, and beginning to work up a draft of my own.

The contracts, when I could wade through the jargon, were fascinating. You wouldn't be surprised with how many people sold their souls, but you might be surprised at how cheaply they did it. Jessica tried to send me relevant contracts, so I saw a lot of people looking for escape clauses from their real lives. It was a combination of people who needed out, wanted out, and deserved a lot worse than they got. Lu said that the bad ones punched their own tickets, but it looked like some of them signed on the dotted line instead. There were "good behavior" clauses in a few, which I took a lot of notes on, and none of them had any egregious allowances.

I was no lawyer (the most I got was the equivalent of a 101 class in my training) but having this much historical information to go on was helpful. By Wednesday, I had a good working copy, and on Thursday morning, I handed Jessica the latte along with a hard copy of my draft. She gave me a raised eyebrow but took the pages and told me to come back that afternoon. I busied myself until lunch and then popped downstairs to see her. She greeted me with the same raised eyebrow that she sent me off with.

"It wasn't unsalvageable." She nearly smirked, which I took as high praise.

"So it could work?" by her face, I sounded a little too enthusiastic.

"I made some edits, a few additions and subtractions, your language was too non-specific in a few places, so I tightened the whole thing up." She handed me the sheaf of paper, full of red pen and sticky notes. "You're welcome."

I took the packet from her gratefully. "Thanks a lot for your help."

"You're one of the better ones, Nick, you did most of the work yourself. Half the people Les brings to visit expect us to do the research *and* write the contract. Like we're not already doing that for *our* bosses." She peered over her glasses at me, down at the papers. "You've got it out for this guy, don't you." It wasn't a question.

"Reap what you sow, right?"

"I guess. Come see me next time you need help with something. You owe me for this." She turned back to her computer, enjoying the last word.

CHAPTER 17

"Handshake deal?" Lu was reading my freshly printed final draft, while I sat nervously across from him at his desk. I used all of Jessica's comments to revise it into as air-tight a contract as I could and then scheduled a meeting for Friday to talk it over with the boss.

Handshakes were how all the old contracts used to be sealed. Parties would discuss the terms and then shake on it, simple as that. One party would get what they asked for, and Lu would take custodianship of a soul. Sounded pretty straightforward, right? Except with the advent of the printed word, and then computers, his legal strategy got to be as complicated as any in the modern day. People wanted to see contracts and nitpicked every clause and paragraph. Well, the smart ones did. Some even employed lawyers to read the fine print, if they could get one to believe them. I found a reference in one of the samples from Jessica to an agent putting a handshake clause into the contract. The whole thing was on paper, provided to the client, and the terms written down were executed by a handshake. In the sample case, it was all above board. The client was an elderly gentleman from the country, and that's how he liked to make his agreements. The agent in charge of that case didn't see any problem with it, so he wrote it into the contract. It wasn't that you couldn't have a verbal agreement and seal it with a shake these days—it's that no one wanted to. I thought I might be able to use that to my advantage.

"Old-school. Smart. I like it." Lu finished speed-reading the contract and set it back on his desk. It wasn't too thick, but still hit the surface with a meaty thump. It was nearly a week of work in the making, and I hoped it would be substantial. "You sure you want to go this route?"

I twisted my hands together. "The more I thought about it, and what Samuel wanted, the closer I got to this. It's less than he deserves."

"Hey, you're not going to get any arguments from me. I just want to make sure you're clear on the consequences."

"Yes, sir," I said, picking up the contract. "And it'll happen? All I have to do is get him to read the contract and shake hands with me?"

"Bingo. Good work. Take the rest of the day off, you've been working too hard." Lu leaned back. "I assume you're going to try and catch him this weekend?"

"Right," I stood up, "I know where he'll be."

I left the office and went home to change into my street clothes. After bailing on Amy for coffee last Sunday I messaged her, asking if she wanted to grab a bite to eat on Friday. Given that I had the rest of the day off, I figured to surprise her at work, and then bum around downtown until she was off. I had until Sunday, and even that was a self-imposed deadline, so I might as well try to enjoy the start of my weekend.

I walked into the Off-Campus Bookstore, which was a cute tautological name for what it was. A bookstore. Off campus. Amy liked it because it was hip, compared to working at the actual campus bookstore. Also, because it was independent, they had shop cats. She loved shop-cats and always said it was like shopping in someone's living room with the cats flopped all over the place. When I walked in there weren't a lot of customers and Amy saw me right away. She also saw something in my face that worried her and immediately looked concerned.

"Nick! Hey, what's wrong?"

"What?" I brushed it off. "Nothing's wrong. Can't a guy come see his friend when his boss surprises him with an afternoon off?"

"That job's got perks," she grinned at me, "right? Well, you just look... maybe you look like you need a friend. So I'm glad you came. Wait!" She ran behind the counter and came back holding a large, orange tabby and pressed it into my arms. "Hold this. She's very sweet."

Few things instantly melted away worry, even worry that I didn't realize I was holding onto, like a fuzzy animal being thrust into my arms. Amy was right, I needed that. I held the cat gently, and when she didn't seem to mind me holding her, I buried my nose in the soft fur on the top of her head. I mumbled some thanks to Amy, and she busied herself behind the counter.

I put the cat down after a minute and leaned up against the counter. "I didn't plan to stay long, I'm sure you're busy, but I wanted to say hi before wasting the rest of my afternoon somewhere."

"I'm glad you came in," Amy suddenly looked shy. "We're still on for dinner, right?"

"Yeah, I wasn't planning anything fancy though."

She looked a little disappointed. Sometimes I just didn't pay enough attention, and this was one of those times where words came out of my mouth before my brain could catch up to say, "It's a date, stupid!" I was still thinking like a poor coffee slinger but realized it was the end of my second week and I probably should have gotten paid at this point. "Hold that thought." I held up one finger and took out my phone. A quick check of my bank balance weakened my knees, and I nearly fell over.

"Never mind," I croaked, clearing my throat, "we're going wherever you want."

"Sushi!" Amy called out, clapped her hands together, and smiled until she squinted. "That place on Howe!"

"Sushi it is. I'll make a reservation before you're out of work. Meet me there at, what, six?"

"Yay!" She jumped up and down a little, which was insanely adorable in her black granny boots.

I went back to my car and sat in the driver's seat for a few minutes, then I took my phone out again and looked at my bank account. I didn't think I'd ever had that many zeroes. I mean, I wasn't suddenly rich, but Lu apparently believed in a comfortable living wage. Very comfortable. When I had been living check to check for as long as I had, I didn't know what to do with a surplus. So after making the reservation, I spent the afternoon doing things I would have done anyway: wandering around the Green, checking out shops but not buying anything, grabbing a snack, and contemplating the past couple of weeks. Then I reflected on the months leading up to it, and couldn't decide if I was blessed or cursed.

The afternoon passed faster than I expected, and I ended up rushing to drive home in time to change and get back to the restaurant. I thought about the look on Amy's face when she saw me in my work clothes and decided to dress up a bit: slacks, collared shirt, vest, no tie. Artfully tousle the hair, by which I mean leave it as messy as it was earlier, and I was all set.

Hanzo was Amy's favorite restaurant, or so she told me. I wasn't sure if it was her favorite restaurant or just one of many, but I wasn't going to argue. It was a cute little place on Howe Street, just a few blocks from York Square. It wasn't the trendiest place (that was two blocks over), but it was a homey restaurant and featured organic sprout salads from one of the local farms in addition to their regular food. I'd never been huge into the local food movement, mostly because I couldn't afford it, but I decided to try it. Hell, with my most recent paycheck, I could probably try everything at least once.

I rushed to the restaurant and managed to find parking, but still couldn't get to the door until it was five past six. Frustrated at myself for running late, I rushed in with my head down and almost collided with a beautifully dressed woman.

"Excuse me," I looked up. "I..." Whoa.

"Hi, Nick."

I wasn't the only one who had changed, and now I was especially glad that I had. Perhaps I underestimated the date-ness of tonight. I'd mentioned that Amy was pretty, but I had never seen her dressed as elegantly as she was. She was usually a circle skirt and boots kind of woman, but tonight, she was something else. It was simple. Just a 'little black dress' accented with silver jewelry, her hair put halfway up, and a little bit of makeup just to enhance the color of her eyes. Simple, and breathtaking.

And then she smiled at me. I didn't know which of us blushed first, but within moments, both of our cheeks burned. Neither of us said anything. I just held the door for her and asked for our table. We were seated and having tea poured before I could crack my jaw open and break the silence.

"You look amazing," I stage-whispered, trying to be funny and charming. I hoped I would pass for either of those.

"I said it before, Nick," Amy was still blushing slightly, "but you clean up pretty good."

"Well," I sniffed, tucking my thumbs into the shoulders of my vest like a pair of suspenders, "when you're an important guy like me, you have a certain standard to uphold."

We both laughed at that and sipped at our tea. The silence, now broken, passed into a comfortable rhythm of conversation. We ordered a three-course meal, splurging on a bottle of unfiltered saké to share, and then I asked about her week. Amy smiled as she told me about her new job at the bookstore and the interesting things she had been learning. Amy was a library science major. First, forget all of the librarian comments you were thinking, naughty or otherwise. I'd never met someone who decided to major in library science who wasn't amazing at finding information, which was what a lot of the program was about. It also exhibited her interest in just about everything, so it made sense that she'd want to work where she could get her hands on any piece of literature she wanted. A library might have been a little better, but she liked the retail experience. Far too chipper.

We talked our way through the appetizers and toasted to our new opportunities. I told her about my week, sharing details within reason, and the more I talked about it the more it sounded like an interesting and dangerous story. Like a spy thriller, or something close enough. I got caught up in the details, and ignored all of the boring parts, as if I was telling someone else's story rather than my own. It sounded important, even righteous, to investigate a family and save them from a monster lurking within it. I had gotten to the exciting part where I had to cover my discovery, by stealing the sandwich and running for my life, when the food arrived.

We had ordered a sushi boat. I always wanted to order one but never had either the money or the person to share a boatload of sushi with. The conversation came to an abrupt halt and we spent the next half hour ooh-ing and ahh-ing over the food, comparing notes, and suggesting tidbits to each other. I decided that this was something I could get used to, on many levels. After a short break and green tea ice cream for dessert, I declared a walk was required and asked if Amy would accompany me. We strolled down Chapel Street toward the Green.

"I didn't get to tell you the rest of my story," I said, turning to look at Amy's face, "because it's not over yet. The next part is more... complicated."

"It already sounds pretty complicated, Nick," she raised an eyebrow at me, "I'm curious what's going to make it more so."

"Well," I started, "let's say for starters that I've got as definitive proof as I need to go on."

"That's great!" she exclaimed. "I mean... not great that it's happening, it's physical abuse, but great that you can do something about it."

"Right, so how do you think I'm going to be able to do that?" It was a rhetorical question, and I was eager to finish my story, so I rushed on to explain the contract to her, and how I needed to get Daniel to sell his soul in exchange for what I would offer him. "This whole thing should have been handled a long time ago by the police, Family Services, the school, someone! People tried, but it fell through the cracks and never made it through the system."

She stopped me with a hand on my shoulder. "But now *you* can do something, right? Oh my God, that sounded so trite. I mean, you've got a solution."

"That's the part that worries me." I put my hand lightly on hers, squeezing it gently. "I can help, but to do that I have to convince someone to give up their soul. Even worse? He's a monster, so I don't have a problem with that. I'm having a hard time recognizing myself these days."

"Let me play Devil's advocate," Amy volunteered.

I laughed.

"I'm serious!" She stomped her foot, which was quite charming.

"Okay!" I relented. "Have at it."

"Fine." She walked around me in a circle like a shark, or a prosecuting attorney. "If he sells his soul, what happens?"

"In theory or practice?"

"Both?"

"Well," I nodded my head side to side, weighing my thoughts, "I don't know the practice so the *theory* is that he gives up his free will. That's it, if I can trust Lu. That's a weird statement, but he hasn't given me a reason not to trust him. He's probably been one of the most straightforward people I've ever met."

"Right," she continued the cross-examination, "and what happens if he went to prison?"

"He'd be in prison," I answered dully.

"Very astute, Sherlock." She slapped me lightly on the chest. "Play along. If he went to prison, would he be able to do whatever he wanted?"

"No." I was skeptical but could sense where she was going.

"Would he," she asked again, "be able to do anything that wasn't expressly permitted by the prison system?"

"No..."

"So even though he'd have this free will, he wouldn't be able to use it, unless he wanted to pick which book to read from the library, or pick a fight, or something like that."

"I see what you're doing." I shook my head, "I know you mean well but it's more existential than that."

She grumbled at me. "Of course I know that, Nick. I was just trying to show you it doesn't even sound cut and dry from where I'm standing."

"I just don't want to make the wrong choice. I want to help them, Eric and Sarah. But what does that make me? If I do this, even if it helps those two people, doesn't that change me? To make that kind of decision for someone else?" I realized I was losing it a little bit. *Way to keep cool, Nick.* "If I do this," I turned and looked straight into Amy's eyes, "who will I be afterward?"

"Oh, Nick." Amy took my face between her two small hands. "You'd be yourself, wonderfully flawed. Human, just like the rest of us."

Then she kissed me, lightly on the lips. We were having a pretty heavy conversation, so it stopped my brain completely in its tracks. I let my hands rest lightly on her waist, and just stood still, letting it last for as long as she would stay there. It was probably no more than a second or two but after that small eternity, she looked into my eyes again. I could barely breathe, but I made a valiant effort so I wouldn't hyperventilate on her at this close range.

"I believe in you, Nick." She let go of my face, and I let my hands fall to my sides. "You'll make the right choice, whatever that is."

I walked her back to her car, parked near the restaurant. Halfway back, our hands seemed to find each other, and we spent the remainder of our stroll in silence. I waved to her back window as she pulled away; then floated back to my car and headed home.

It was the first night in more than a week that I slept easily.

CHAPTER 18

Let's skip Saturday, shall we? Nothing important happened on Saturday. After a good night's sleep, I spent the day repeatedly reviewing the contract. That's also what I did Sunday morning... and Sunday afternoon.

They say you can never prepare too much, but my stomach begged to differ as it was filled with acid for the entire time. I was worrying myself sick going over the maybes of the situation. Daniel could just not show, he could somehow magically know that I was coming, or he could say no.

I couldn't let him say no.

I followed the same pattern as the week prior, parking on the Green and walking over to the Cornerstone. Sal manned the bar and lifted a hand in recognition as I walked in the door, apparently recognizing me from last week. I took the same initial perch as last time, a table on the wall, and ordered a beer to nurse until Daniel arrived. Assuming that he was coming, of course. It was early so I killed some time watching whatever was on the one television above the bar, which looked like some off-channel dirt bike racing. The early birds cheered whenever someone hit the dirt or wiped out. I told you what kind of crowd this was, didn't I?

I was halfway through my beer when Daniel walked in. He headed straight for the bar and, as he sat down at one of the stools, a double whiskey and beer chaser was placed in front of him before he even asked. Daniel looked at the drinks, then to Sal, who pointed in my direction. While killing time I also placed an advance order, my treat, for Daniel. His favorite. I needed to get his attention somehow, so I led the horse to water. He raised the oversized shot glass in my direction and belted the whole thing in one go, then grabbed his beer and wandered in a not-entirely-straight line over to my table. Dropping heavily into the chair opposite me, he offered his hand which I shook as hard as possible. He gave me that look of grudging approval, the look of a man who felt he might be in the company of other men.

"I think I recognize you." Daniel pulled at his beer.

"Bob." I pointed my thumb at my chest as if I were wearing a name tag. "We met last week."

"Wife problems," he chuckled, "right. Well, Bob, thanks for the beer. To what do I owe the generosity?"

"Well, I hoped that I'd be seeing you here. I know we talked last week," I motioned between us, "and it sounded like you had it pretty rough. Man deserves a drink, so I figured I'd get you started."

Daniel nodded along with what I was saying. I think he had already pre-gamed before he got to the bar. "I do appreciate it, mighty nice of you." You would be surprised how many people think they deserve all sorts of things.

"Things improved at all this week?" I couldn't just get right down to business, the snare needed a light touch.

"Not even a little bit." He leaned back, arms draped over the chair. "Kid's doing all right, but my wife? She went and broke her damn wrist."

"Really?" My face started to burn, but I did my best to keep the rising concern from my eyes. "What happened?"

"Oh, she says it was just a stupid accident, hell if I know. Probably did it to herself, dumb as she is. Now I've got ER bills to pay on top of dealing with her whining ass for a while. Not sure what I did to deserve this."

"I can hardly believe that." I seriously couldn't.

"Yeah, well, I'll just have to deal with it like I normally do. What about you?" He pointed at me with his glass. "How's your brood?"

"Truthfully? I'm not married anymore." I paused and sipped my beer for dramatic effect.

"Divorced?" He whistled through his front teeth. "Damn, that was fast."

"Not exactly." I leaned over the table and spoke in a quieter voice. "Actually, Daniel, it's part of why I'm here tonight. I found a way out. A loophole, a catch, and I thought you might be interested."

"What," he snorted, "you kill somebody? Not interested in going to jail, friend."

"No, no, you've got it all wrong," I held up my hands in mock surrender, "no one's dead. Everyone's happy."

"What kind of magic pills are you selling, Bob?" Daniel drank more beer, looking dubiously at me.

"Are you a religious man, Daniel?"

"Only so much." He shook his head. "Church on Sundays and the like."

"What if I told you it was true? That there's a god and a Devil, and they're competing for your soul." I motioned around the bar. "We know who's winning at this point."

"You're crazy, man." Daniel stood up from the table and moved to head back to his bar stool.

"Leave this table," my voice was neutral to the point of apathy, as if it didn't matter to me what happened next, "and you'll never get another chance." I didn't stand up, I just looked him in the eye from where I sat.

He hesitated, and I knew that I had at least hooked him into the conversation. Daniel was a man desperate to escape his own choices. He sat down again, if slowly.

"All I want you to do is hear me out."

"You bought me a drink," he said. "Least I owe you is that, even if you are nuts."

"I met a man yesterday. He looked like a lawyer, all sharp-dressed. He saw me sitting on a bench at the mall, watching my wife spend all my money, and he sat down next to me. You know what he said?" I paused, waiting for Daniel to fill the silence with his own desires.

"He said he could fix it," Daniel said easily, investing himself into the story.

"Damn right, he said he could fix it. Said I'd live out the rest of my life in comfort and happiness, doing what I wanted…" I paused again, smirking at Daniel, waiting.

"When you wanted," Daniel finished my sentence. I was leading the witness again.

"Exactly. See, I *knew* you'd understand. He had some papers with him, and by God, didn't it say that I'd be free and taken care of." I paused, taking another drink.

"What did you have to do?" Daniel leaned toward me, hands on the table, beer forgotten. He may not have believed me, but the hook was set deep enough that he *wanted* to believe.

"I read the papers, and then I just had to shake his hand." I held out my hand in pantomime. "And poof, done."

"Bullshit," Daniel said, but it didn't have any conviction behind it. I didn't know if he was already drunk, or just intoxicated at the thought of his own freedom.

"I'm telling you," I leaned back, "it's true. More importantly for you, there was an added bonus." Casting out the line… "I could pass this on to someone else, someone who deserved the same thing. He didn't care who it was, left it up to me."

"Me?" he said, incredulous. "How could I even believe you? This is ridiculous. Even if it was true, you don't even know me."

He made to get up again, but I had his attention when I took the stack of papers out of my messenger bag and slid them onto the table. "Why you, Daniel? Why not? The moment I met you, I felt a kindred spirit. A man with too much weighing him down, who might appreciate the same second chance that I was offered." He eyed the packet, which was visually impressive. High quality, heavy stock paper, embossed and gilded letters, everything I needed to catch someone's eye. Daniel didn't get two inches out of his chair before he sat down again.

"You can't be serious," he said, with a hopeful voice.

"Dead serious." I slid the pages to the middle of the table, but let him be the one to reach for them. He picked them up and glanced through but seemed to get a little dizzy by the time he reached the fifth "party of the first part." I buried the terms inside so much legal mumbo jumbo that he'd need an actual lawyer, and a few hours, to decipher the contents. This meeting wasn't about the paper; it was about the promise.

"Let's say I'm giving you the benefit of the doubt," he swallowed heavily, "what did he want from you, in return?"

"Nothing I was using anyway." I tried to sound as casual as possible. "What are we doing with our souls these days anyway?" I needed to be careful. Daniel looked a little fragile around the edges, and I couldn't have him crack and run away. "Look, Daniel, I was the same person before as I am now. Except now, I don't have to worry about a wife and kids, and I'm spending my evenings in better company with more money in my pocket than I ever had before. I thought you'd be interested in that kind of proposition."

"But, Bob, my soul? That doesn't even sound right."

"I'll break it down the way it was explained to me. Our souls are just free will. Giving up your soul to the man downstairs lets him take care of it. Where are you now, Daniel?" I needed to amp up my argument. "What's free will doing for you? You're stuck in a marriage you hate, with a woman you say is dumb as bricks, and a kid who's nothing but a disappointment. Sounds like you've pretty much given up as it is, without getting anything out of it besides bills and a headache."

I saw something from my eyes reflected in his, and it stopped me cold. A tiny flame. I didn't know where it came from but it was apparently a sign he could accept what was happening. He was hooked.

"I need a minute." Daniel took some deep breaths.

"That's fine," I smiled, "it's a big decision. But you and I know it's what you want. Take all the time you need."

Daniel was sweating now, leafing through the contract, trying to hastily digest all of the details. I didn't expect him to find any of the most important stipulations, and he didn't disappoint me.

"And I'd be free?" His voice was plaintive.

"Free. It's not a genie's lamp— you won't be rich and powerful. But you'll have money to spare, never be without a place to call your own, and only need to work if you want to." I tried to offer him a lazy bachelor's dream. "Besides, if I'm out of my mind, what's the harm?"

My logic seemed to hold up, and Daniel stopped paging through the contract.

I held my hand out, in the middle of the table. "Shake my hand and you'll either be a free man, or you'll be in exactly the same situation you're in now, but with a hell of a story to tell your friends tomorrow. Sounds like a win-win to me."

Daniel's hand left the table, but it was an eternity before he decided to hesitantly grasp mine. As soon as we shook, the tiny flame that I had seen reflected in his eyes spread through my pupils, and for a split second, I stared through the fire of hell itself. And then it was gone.

Our hands parted, and Daniel's shook. He did not like what he had seen in my eyes, but it was too late.

"Hey, uh," he stammered, "let's drink to it."

I smiled, a little smugly, and clinked glasses with him. I savored my sip of beer, and watched over the rim of my glass as he drank his. As soon as the liquid touched his mouth, he spat, spraying warm beer all over the table.

"What the hell, man?" His glass slammed down onto the table. "That burned like a son of a bitch."

"Oh." My face was blank as I leaned toward him. "Your soul paid for the creature comforts, but the Devil is always in the details. I probably forgot to tell you a few things, but I was so excited to share that it must have slipped my mind."

Daniel jumped out of his chair and charged at me. "You bastard!" He cocked back his arm and aimed at my face, but as soon as he did that, his eyes shot wide open. He gasped and fell to the floor, grabbing and thumping at his chest.

Sal, the dutiful employee that he was, shouted over asking what the hell was going on. I yelled back something about Danny having too much to drink already, and that I'd make sure he was all right. Sal turned back to another customer at the bar without a second glance.

I left my chair and kneeled next to Daniel, my face close enough to his that he could hear me whisper.

"Let me fill you in. First, the good news. You really will get those creature comforts I talked about. Money, house, car, whatever. All that's taken care of in trust and I couldn't care less about it. Or you. Next, the bad news. You'll probably never want to drink again. If you thought that burning sensation was an accident, you're mistaken. Drunk Daniel is a danger to himself and others, so we can't have that happening anymore now, can we?"

He tried to raise himself up on his elbows, but I placed my right hand on his chest and pushed downward holding him to the floor. His eyes were wide with shock and pain, still trying to process what was happening.

"Now, let's talk about this bit right here." I smiled and continued. "I'm sorry that happened. I didn't expect you to try to hit me, but I guess now is as good a time as any to have an object lesson. Let me reassure you. You're not dying. Yet, anyway. I think they call this angina. Acute chest pain. I don't know, I'm not a doctor. Anyway, attack another human being in anger and you'll end up on the floor again. I imagine if it was with someone else in some other bar, you'd have the shit kicked out of you by now, so consider this a blessing." I eased up the pressure and tapped my finger on his chest, right above his heart. "I'll make a sports analogy, so it's easy to understand. Three more strikes and you're out. You would have had four, but unfortunately, you decided to use one just now. Not my problem, but you should be more careful. We're not leaving you helpless; you can still act in self-defense. We're not monsters. You just won't be assaulting anyone that isn't a threat to you."

I leaned back, sitting on my haunches. "That brings me to the best part. You're definitely free from your wife and child, by which I mean they're free from you. Not only will you have enough money to live comfortably, the alimony that your wife receives from that same trust, for the rest of her life, will be more than enough to make up for the fact that you'll be out of the picture. See? Everyone wins."

Daniel leaned his head back, regaining some of his breath finally. I stood up and gave the all-clear sign to Sal, picked up my glass, and drained the contents.

"Cheers, Daniel. And don't thank me. You deserve this."

CHAPTER 19

Berserkers were an interesting part of Norse mythology. They were fabled warriors who entered a trance state to fight and became unstoppable forces on the battlefield. I bet you felt something like that once, even if you didn't realize it.

Imagine this: You're talking with someone, and they say something that you don't particularly like. It's something that infuriates you. You're livid. Instantly, instinctively, your body responds to this perceived threat, without even a fired neuron of conscious thought. You lash out at them, whether you're throwing fists or words. Your face is hot, time slows down, and you feel like you're in the most control of yourself that you've ever been. Except you're not making any choices. Things are just happening, coming out of you with fiery intent and you mean every punch or insult. The problem is, there aren't any brakes, any slowing of thought or action, anything keeping you from doing whatever it is your body has decided to do on your brain's behalf.

It's not exactly the same as going berserk, but do you think for a moment that anything other than a full-body tackle at that moment would have stopped you? What do you think a trance state is? A state of no mind, unthinking, you just happen to be moving and talking while it's happening.

I didn't know what I was going to say to Daniel until it had all run out of my mouth and I stood, shaking and close to vomiting, outside the bar. I went from the super-controlled salesman in the bar, doling out a ration of comeuppance to a monster masquerading as an average Joe, to a shivering wreck. Adrenaline did that to a person.

I walked jerkily to my car and miraculously managed to get home without hitting anyone or anything on, or off, the road.

I woke up to Odin's paw in my mouth, fishing around for the mouse that had apparently died there while I was sleeping. Clothes from last night? Check. I was exhausted when I got back, still coming down from the encounter with Daniel, and passed out without changing. The alarm was going off, for how long I couldn't have said. I vaguely remembered setting it before lying down, but I didn't recall anything after that. Stopping that horrible beeping noise? Check.

It wasn't until I was in the shower, scalding water pounding the sleep out of my eyes, that I remembered why I would have made sure to set the alarm before dropping off.

Eric and Sarah.

I jumped out of the shower, half of the conditioner still in my hair, and got dressed as quickly as possible to get out the door. Odin meowed at me, apparently to remind me to shut the water off before I left. Good kitty, extra mush for you later.

I flew on four wheels to Amistad and arrived in time to park and watch the parents sending their children off. My eyes burned before I remembered to blink again, this happened more than once. I didn't see the van, but it took me a minute to remember that I wasn't looking for a van, not this time. I recalibrated and looked for the people, and caught sight of Eric just before he walked into the school. Scanning the line of cars, I managed to just make out Sarah's face as she pulled away in her own vehicle.

She was smiling.

She. Was. Smiling.

I let out a breath that I didn't recall holding and leaned back against the headrest with my eyes closed.

"That seemed to go well."

I jumped and smashed my head into the driver's side window, looking next to me to find Lu sitting calmly in the passenger seat.

"Jumpy?" Lu passed me a paper cup filled with what had better be coffee, after scaring me senseless like that.

I reached for the cup with a tremor that didn't disappear until I had grasped it. "What the hell, Lu? Haven't you heard of a door?"

"Of course, I have," he scoffed. "I was just excited for you. Oh, and what kind of way is that to talk to your boss?"

"Sorry," I muttered, sipping gratefully at what was, in fact, the coffee I hadn't had time to get for myself. "I just... I mean. Seriously, you needed to be that dramatic? You startled the crap out of me."

"Right, right, I get it. But focus on the important stuff, this went great! Daniel's out of the picture and, incidentally, the town. Sarah received word late Sunday night that a formerly unknown relative had passed away and left her as sole executor of their estate." Lu raised his own materialized cup in salute. "The legal fund is covering all of her expenses while it's getting ironed out, so she doesn't need to worry about working right now. Eric will only need a moderate amount of therapy when he's older. Probably. Less than he would have if it all continued, anyway."

"Right," I sighed, "and all I had to do was lie, cheat, and steal."

This earned me a raised eyebrow and a clucked tongue. "That's a little melodramatic, isn't it?"

"But true," I countered.

"True," Lu conceded, "but this is where I give you a pep talk about the greater good, right?"

"Probably wouldn't hurt."

"Well," he cleared his throat, "imagine that I did that. It was rousing. I'll see you back at the office."

I blinked, and he was gone. At least he left me the coffee.

Everything had gone according to plan. According to *my* plan. I probably shouldn't be sulking in my car, now that I had proof that I had helped Eric and Sarah. Why else did I get involved in this, if it wasn't to help people? Sometimes to make an omelet, you had to break a few ethical constructs. Eggs were too easy.

I made my way to the office, contemplating my recent actions. I stood, staring at the ticker above my desk.

500 out of a thousand. Halfway to... what? I had a hard time feeling different despite any prior assertions.

There are two sayings: No rest for the wicked, and the reward for a job well done is more work. Both of these were true, working for the Devil. Putting everything in motion with the Diggers wasn't hard enough, apparently, and I needed to be involved in the post-processing as Jessica called it. She waited for me at my desk. Lester had informed her that I executed the contract over the weekend so she was there to make sure I didn't bungle the whole thing after the fact.

Think about your everyday wish fulfillment. Rather, think of it as if it really happened. In this case, it mostly did, with some caveats. Who made all those little details fall into place? Do you think Lu just snapped his fingers and everything changed? I had hoped, even expected, that was the case but other than delivering me coffee straight into my car it wasn't working out that way. The metaphysical effects took care of themselves; that was somehow easier than the practical things. The magical heart attacks? Easy. The nitty gritty? Much more complicated. There were trust funds to establish, imaginary lost relatives to document, and then kill off, it was all quite a lot of work as Jessica was more than happy to explain to me.

The long and short of it was that I was expected to monitor the situation for a period of no less than two weeks before handing it off to some sort of account manager who would make sure the foundation we had built didn't fall apart and everything worked in perpetuity.

One happy side effect was that I volunteered at the soup kitchen twice over the course of those two weeks, mostly to check up on Sarah. The bruises faded, and she even cursed her "husband who had run off" a few times, but there was a lightness to the way she carried herself that took some of the sting out of what I had done to Daniel. Did I need a pep talk? I wasn't sure. I had given a man his freedom, with some unexpected fine print, and set up his family in comfort without him. All for the price of that one mostly worthless soul, and perhaps a portion of my own.

I was getting good at this rationalization thing.

It was a fairly easy two weeks, and I finally buttoned up the details on the Digger project to hand off to the next department. It was Friday, conveniently, so I called Amy and asked if she wanted to meet me after work for noodles. There was a delighted "Sure!" and I had myself a plan. A date? Amy and I had texted a few times back and forth, but I was so busy working on my case that we hadn't been able to meet up since our first date. I finished up the day, got an official "good work" from Lu, and headed off to York Square. There was a noodle house on the corner, the only place I knew around to get dim sum and spicy noodle soup. Amy had beaten me there (it took longer than I thought to get parking), and she had a dim sum platter on the table waiting for us.

"I thought I'd get us started," she said while popping shumai into her mouth.

"Thanks, I'm starving!" I dug into the plate, and neither of us said anything for a few minutes as we consumed heavenly calories.

I went up to the counter and ordered some soups for us, then went back to the table where Amy looked at me thoughtfully.

"What?" I asked. "Do I look different?"

She shook her head. "No? I think I was curious if you were going to. I don't see any horns or anything. Did everything go okay with that family?"

"Surprisingly well, actually." I leaned back in my chair. "The road to hell is still paved with good intentions."

"So now you've finished one for him," she held up one finger, "does that mean you get to do something for yourself now?" She held up a second finger, wiggling them both.

"I hadn't thought about it. I guess so? I wasn't expecting the first thing to be humanitarian, so I'm a little out of order thinking about it."

Our number was called, so it gave me a minute to think more about it. I brought the steaming bowls back to the table and Amy's eyes lit up. She breathed the fragrant broth in from her bowl before digging in with both chopsticks and a spoon. I watched her eat greedily for a moment, smiling.

She looked up at me, mouth still trailing noodles. "What? I like noodles?" It sounded more like "Wut? I wike nurdles." I laughed, and she managed not to choke on her soup when she started to laugh with me.

"Things have been serious lately," I said after I finally stopped laughing, "I needed this."

"You needed me?" She struck a pose with her hands against her cheek. "How sweet!"

"Ha ha," I chuckled, my face turning a little red and not from the spices, "I see what you did there."

We ate in silence for another few minutes before Amy asked, "So what do you think you'll do now?"

"I'm not sure how this works, if I get to pick my own project," I admitted. "It was easy when I was handed an assignment. I assume I'll need to figure it out myself, about who I decide to try to help."

"That's vague."

"You think?" I flicked a drop of soup at her. "I didn't say it'd be easy, I just said I'd have to do it myself."

"I could..." she thought about it, "look in the newspapers or online, for needy people or something?"

"I'm not going to tell you no," I said. "I'll take all the help I can get. But I'm still getting paid, as far as I know, so don't stress yourself out trying to find me a willing victim."

"Don't you worry. I'll find you the saddest, sorriest, neediest person that ever existed." She held up her fingers in some kind of made-up scout salute.

"Let's not get carried away, okay?"

"Sure."

My hand found hers on the table. Luckily, she didn't recoil in horror. Despite our date the other night, I wasn't sure what to expect. It could have been a fluke. "What are you up to this weekend?"

"Oh," she turned her hand and laced her fingers into mine, "watching some movies."

"With me or by yourself?" I grinned.

"You're the one with the teddy bear cat that I owe a visit to. I figured I'd swing by your place tomorrow." She looked at me with very innocent eyes. "If you're not busy? I'm sure Odin misses me terribly."

"He does. He even got off my chest and let me go to work when I told him that you might come by this weekend." When the girl said she would come by my apartment, I made that sound like the best idea ever. I mean, it was, but marketing didn't hurt.

We set a time and then parted ways outside the shop. Amy stood on her tiptoes and gave me a quick kiss on the nose before darting off in the other direction. At that moment, I was reasonably certain I could not predict the trajectory of whatever this relationship was going to be. I was also pretty comfortable with that, given recent circumstances. When my whole life was bizarre? Mildly confusing things were perfectly normal.

I walked back to my car and, when I was about a block away, noticed someone leaning against my passenger door. As I got closer, I recognized the face but couldn't understand what he was doing there. It looked like he was waiting for me.

"Hey, Rob," I waved from about ten feet away while walking toward my car. "What's going on?"

"Hey, Nick." Rob didn't look so good. "Haven't seen you since that night at the graveyard." His hair was stringy, clothes shabbier than usual, like he had been on a bender. It was Friday, so I wasn't sure where or what he had been doing that would put him in this kind of state. He was usually put together pretty well, dorm-room posters in his apartment aside.

"Not exactly the kind of greeting you hear on the street." I laughed a little awkwardly, remembering what Amy had said to me that first night over coffee. "You doing okay?" I walked a little closer, it was my car after all and I intended to leave in it shortly.

"You're looking good." He straightened up from his lean and came closer to me, brushing invisible lint off my shoulder. "New job treating you well?"

"Uh," I paused, "What new job?"

"Don't play dumb with me, Nick." Rob stared at me intently, making me decidedly uncomfortable.

I held up my hands, "What? Can't a guy dress up nice for a dinner date?"

"Oh, I know you were here seeing Amy, but I know that's not why you're dressed like an office drone." Rob's voice dropped low so no one on the street could hear him except me. "I want to meet him."

A drop of adrenaline and mental defenses kicked into overdrive. "Meet who?"

"You know who. That's even what some people refer to him as when they don't want to call him by name. *You know who.*" Rob chuckled at his own double entendre.

"You're freaking me out a little, Rob." I edged toward the front of my car.

Rob closed the distance between us and drove a finger into my chest. "Don't!" he hissed between clenched teeth. "Don't pretend it's not true. What you did. I've been following you."

"I..." My mind reeled. How long had he been following me? Did he know what I did to Daniel Digger?

"I want what you took from me."

"Rob," I started sounding exasperated, "I don't know what you're talking about."

"What you *stole* from me!" Spittle flew out of Rob's mouth, and his eyes were wide and wild.

It took a second, but the adrenaline sharpened my thinking enough to realize he had told me in the beginning what this was all about. The cemetery.

"That's what this is about?" I pushed his finger away, "The Devil? You're crazy, Rob."

"Am I?" His breathing was ragged. "You stole it, my chance at being great. I did the work, I brought the people, I said the words, and *you took it.*"

"Look, man, you need to chill out." I backed toward the street, off the curb, trying to head to the driver's side door of my car.

"It was my right," he was nearly screaming at this point, "you owe me, Nick! You took the chance that should have been mine, and now you owe me!"

He wasn't following me into the road, so I unlocked and opened my door. "We don't have anything to talk about, Rob. You were playing games in a graveyard with delusions of grandeur. I'm leaving now, talk to me when you're less strung out." I got into the car and locked the door as I shut it.

There was a resounding crash as glass sprayed into the passenger seat. Rob pressed himself into where the window had been moments ago and screeched as I tried to pull the car into the street, "You owe me, Nick! YOU OWE ME!"

I managed to drive away without taking Rob's torso with me and could see him running after my car as I sped down the street. My heart was pounding, and I was covered in shards of safety glass. I couldn't remember if Rob knew where I lived, but as I looked next to me and noticed the brick that was sitting in the seat next to me, I sure as hell hoped not.

CHAPTER 20

I was torn between telling Amy about what had happened with Rob and ignoring it like a bad dream. When I woke up the next morning and headed to the parking lot to run some errands, the chill that ran up my spine, looking at the broken window, reminded me that the bad dream was reality. I had hastily taped a garbage bag over the broken window the night before, to keep the bugs out, and thankfully that was still in place. I found a local glass repair shop that was open and taking walk-ins, and my car was generic enough that they had a passenger window available to replace mine. It would be done in a few hours, but even with that eyesore fixed, I assumed I'd have to tell someone at some point. I decided to at least talk with Lu on Monday but didn't plan to ruin a perfectly good Saturday worrying Amy.

This was probably not my smartest idea ever, but I was a little distracted on multiple fronts. They say you shouldn't mix business with pleasure, or never start a land war in Asia. You can almost certainly add "Don't start a relationship while maybe selling your soul to the Devil." It doesn't flow very well, as an axiom, but seemed fairly accurate.

Insert a cleaning montage leading up to Amy's visit to my apartment, with Odin running from room to room escaping the rampaging monster sucking up all his fuzzy tumbleweeds. She hadn't been there since I invited her for dinner, so I reverted to a state of bachelordom. I actually cleaned though, instead of throwing everything in the closet. I considered this a sign of my growing maturity.

Amy arrived in the afternoon and we spent the rest of the day talking and watching movies. Sitting next to each other holding hands, then leaning, then cuddling on the couch, and getting to know the lazy weekend habits of the other. I wasn't the only one vying for Amy's affection, Odin was some serious competition. He also liked to play hard to get, mostly because he was a cat and therefore extremely fickle. He made Amy chase him around the apartment before finally letting himself get picked up and placed on the couch next to her. Add some pizza delivery to the equation, I was paranoid enough about the Rob situation to not want either of us to go out that night, and it was a very pleasant evening.

All good things must come to an end. We were still on the couch, but it was getting late, and Amy made noises about heading home soon. She saw something in my eyes, I was worried about her getting home safely, and debating telling her about Rob.

She punched me in the shoulder. "I'm not staying the night, Nick."

I guess it didn't look like worry. "I wasn't making eyes at you about that." I placed both of my hands over her right, holding it gently, though partly to stop her from hitting me again. "I like you, Amy. I like you a lot. Things have been complicated, and you've been the only person I could talk to. That's not why I like you, but that's why I want to make sure we keep our eyes wide open walking into whatever this could be. Things are going to settle out for me, one way or the other, and I want to make sure you still like whoever is on the other side."

Amy scooted over and laid her cheek against my chest, over my heart. "I'm sure you'll still be the same. All of this is overwhelming, but it seems to be helping you figure out who you were inside, the whole time, rather than changing you." She sat up and put her hand on my cheek. "But I appreciate what you're saying and that you don't have any expectations."

"None, other than that I'd like to see you again."

"After a day like today?" she stretched, as languidly as a cat, "You bet. So what was the face for?"

The face in question shifted to a look of worry. "Well..." I twisted my hands together a little. "I'm worried about you."

"I've lived here for a while, Nick. I'll be fine getting home." She looked genuinely confused.

"No," I shook my head, "it's not that. It's just... I ran into Rob last night." Her eyes grew wide, and she opened her mouth to say something but I interrupted her. "Before you say anything, you're right, and I should have told you sooner. But that's why I'm telling you now. Because I'd rather it was out in the open, and you could watch out for him. I also hated keeping it from you. It felt dishonest, and that's not who I am."

Amy's mouth stayed open for a moment, but then she closed it and looked at me appraisingly. She was obviously waiting for an explanation. I told her about the encounter with Rob, and she looked pretty horrified when I explained how terrible Rob looked and what he thought had happened to me. When I described the broken window and nearly pulling Rob down the street with me, she placed her hand over mine and her face was filled with worry. A weight lifted from my chest, and a knot uncurled from my stomach, when I finished.

"I'll forgive you for not telling me sooner," she said, "this time, because you decided to be upfront with me."

"You've believed me and trusted me when I've told you about some truly unbelievable stuff. I figured it would be bad if I stopped now."

I opened my arms, and she wrapped her arms around my waist to give me a long, strong, hug. I needed it. I kissed the top of her head and breathed in the scent of her hair, a subtle vanilla, wishing that moment would never end. I walked her to her car, it was both romantic and the sensible thing to do. "Thank you for spending your day off with me."

She turned on the curb to face me and grabbed me around the middle again for a tight squeeze. "My pleasure, and thank you for letting me invite myself over."

I put my arms around her, and she looked up at me with her pixie face. I kissed her deeply, and we melted into each other. It was a long moment before we finally separated.

Amy smiled and walked to her driver's side door. She opened it and leaned over the roof of her car. "Good start," she smirked at me, "and good night, Nick."

Chapter 21

"Nick? Are you with me?" Lu snapped his fingers in front of my face and I came back to attention. I had been telling Lu about what happened with Rob, but then I got lost in remembering Saturday night with Amy. Can you blame me?

Lu leaned back in his chair and steepled his fingers under his chin. "Tell me again why you're worried about this?"

"It was just weird," I said, which sounded like the lamest reason for Lu to care, "I mean, he was pretty deranged and yelling at me. He thinks it should be him... doing whatever he thinks I might be doing. Instead of me."

"I followed you on that, but I still don't see why you're worried."

"He broke my car window," I said flatly, "isn't that enough?"

Lu tutted, "I told you to get that jalopy replaced anyway, didn't I? Take it as a sign that you can finally trade that heap in for something respectable, and maybe Rob won't even recognize you around town."

The Devil was still giving me hell about my car. "He could cause more trouble?" I ventured but didn't sound very confident in my assessment.

"I suppose he could, but what's he going to do?" Lu smiled broadly. "Call the police? Report you to the Better Business Bureau? Come on, Nick. We're playing at an entirely different level at this point."

"So you just want me to ignore him?" I asked.

"Exactly that," Lu replied. "Ignore the crazy man and maybe he'll get tired of not bathing regularly and go back to business as usual."

"This doesn't feel like a very good plan, Lu," I accused.

"This doesn't sound like a very big problem, Nick," Lu retorted, "if he breaks another car window, call the police and have him arrested. If he raves at the cops like that, he's not going to make many friends."

I gave up. "Fine, I get it, okay. But answer me something, would you?"

"Shoot." Lu leaned forward, elbows on his desk.

"If he's such a small problem, why couldn't you just make his wish come true? He tried to summon the Devil, which succeeded." I gave a double thumbs up for the achievement. "Why won't you meet with him? Especially now that he has some sort of proof."

Lu held up one finger. "First, that was a great excuse to show up, but *no one* summons me. Second, I told you before that he was a non-believer."

"He believes now," I snorted, "that's for sure."

Lu sighed. "He believes because now he thinks he can get something out of it and because he thinks he was cheated. Could I meet him? Sure. Could I sell him on a deal? Absolutely, and probably for much less than most. But what would I get? I need dedication; I don't need a zealot. No, Rob can wait until he's matured a bit more. Some people are like fine wine and need to age before they can become approachable. That was you, Nick, and look how you're turning out now that you've had room to breathe. Rob? He's not done fermenting yet."

"So you're leaving this all alone because he's too easy?" I goggled at Lu.

"You make it sound tawdry." Lu snickered at me. "Cheap, even. Look at it from my perspective, yes? I'm how old? I've literally seen it all. I like a good challenge as much as the next personified deity, and who could blame me? I like to work with people whose minds are their own, unclouded, thinking about what they want and why they want it. Rob? He's over the edge to crazy and even I, the Devil, don't intend to take that advantage."

"You're all over the map on this." I cocked my head, trying to digest what I was being told. "Now you're noble about it?"

Lu looked slightly impatient. "What's the real concern here, Nick? We're beating around the bush, and you haven't told me what issue number one is."

I stared at him, my eyebrows furrowed. "I don't want Amy to be in danger, and I'm worried that Rob could cause trouble for her."

"Ah." Lu grinned, slightly smug. "I've noticed your confidence, Nick, it's been improving by leaps and bounds since you've come to work with me. I'm glad that you're getting along well with Amy. I'd like to think your progress here helped with that."

"You're changing the subject." I blushed red to the tips of my ears.

"Yes, I am, unapologetically." Lu waved his hand as I tried to argue. "Look, Nick. Rob could be a problem, but I'm not sold on the concern. Keep an eye on it but, otherwise, I'd get focused on the task at hand. You did a job for me, and quite well at that. Samuel sends his regards, by the way."

"Thanks," I said, quietly. Every time I thought about that first job, I tested myself internally to see how I felt about it. Guilty? Self-Righteous? Sad? Happy? I wasn't trying to label it. I was just trying to figure out what halfway to being ripe for the Devil's picking felt like. The ticker over my desk was a constant reminder, and I had glanced at it before coming in for this meeting. Luckily, I hadn't kicked any puppies on the way to the office, and my total remained as it was on Friday.

"The task at hand now," Lu continued, "is to figure out what you're going to do next."

"Right, next." I took a deep breath. "Well, I was trying to do some research over the weekend to find someone or something in the local community that I could help with."

"Sounds charitable. I'm not against it, categorically." Lu made a few notes, I didn't know if it was about me or not.

"Uh," I stumbled, "good? You said I'd have all the same facilities at my disposal for the personal project."

"Which continues to be a true statement." Lu held his hand over where his heart would be. "I am nothing if not a man of my word. Think carefully about the size of the project. Resources, and facilities, all of which will be provided *within reason*. Granted, you have some understanding of the level of reason I'll accept, given your last assignment, so I trust you to make a sound judgment yourself before bringing anything to me."

"So," I tried to continue, "I was planning to do some more field research and then make a decision mid-week about where I would focus."

"There are worse plans," Lu put his pen down, "I'm fine with it. Bring me a short proposal by Thursday, okay? And if it's to end hunger or enact world peace, I'll be cross with you."

"Sure thing, boss." I headed back to my desk.

I spent a few hours surfing the internet, going from local news site to news site, trying to find something that would catch my eye. Things like 'family house burns, total loss' led to scanning the articles. Scanning the articles led to some being passed over, especially any that said insurance or disaster relief would be handling one hundred percent of the recovery. Some were less clear so I made a few calls, representing myself as a charity organizer, and found that other situations had similar benefactors and didn't need a public fund or anything like that.

More than once, my searches had shown me the website for the community soup kitchen. I kept passing it over until I had been down the local news rabbit hole for four hours. I needed to grab something for lunch anyway. Home cooking had been the last thing on my to-do list lately, and the refrigerator had a fine selection of condiments but little else, so I decided to stop by and visit with Walt. Maybe he'd have some advice for me.

It was late afternoon by the time I had left the office, grabbed a bite, and headed for the church, otherwise, I would have volunteered for a food service just to get on Walt's good side. Not that I expected him to have a bad side, but I wasn't sure how to start a conversation like this with anyone, let alone a priest.

I found him in his office, hunting and pecking at the keyboard of a computer that was five years out of date at least five years ago. What hair he had left was askew, his glasses propped on his forehead. He peered intently at a pixel that had wronged him when I entered the room.

"Nick, my boy!" Walt jumped when I came in and rushed to the other side of the desk to shake my hand enthusiastically. "What can I do for you? I don't think I would ever have expected to see you this evening. Sit, sit!"

I sat in a well-worn wingback chair, one of a set that adorned the office along with a scuffed but serviceable side table. Walt sat opposite me, falling heavily into the other chair with a groan. The chair creaked but didn't give up the ghost, clearly accustomed to the abuse.

"What can I do for you?" Walt asked when he had finally settled into the armchair with another grunt.

"I've ended up with what I can only call a 'good problem to have' and needed some help figuring out how to tackle it." I didn't know where to start, other than vague.

"Well, now." Walt rubbed his chin. "If you share some of the details, I may be able to help. Without that, all I can do is congratulate you on having the right kind of problem."

"Understandable," I nodded, "I'm having a hard time figuring out how to put this. Let me ask you a hypothetical question."

"You've saved me from an evening going over the church's finances, so take all the time you need to explain," Walt grinned at me, "I am all ears."

"Okay. What if you were given enough resources that you could help with one *thing*?" I put 'thing' in air quotes. "That one thing could be a family in need, a business needing help, a person down on their luck, anything that you thought would be a good investment of time and money aimed at the greater good. With me so far?"

"Sure I am, sounds good. Keep going." Walt nodded as he listened.

"Right, so you need to decide what that thing you're going to invest in is. But how can you pick? There are so many people, so many projects, so many *things* that need help and you can't decide which one needs it first." I spread my hands and looked at Walt, hoping he could take that small pile of junk I just handed him and massage it into something that made sense.

"Nick," Walt patted my knee in a fatherly manner, "first off, I'd just like to say that a young man like yourself even thinking about charitable works is just a fantastic thing to see in this day and age. I recall quoting Corinthians at you once before, a coincidence that it's so appropriate again. 'And now abideth faith, hope, charity, these three, but the greatest of these is charity.'"

"But you see why I have a problem, right?" I asked. "There are so many people who are getting helped by various systems, who don't need as much of a hand as those that aren't. Then you've got the rare people who are just scamming the charities, and they're not always easy to see, but you want to make sure you're not giving to the wrong cause."

Walt nodded emphatically now, almost tipping forward out of his chair. "Yes, sir, that's often the trouble. But sometimes you must give aid to all so that the few who have the least will get their fair share. So many people come to a place like this and they don't see it for what it is. I think you did, and that's why you've come back with this dilemma. I appreciate the faith you've placed in me, my friend."

"So you'll help?" I asked.

"Most certainly, though now we need to get into some of the nitty gritty. I hate to make things about money, for as the Bible says love of money is truly the root of all evil, but what sort of budget does your 'good problem' have?"

Walt's enthusiasm was infectious, and I found myself becoming excited. "For right now, let's call it an anonymous source. The sponsor doesn't want to be named and hasn't set a limit on the budget. They're more interested in seeing a proposal and then telling me whether they'll fund it or not."

Walt straightened up slightly. "Now, Nick, I hate to be selfish at a time like this, but this church has done a lot for the community. You've even been a part of it, seen the people it can help." Walt looked a little bashful as he continued. "I haven't announced the drive yet, but I was going to start a fundraising effort to refurbish the kitchen and dining facilities that serve the soup kitchen. We very nearly failed our last inspection, not for lack of effort but lack of funds for necessary repairs."

I started to feel guilty, and maybe even a little uncomfortable, about not sharing the truth of my benefactor with Walt.

"Walt," I held up my hand to stop him from going on about the works of the church, "I know you're doing good things here, and yeah, I've seen them firsthand. I left something out about the sponsor, I mean besides being super vague about the whole thing."

"Well, spit it out, young man," Walt chuckled. "Anyone willing to do good works like these deserves credit for it. Though the humble man will hide from the praise given to his deeds."

"Funny question," I laughed weakly. "What if the source of this funding wasn't the kind benefactor you think it is? What if it came from a more sinister source?"

"You can stop right there, Nick." Walt's face had become very serious. "We don't take money from any drug dealers, so if you're talking about some sort of illicit fairy godfather, we'll just stop this conversation right here."

I burst out laughing, which confused Walt. "No..." I wheezed as my laughing fit finally slowed down, "not drugs. Wow, I didn't even think about how that would sound when I said it aloud."

Walt looked at me sideways. "You're not making a lot of sense."

"I've been told that a lot lately." I leaned down in my chair and shook my head to clear it. "Walt, I'd like to level with you. How open-minded are you feeling tonight?"

"I haven't had my supper yet, so other than a little hypoglycemic, I should get on just fine." He waved toward himself, inviting me to talk to him.

"Okay, can I ask for whatever the whole client-patient privilege thing is that priests do?" Walt nodded his head, so I rubbed my hands together and started talking. "I'm going to skip over the first question, which would have sounded a lot like, 'Do you believe in God?' Because I think we've got that covered. Do you believe in the Devil, Walt?"

Walt cleared his throat and looked thoughtful for a moment before answering. "I believe what scripture and my meditations have taught me about the state of our world and the ear we leave open to hear the voice of God. If I believe in one, then I suppose I should say that I believe in the other. Though, and it pains me to say this, I have seen such things in this city alone that I barely believe in Satan. What our people do to each other here on this Earth is enough."

"You're almost proving his point..." I muttered, not directly to Walt.

"Whose point?"

I looked up at Walt. "Look, it's going to get either more, or less, complicated when I tell you this. More if you believe me, less if you don't."

"This is the troubled young man I remember meeting," Walt leaned back into the wings of his chair, "I'm here to listen."

"I met Lucifer."

"Nick, we all face the Devil and his trials in our lives. Just the other day..."

"No," I said, cutting Walt off, "you don't get it. I met Lucifer. The Devil. The man in black. Whatever you want to call him, I met him. More than met him, he gave me a job."

"Are you feeling alright? I could give someone a call?" Walt looked a little nervous now. It took me a second to remember what happened in the news when people said that "the Devil spoke to them."

"No! Jesus," I winced, "I mean, sorry. No, not like 'go bury your dog in the backyard' kind of job. I can prove it to you."

"I'll certainly hear you out."

"Sarah and Eric," I said it like it should mean something, but it obviously didn't.

"Mrs. Digger and her son? What do they have to do with this?"

"Haven't you noticed how Sarah has been happier lately? More relaxed? Her husband isn't around to beat her or her son anymore."

"Well, it's been obvious how much lighter Sarah's load has been lately, I expect she said something to you about it. I'm not sure what that proves." Walt had crossed his arms over his chest. Not exactly an open listening posture.

"But I doubt she'd tell me that it was her great aunt who had passed away, leaving her as executor of her estate." I ticked points off on my fingers. "Or that there was a legal fund in place to cover her living expenses while everything cleared probate, or that the next place Daniel Digger is going to be spotted, unsurprisingly, is Las Vegas."

"How do you know all that?" Walt looked stricken.

"The first two are because I wrote the paperwork and convinced Daniel to sign over his soul, the last one because I brought a macchiato to the account manager that I handed this whole damn thing off to and he told me about the Vegas thing." I leaned forward with my hands on my knees. "I am very serious about this, and I'd like it if you gave me the benefit of the doubt at this point."

Walt swallowed loudly, brought a handkerchief out of his pocket, and dabbed at his forehead. "Daniel Digger sold his soul to the Devil, brokered through you, to go to Las Vegas while his wife was set up in financial comfort?"

"Walt," I shook my head at him, "that's just the takeaway right now. Daniel Digger sold his soul to be free of a marriage he hated, and I just made sure there would be no collateral damage when he was given that freedom."

"Just like that?"

I snapped my fingers and ignored two solid weeks of work that put it all together. "Just like that."

"And you," Walt stuttered, "you were looking for new... what, victims? Clients?"

"I made a deal with the Devil," I went on, "and did something for him. Now he's put his resources at my disposal to do something that I choose. I was looking for help figuring out what that was."

"And the price for this help? Since I was almost on your hook, greedy though I was."

"On the house."

"Even if I believed you," Walt scooted to the edge of his seat toward me, "nothing coming from the Devil is free, Nick."

"Free? I sweated for that deal, that's what's paid for this next opportunity." I stood and paced the office. "I helped stop an abusive bastard and helped make his family safe. Now? I get to do something good, something bigger than myself, something hopelessly idealistic. All I wanted was to figure out what that was." I stopped in front of the window, looking out into the alley. "I've never been any good at this stuff, and now that I have the chance to put my own mark on something, I can't even decide how to do it. There's so much injustice, so much hate and violence, so many people in need, and I can't even pick one out of the newspaper to help."

I felt a hand come to rest on my shoulder. "Oh, Nick." Walt's voice was gentle. He must have gotten out of his chair while I was talking and come up behind me. "You're the price."

I spun and looked at Walt, and saw sorrow in his eyes. "What?"

"You," Walt placed both of his hands on my shoulders and stared me in the eyes. "You're the price, Nick. 'But each person is tempted when he is lured and enticed by his own desire.'"

"But..." I broke away from Walt and sat down again, "I did good! I helped someone. He was just a child, he didn't deserve any of that, and now he's safe. Aren't there any Bible verses about the ends justifying the means?"

"Proverbs," Walt replied, "'Men do not despise a thief, if he steals to satisfy his soul when he is hungry.' Though it may not mean what you think it does. Even I would not argue with your results. Sarah is happier and safer. Eric, a child who I agree never deserved a finger to be laid upon him, is safer though perhaps not yet happier. Children don't understand when a parent leaves, no matter how bad they are for them. Yes, your ends are undeniable, but your means?"

"He was a bad man," I countered, "and it was his choice to make. He made it willingly and got exactly what he asked for. What he deserved."

"And now?" Walt sat across from me once again. "If you were to renovate our kitchens, you say there is no price. On the house, yes?"

I nodded.

Walt continued, "The price is your pride, your desire, your hubris. The Devil has his claws in you, I see it as clear as day."

"After that? I could walk away."

"Could you?" Walt tilted his head, appraising me. "I wonder if you could. I am not in your shoes, nor could I be. We each face our own trials, and you're swimming deep in yours."

"So you're saying it's a test, this freebie I'm trying to give away?"

"Isn't everything?"

Chapter 22

After my meeting with Walt I could barely sleep and, in the morning, decided that I was probably developing an ulcer based on the way my coffee hit my stomach. That or I was becoming a hypochondriac. Maybe I was a hypochondriac with an ulcer. Did I mention that I hadn't slept well?

Walt's advice had left me feeling duped, like everything I had done was as a pawn of Lucifer. It made sense, he wasn't supposed to be a nice guy. He was manipulative, slick, and out for his own benefit. That put me in a mindset to dissect everything I had done over the past few weeks, laying it out under a mental microscope.

All that was left for me to do was confront Lu. Sure, I could quit now, but what was self-doubt without the doubt? How could I be sure that Walt was right? Just because he was a godly man didn't mean he was right. God let all sorts of religious people do terrible things to each other, so there were rounds of doubt all around.

When I walked into the office, Lester was at the front desk. He seemed surprised to see me, but that barely registered as I barreled through the halls toward Lu's office. I barged into the room, opening the door sharply in front of me. I looked up, expecting to find Lu, but the room was empty.

"The knock is usually my cue to show up." Lu's voice came from behind me.

I spun a little too quickly and felt dizzy as Lu passed me into the office and took a seat at the desk. My walk to the chairs opposite him probably looked slightly drunk.

"I don't get it." I probably sounded a little drunk too. Tough to say, but insomnia did not become me.

"Don't get what?" Lu asked. "Don't get what you have to do next? I told you, just find something..."

"No, not that." I cut him off. How many people could say they shut the Devil up? He didn't look particularly pleased, but I didn't care. "I don't get why you're doing this. For me."

"Nick," Lu's face softened, "we've been over this time and time again. One more time, then I'll ask you to record the conversation so you can play it back to yourself when you need a pep talk. I saw something in you, something that needed nurturing. You had a lot of untapped potential, and I hate to see something like that go to waste."

"If I'm so special, why was I such a loser?" It hurt to ask that, but it was the truth.

"I blame God," Lu said sarcastically. "He's the one that gave you free will," Lu said softly as if it were so simple. "It's a blessing and a curse, isn't it? If destiny were real, you'd have been something great by now. A politician, a scientist, something ambitious? Rich, powerful, philanthropic? Name it. Your kind of potential would have led you to great things. If I were pulling your strings, you'd have been there years ago. But with Him handing out all that free will? You would have had to care to try."

"But..." I tried to respond, but this time Lu cut me off.

"Oh." He rose from his chair and paced behind the desk. "You wanted things. Who doesn't want things? Toys, cars, girls, good grades, decent jobs, families, friends. We all want them. You just didn't care enough to use your God-given potential to achieve them. I don't mean this to insult you, it's just the facts. You were a loser before I found you. Before I gave you that chance and reason to shine. You had more than enough free will to waste your life away latte by latte. You didn't have the toys, the friends, or the girl. You. Had. Nothing."

He wasn't yelling, or even intimidating. He was just talking to me like he normally did. I felt my righteous indignation melting away under his calm onslaught. I could remember how I felt, talking with Walt, but how could I argue with what Lu was saying?

"I don't need to quote the Bible at you, Nick," Lu continued. "Let me quote an old friend of mine. Maimonides said, 'Give a man a fish and you feed him for a day. Teach a man to fish and you feed him for a lifetime.' I taught you how to fish, Nick. You barely knew how to balance a checkbook, and now look at you!" Lu walked around the desk and grabbed me by the shoulders, smiling triumphantly as he looked into my eyes. "You took it! You took the chance I gave you, and you're making something of yourself. Sure, I spoon-fed you the parts you needed but you've had drive, ambition, and savvy since you started working independently. What's that worth, Nick?" He let go of me and leaned back against the desk.

"But," I stammered, "isn't all of this a test?"

"Sure it is, but it's not the kind you think." Lu crossed his arms over his chest. "It's for you to test yourself, test your limits, see what you could do. Take the car out and open it up on the highway, see how it handles. What do you think this is all about? We haven't made a deal, you and I. It was free and still is. You could walk away now, and I'd have no hold on you. Free will."

"Free will." My mind raced. "That you'll take from me when this is all over; if I choose to stay and work for you."

Lu's face dropped, and his eyes became sad. "Nick, you think that poorly of me? Yes, I would have custody of your soul, and yes I could make you do what I wanted. There is a vast ocean of distance between 'can' and 'will.' That doesn't mean I wouldn't let you make your own choices. I don't need worker bees, I need independent agents. I need people I can trust to keep their own reins, even if I'm taking care of their souls. Think of me as a caretaker, I want my flock as much as the guy upstairs. I'm just willing to do more to keep them happy, to help them flourish."

"And you want me to be happy?" I pulled the conclusion from his words, but I wasn't sure how I felt about it.

"Very." Lu grinned at me. "I don't want you to worry about all this. You still take the time you need to figure out your first philanthropic act. Don't even run it past me, just go with it. Resources of the office are at your disposal. Talk to Lester if you need anything specific, and you won't hear from me until you're finished."

"Uh," I said, dumbly, "okay."

I let myself be ushered out of the office and heard the door close behind me. I doubted Lu was even still in the room and bet myself money that he wouldn't be there if I opened the door. I was too numb from the conversation to test my theory and instead, walked out of the office like a zombie and went home. Some people say you can never be too introspective, but I started to think they were wrong. I felt entirely out of sorts, confused, and wanted some sort of comfort. Odin tried his best, but mostly just tried to put his tail up my nose, so he wasn't much help.

Someone was looking out for me somewhere, though according to Lu it wasn't fate, because Amy texted me wanting to know what I was doing. Remembering that I kind of, sort of, maybe had a girlfriend-type-person, I jumped on the chance and told her that I needed fifty cc's of distraction. Stat. She told me to meet her at The Fix at five o'clock, and she'd take me walking somewhere.

I let that thought distract me until it was time to leave. I got to The Fix early, ordered two coffees, and set myself up at *our* table in the corner. Five came and went. By five-thirty, I had finished my coffee. By six, I had finished hers, sending a nervous text message. It hit six thirty, with no response, and I was starting to get worried.

Finally, seven o'clock and a double espresso rolled around. I was done waiting.

I didn't actually know precisely where Amy lived, just the neighborhood and building, so I started with what I did know. The first stop was the bookstore. As far as the staff there knew, she had left after her shift ended at three and went home. Not much to go on there. Luckily, they knew me from occasional visits to see Amy at the bookstore and reminded me which apartment she was in. Next, I was knocking on Amy's door. I tried to call her cell phone, to see if I could hear it ringing in the apartment, to no avail.

Maybe I was just being blown off, you say? While possible, I didn't think it was very likely. We were taking things slow, so I doubted I scared her off. She was the one to invite me out so it seemed extra weird for her to bail on the date. I wouldn't have been so worried, people forget things all the time, but my encounter with Rob sprang to mind soon after I decided that I hadn't been stood up.

I wasn't always an action-before-thought kind of person, but I headed straight for Rob's apartment. I hadn't been there since the night of the summoning, but I found my way to his door in what felt like a heartbeat. I knocked, then thumped, then pounded at the cheap entry door. The upstairs neighbor finally poked his head out of the door into the hallway and yelled down that he didn't think Rob was there. He hadn't seen him since the day before, either.

It was getting late, but I had to do something. I called the police and made a missing person's report. I wasn't kin but they accepted that I was her boyfriend, and was concerned that she had missed our date and couldn't be reached. They said they would look into it once she was missing for 48 hours, but I didn't have any confidence that it was at the top of their priority list. I gave them Rob's name and address as someone who might know her whereabouts, hoping they could put their hands on him quicker than I could.

For good measure, I added Derek's name, but didn't know where he lived, so I couldn't give that much information.

I was finally at home, sitting on the couch, with Odin curled up on my lap. I wasn't planning on sleeping, but with insomnia from the night before, I couldn't help myself from falling into an exhaustion-induced slumber.

Beep. Beep. Beep. The alarm went off somewhere, and when I tried to move, pain shot through my body from my numb backside to the top of my head. I lurched off the couch and stumbled into the bedroom to turn off the alarm. Why was the alarm going off? What day was it? Why did I fall asleep on the couch?

I continued to ask myself the kind of stupid questions that occurred to you when you were still seventy-five percent asleep. Finally, I came back to myself and remembered what had happened the night before. I checked my phone and saw a missed call from the police department. They had gotten in touch with Rob but he claimed to not have any knowledge of Amy's location. He sounded concerned, they said, but that didn't convince me he was innocent in this.

It had been another night of accidentally sleeping in my day clothes, so I was delayed getting into the office by way of the shower. I was getting into the habit of marching into the office and barging into Lu's office. He wasn't there. I waited a few minutes, occasionally turning around to see if he would materialize behind me, but he never showed up. I walked (marching in had used up my steam) back to the front desk where Lester sat.

"Where's Lu?" I asked.

"Good morning to you too," Lester replied with more than a generous dollop of sarcasm. "Am I the Devil's keeper?"

"Actually," I leaned against the wall next to his desk, "yes."

"Right. Fair point." He turned to his computer and tapped at the mouse and keyboard for a minute, checking calendars and reviewing email. "For you? He's not going to be in."

"What?" I stood straight up again, indignation was like an electrified steel rod in my spine.

"Calm down there, tiger," Lester turned in his chair to face me. "He told you that he wouldn't interfere with you until you finished your project. Says so right here on his calendar."

"Things changed," I was getting impatient, "Amy is missing."

Lester adopted a look of concern, and it seemed pretty genuine. "That's horrible! What happened?"

"I don't know," I said, shaking my head. "I just know that she was late for our date and then I couldn't find her at her apartment, or reach her cell."

"Lu's a man of his word, Nick," Lester replied, "and if he says he's not going to bother you, he meant it. You know how he always seems to know when you need to see him, or when he should show up for something? He has this way of tuning a person out, so until there's a kind of trigger, you won't be on his radar."

"Seriously?" I was incredulous.

"Seriously," Lester continued. "But the same note says that you've got the run of the shop here. Maybe someone else can help you?"

I thought back to my introduction at the office, and the little bit of video surveillance I watched when Lu wanted to illustrate a point.

"Sonia." No sooner had I said the name than my feet carried me to the IT department. I tried to reach the surveillance room, but a burly man stepped in front of me shortly after I entered. We exchanged as many pleasantries as I could stand, which was about one, before I launched into what I needed. He called Sonia and she arrived shortly after. I immediately started running at the mouth, trying to explain.

"Whoa there," Sonia put her hands up to stop me, "you need what?"

"My girlfriend," I repeated, "Amy, has gone missing. I need you to help me find her."

"It's not magic, Nick," Sonia showed me to a bank of monitors. "No matter how easy Lu makes it look. We have teams scouring hours of footage, analyzing tons of data, and even developing algorithms to help predict likely locations for bad behavior. It's not a sure thing. If she's in a private residence, out of the range of cameras, or isn't noticed by our agents, we'll get nothing."

"What if you kept surveillance on likely places where she might go? Work, home, regular haunts, stuff like that?" I grasped at straws. If she was kidnapped, why would she show up at any of those places? I couldn't even support my own logic.

Sonia sighed. "We can try. I can ask the team to set up some recordings on those local spots, and ask the field agents to keep an eye out for her description."

"And Rob," I added.

"We can keep an eye out for Rob," she agreed, "and watch for any suspicious activity."

"I can help too." I couldn't imagine sitting out on this. "I won't be able to focus on helping anyone else until I find Amy."

"Noble," Sonia nodded, "but not super helpful to me in the field. You can at least help keep an eye on those cameras you're asking for. It's boring, but useful."

"Count me in."

Chapter 23

What was boring about it? Boring was a chair in a surveillance room watching people do absolutely mundane things, with all the bad coffee I could drink. No company, either, because no one else volunteered to do this. The company didn't make it a policy to stop bad behavior in progress, it was more about identification and categorization. Analysis and comparison of acts of free will. This? This was live, and I was the only person interested in the subject.

Every hour made me more nervous and agitated, and thirty-six of them had passed by this point. I eventually took a break and went home to sleep poorly for about three of those hours before going back to the office. I watched a bank of monitors showing multiple scenes that I became intimately familiar with. I tried to keep it to likely locations and common haunts, like Amy's work, her apartment, Rob's place, The Fix, anywhere that I might catch a glimpse of something to give me a clue.

It was evening on the third day of Amy's disappearance when I finally saw something suspicious.

Derek.

Much like Rob, I hadn't seen Derek since the night in the graveyard. He was pretty much Rob's right-hand man, which was why I had given his name to the police, but I started kicking myself when it dawned on me that I hadn't tried harder to get a bead on where he was or if he was involved.

I noticed Derek standing outside The Fix, very obviously looking for someone. He went inside, and that was where my vantage was lost. The office wasn't so far from the shop that I couldn't make it there before a few orders hit the counter, so I bolted for my car and drove to the store. I walked inside and scanned the place, seeing Derek in the back at the table I normally sat at with Amy. His eyes widened when he saw me, but he didn't get up. I walked straight back to the table and sat across from him. His eyes were bloodshot and there were bags, heavy as his apparent conscience, underneath. He hadn't been sleeping well, and I probably didn't look much better.

"Look, Nick," he stammered, "before I say anything else, I need you to know that I didn't want anything to do with this."

"To do with what, Derek?" My voice was low, dangerous.

"With," he stuttered more, "with A... Amy."

"Where is she?" I demanded. "What did you do to her?"

"Rob," Derek fiddled with the cup that was in front of him, "he wasn't this bad at first." He looked up at me, gauging whether I was going to ask him more questions.

I decided to let him talk. If he needed to explain his innocence, I'd let him do it. So long as it got me the information I needed.

"He told me something had happened," Derek's voice gained some confidence when he realized I wasn't going to jump on top of him, "that night in the graveyard. I mean, you always *want* something to happen, but nothing ever does. But he said that this time was different, that he had felt it, and that he was sure we were going to make some sort of contact. But then nothing materialized, and Rob got disappointed. We didn't talk about it after that so I thought he must have given up on the idea. Then he called me and asked me to come by his apartment, he had something to show me." He trailed off and took a sip of coffee to help steady himself, his hands had a distinct tremor. "They were pictures, Nick. Of you, you and Amy, the office building you worked in, stuff like that. He told me that when we summoned the Devil, you stole his attention. That he made a deal with you, instead of with us. That you owed us something. I didn't like it, because it sounded like he was losing it. Real lunatic fringe kind of conspiracy theory, right? So I ignored it. He's my best friend, you know? What am I supposed to do?" He smiled sadly at me, and I was glad I had chosen to listen. This was more, and worse, than I expected. "Then yesterday he called me and told me that he'd found a way to get what *we* wanted. To get the attention of Lucifer back from you." His eyes watered, and he sniffed a few times. "He took her, Nick. He kidnapped Amy after she got off from work. I don't know what he's planning to do, but I know where he has her."

"What were you going to do, Derek?" I didn't want to look a gift horse in the mouth, but I had questions.

"Rob told me that you were working for *him,* for the Devil." It was the first time he smiled since we started talking. "I don't know what to believe right now. I didn't have any way to get in touch with you, and I couldn't ask Rob. It would have tipped him off that I didn't want to go along with his plan. So I've been looking for you. I know this is one of your spots so I figured I'd hang out here and see if you showed up. I didn't expect it to be this fast though."

"Where is she?" If Rob had a plan for Amy, I needed to find her soon. I appreciated that Derek tried to distance himself from Rob, but I didn't have time for him to feel better about himself.

"You can't tell Rob how you found them. Promise me." Derek's voice got low and he leaned across the table. "Promise me that you'll keep my name out of it."

"Don't want to be a hero?" I asked, a little sarcastically.

"Don't want to end up dead," Derek replied. "Rob said that if he didn't get what he wanted this time around, someone was going to suffer. He's gone over the edge, I don't think he'll give me a break just because we're buddies."

This upped the ante a little bit, but it's not like I was going to walk away. "I promise. Now, where is she?"

"He's keeping her in a mausoleum in the Grove Street cemetery, I don't know which one. I haven't agreed to meet him there," he shrugged. "I kept making excuses about having to work, and not taking his calls. He wants me to help him."

"Well." The gears turned in my mind, and I had the inkling of a plan laying itself out as I talked, "You're going to have to help him."

"What?" Derek jumped back in his chair.

"No, stupid." I slapped my hand on the table to jolt him back to reality. "You have to *pretend* to help him. You don't know where the mausoleum is, and neither do I. Who does? Rob."

Derek still looked like a scared rabbit, ready to run to ground. "I don't follow."

"I find a vantage point," I pointed above my head, "where I can see most of the cemetery. You call Rob and tell him you want to meet him. Get him to leave, to come to where you are. I watch from above, and then head in wherever I see him pop his head out."

Derek pushed his chair away from the table and looked like he might bolt. "I told you, he's dangerous, and I..."

"And you," I didn't let him finish his excuses, "didn't warn me about this before he took Amy. You knew he was losing it, and didn't stop him before he became a problem. I'm not asking you to do the heavy lifting. I'm telling you that I need you to be a decoy. He thinks I owe him something? Well, you owe me this."

Derek swallowed heavily and slumped in his chair. The situation had obviously taken a lot out of him, and if he resigned himself to helping me, it wasn't bolstering his spirits.

"Fine," he finally croaked, "I'll do it."

I traded phone numbers with Derek and left him to gather his courage. I headed toward the cemetery and scouted for an apartment building tall enough to see the majority of the graveyard. The nice thing about apartment buildings, though a bane for residents, was that it wasn't hard to get inside the building itself. I wasn't looking to get into anyone's apartment proper, so I felt okay with my minor trespassing. I found a suitable building, equipped with a buzzer entry system, and hit buttons until someone buzzed me in.

I texted Derek from the front and told him to start the conversation with Rob before I headed upstairs to the third floor. I found a convenient window in the hallway and scanned the area to mentally tag the mausoleums. The problem with this particular plot was the size. It was more than four square blocks, and trying to find Rob as he left might be like finding a needle in a haystack. I tried to soft-focus on the whole area, to let myself catch any movement, so I was startled when my phone started vibrating.

"He told me to meet him at the corner of York and Grove." Derek sounded nervous. "You're going to have to hurry once you see him."

"Stop freaking out, Derek." I doubted my encouragement helped. "He's crazy enough that he can probably smell fear." He hung up on me, but that didn't matter as long as he did his part.

I went back to staring out the window and caught a glimpse of movement coming from the northwest corner of the cemetery. It took some squinting and focusing before I felt confident it was Rob. I didn't see which mausoleum he had come out of and cursed under my breath as I ran down the stairs, hitting the street. I waited on the corner opposite Rob and Derek's meeting point and, once I saw Rob clear the entrance, I crept across the street and darted through the gate. It was dark but ambient light from the streetlights let me find my way to the back corner I saw Rob coming out of. I didn't know which small stone building to start with, so I just started going to the entryways and loudly whispering Amy's name. It was a risky move, I could be alerting anyone to my presence, but I was worried about time and how much I would have left before Rob came back. I was passing the third mausoleum when I heard a scraping sound. It wasn't very loud, and I wasn't sure where it had come from. I stopped moving and stood stock still to listen more closely, hoping I could home in on the sound. I knew I was in the right place when I tried the door to the crypt and it opened without resistance. Rob expected to be back within a few minutes and, if he had Amy restrained, I didn't imagine he'd lock up behind himself.

I had imagined what I might find once I entered the mausoleum. Amy could be bound, gagged, or otherwise incapacitated. I assumed Rob planned to use her as a bargaining chip so I didn't think he would have hurt her, but the darker parts of my mind imagined the terrible things that he could have done to her. The scene that met my eyes was nothing like I had imagined. There was a bucket in one corner, the purpose for which I could probably assume, and some random camping gear like sleeping bags and packaged food. The most surprising part was Amy. She was standing up, removing a last coil of rope from her hands, and then turned to head straight for the door. Her eyes got very wide when I came through the door.

"Nick!" Amy squealed quietly, if that was even possible, when she saw it was me instead of Rob, and grabbed me in a quick embrace. "We've got to get out of here!" She pulled me after her by the hand, and I was too dumbfounded to do anything other than follow her into the darkness. She took us on a beeline for the west wall, and when we hit that, she scanned the ground. "Look for a grate, some kind of cover."

I helped Amy look, and we silently stalked the perimeter heading south. We moved toward the entrance but nowhere near the gate. It took a few minutes but eventually we found an old iron grate half-covered with grass. We would have missed it if Amy hadn't felt a spot of cool air and noticed that particular draft came from an opening. With a lot of elbow grease, we managed to pull the grate up and climb down into the tunnel. I wasn't thinking about anything other than getting away from Rob, so this solution seemed as good as any and Amy seemed to know where she was going. We dropped the grate back into place above us and headed west, no conversation or agreement was necessary.

The tunnel was made of brick, clearly man-made from a bygone era. I had heard about tunnels under Yale before but had never gone looking for any of them myself. Once we were about a hundred feet from the entrance, I felt more comfortable breaking the silence. We spoke in hushed tones, but with the echo of the tunnel, we could more than hear each other.

"What the hell happened back there?" I asked, it seemed like a good place to start.

"Which part?" Amy replied.

"All of it?" There were a lot of holes in the story as I knew it, and I didn't care where we started.

"Well, if you're curious if I went willingly, the answer is no," she laughed, unsurprisingly bitter. "After you warned me about Rob, there was no way I was going anywhere with him. No, after I got out of work, I drove home. Rob was waiting for me around a corner at my apartment, with a rag soaked in chloroform." She stopped and spun on her heel, jabbing her finger into my chest. "And if you or anyone else ever, *ever*, jokes about whether 'this rag smells like chloroform to you?' again? I'll punch them square in the nose." Her point made, she turned again and moved down the tunnel.

"Never," I promised, "that joke will forever be 'too soon.' What happened after that?"

"I woke up in that stupid mausoleum," she continued, "with my hands and feet tied up, and a handkerchief gag around my mouth. I didn't realize it was Rob who had kidnapped me, at first, but once I came around he wanted to tell me all about the terrible wrong you caused him and how I was going to be his leverage. He promised not to hurt me, and all that, but I never believed him. He was batshit crazy, and I couldn't assume he would do anything of the sort."

"How did you get free?"

"He had to go out a couple of times." She looked around the tunnel, trying to get her bearings, "I had a chance to figure out that Rob was never a Boy Scout. I'd been working on the ropes on my wrists and finally got them loose enough to escape right before you came in. I assume you had something to do with getting him out of there? He got a phone call a few minutes ago, I was happy for the distraction."

"Derek," I replied, nodding, "He called Rob and told him he wanted to meet, but he's helping us. Speaking of us, where are we?"

"I'll have to thank Derek later, but that brings me to the exciting part." She rubbed her hands together. "When Rob told Derek to meet him at that intersection, I knew where I was. I mean, there are only so many cemeteries in New Haven, but enough that I wasn't sure until then. Yale's great for people who like the esoteric, and that's been me in a nutshell. I've been researching the old steam tunnels, and I had heard that there was an entrance in the Grove Street cemetery. I figured if we didn't find the entrance, we could try and scale the wall, but here we are!"

Amy told me more about the steam tunnels as we went along. There were long-standing unconfirmed rumors that it was part of the underground railroad, but newer and more confirmed rumors that it was a popular place for college kids to hang out and drink. The whole labyrinth spidered out from the campus power plant, carrying all the necessary bits through one of the oldest parts of Yale. I had mentioned Amy's knack for finding information, and this was the best expression of that talent I could have hoped for. We continued our subterranean travels for about thirty minutes, the flashlight of my cell phone illuminating the tunnel in an incredibly eerie way. We just escaped from a raging lunatic wanting to meet the Devil, so in comparison, it was a stroll in the park. Well, under the park.

We finally surfaced in the basement of one of the dorms. It wasn't late enough that any of the resident assistants noticed, or cared, when we strolled through the hall and out the front door. We were on the opposite side of the cemetery from the side street where I had parked my car, so it took us quite a while to walk a circuitous route back. We also had to stay vigilant in case Rob was out looking for us. Eventually, we made it back to the car and ultimately my apartment. It wasn't until we were through the door and the deadbolts were slammed shut that I let myself exhale a sigh of relief. Amy headed straight for the shower without even asking. She had been tied up, and relieving herself in a bucket, for three days. I wasn't going to stand between her and the hot water. I did, however, find a pair of gym clothes that I figured she could wear until we could get her a proper change of clothes from her apartment.

When the water ran hot enough for steam to creep under the door, I decided it was time to see how my partner in crime was doing. I sat down on the couch, which had been mostly occupied by one large cat, and took out my phone to call Derek. He picked up after a couple of rings, and I launched right into it.

"Hey, we're out safe. Where are you?" I asked while giving Odin some attention next to me.

"Good to hear from you, Nick." A voice that was not Derek's came through my earpiece, I had never heard my name spoken with such contempt dripping off of it.

"Rob..." My blood ran cold.

"I wanted to thank you for helping me see the bigger picture." Rob sounded more manic than the last time we spoke, which was saying something. "I see things more clearly than ever. I don't need any false friends, I don't need anyone." I could hear the muffled sound of someone yelling around a mouthful of something, probably a gag, in the background.

"Don't take this out on Derek, Rob." Derek may have been an unwilling accomplice, but he had tried to help me right the situation, so I had to try to reason with Rob. "He was just worried about Amy, he didn't want this to come between the two of you."

"Well that's a little too late now, isn't it? I didn't want to do this," Rob said, his voice growing cold and even, "I was going to trade you your girlfriend for my deal with the Devil, but you had to go and screw it up."

"No one wants you to do anything. Just let Derek go and we can talk about this. Just you and me." I was stalling, but I didn't know what I was stalling against.

"It's too late for talking, Nick," Rob grunted and I heard a thump and a groan. "I know Derek told you the consequences, someone was going to suffer if I didn't get what I wanted. For now? That's going to be him." Another thump, another groan, followed by what had to be the sound of Derek whimpering.

"What's your endgame, Rob?" If he was already beating Derek, I needed to get his attention back to me. "What do you want?"

"Want?" Rob asked with a rising pitch. "What do I want? I want what you took. I want to be the right hand of Lucifer, and you're going to make that happen."

"You don't even understand what happened," I tried to explain. "It's not like that."

"You have twenty-four hours," Rob didn't sound like he wanted to talk anymore, "to get me what I want. Call this cell when you're ready."

"What if I need more time?" I had to ask.

"You don't get more time. If you don't make it happen? I'm going to summon the Devil myself," Rob chuckled darkly, "using my very own sacrificial lamb right here."

Click.

Amy, always having a fine sense of timing, came around the corner wearing the clothes I had left out for her and toweling off her hair.

"Was that Derek?" she asked. "Everything okay?"

I looked from the phone in my hand to Amy. "It was Rob. He's got Derek... and he's going to kill him."

CHAPTER 24

A nail-biting phone call from a crazed former friend threatening to sacrifice his best friend, unless I did something to stop it, would normally be something that would keep a person awake all night. Color me surprised since Amy and I fell asleep on the couch for a few hours, out of sheer exhaustion. Once we woke up and got over a minor freak-out for the lost time, I drove Amy to her apartment and escorted her inside. She could take care of herself, but we both agreed on a buddy system at this point. I told her that I'd call if I needed her to meet me somewhere, otherwise she should stay inside. If she needed to go anywhere she had a metal Little Slugger bat that she'd take around with her. It was enough to either keep someone at a distance or make sure they couldn't find all the pieces of their kneecaps to chase her with.

I had vanishingly few options and a scant twenty-four, make that twenty-two, hours to make one of them happen.

Option one: Do nothing. Okay, that wasn't an option, but it was still tempting to think about. I would say to myself, "Derek was Rob's friend, he wouldn't kill his friend." Then I'd remind myself that I heard the sound of what was ostensibly Rob's boot connecting with a meaty part of Derek's body. So the first option was off the table.

Option two: Rescue Derek. We did pretty well on Operation Amy's Freedom, ignoring the fact that she was nearly free before

Derek and I even got there. I smiled to myself, thinking about stepping into the crypt to see the kidnapped princess in the process of rescuing herself. The successful distraction was mostly due to Derek coming clean about what he knew of Rob's intentions. I didn't think I'd get another informant like that, so unless I wanted to let Rob try his hand at summoning Lu again, I would have to come up with a better plan than waiting on surveillance.

Option three: Give Rob what he wanted. This last option didn't appeal to me as much as the second one, mostly because it involved Rob getting what he wanted. It would solve the problem, readily enough, but I didn't think he deserved to be rewarded for this amount of bad behavior. I imagined he was well on his way toward punching his own ticket if he hadn't done it already, so giving him a benefit seemed out of the question.

That left option two, coming up with a better plan and rescuing Derek. I called Amy and talked through the options, and she was on board with helping in any way that she could. I told her I was going to the office to see what I could put together before coming to get her.

Lester was getting used to seeing me in street clothes, he only slightly raised an eyebrow as I came through the door of the suite.

"My," he chuckled, "you're up bright and early. Everything work out with your girlfriend? You look like a wreck, by the way."

"Thanks, Lester," I drawled. "I got Amy back but now there's an even bigger problem. The guy I found, Derek, who helped me find Amy? Yeah. He got himself kidnapped and Rob's going to kill him. Sacrifice him in a summoning, to be more specific, if I don't get him a meeting with Lu."

Lester sucked air between his teeth. "That's ghastly. What are you going to do?"

"Me?" I asked. "I'm going to try to find Lu." Lester's eyes got wide, I stopped him before he opened his mouth. "No, not to have him meet Rob. I don't have any idea where Rob is holding him, or how to get him out. I need help."

"Honey," Lester rolled his eyes at me, "you need more than that. You need some perspective. This guy helped you free Amy, yes?"

"Right."

"And after you got Amy," Lester continued, "he got himself kidnapped, right?"

I was getting impatient. "You're telling me what I just told you, Lester."

"And you're missing the point." Lester placed his fingertip on his desk for emphasis. "What happens if you save this Derek guy?"

"Then I pop the cork on a bottle of champagne," I said sarcastically, "for a job well done."

"So what happens to the next person he kidnaps and threatens to kill, to summon our boss?" Lester tilted his head to the side. "How many brilliant plans and bottles of champagne do you have?"

I opened my mouth to answer, without thinking, and the sudden comprehension left my jaw hanging open without any sound coming out. He was right. I was ignoring the real problem.

Rob. He was the problem, and even if I managed to rescue Derek, it wouldn't stop him. I was so focused on the symptoms that I didn't even think about the disease.

"Glad to see you're with me now." Lester smiled at me.

"Fine." I leaned up against the wall and closed my eyes for a moment. "I have a bigger problem than my 'bigger problem.' I still want to find Lu."

"Lu." Lester cleared his throat. "I'm sure he would be able to help with the situation, but is otherwise occupied. If you'll recall, I mentioned that he would be inaccessible until you finish your current assignment."

I left the wall and leaned over the counter above his desk. "I believe this would be extenuating circumstances."

"If he hasn't shown up by now, I doubt he sees it that way."

"So what do I do?" I slammed my fist against the counter. "I still don't know where Rob is!"

"Whoa!" Lester waved his hands in the air. "You keep that macho bullshit to yourself, we're professionals here." He adjusted his tie and continued. "Are you telling me that with the entire office at your disposal, you need the intervention of the actual Devil to fix your problem?"

"You're goading me?" I asked, incredulous.

"Is it working?"

"Actually..." I thought about it. "Yeah."

"Then stop abusing my desk and get to it." He shooed me away. "Whatever 'it' is."

I couldn't argue with him, especially after he had given me an unexpected but entirely necessary head check. I wandered back to my cubicle and sat in my chair, staring off into oblivion, trying to find some sort of inspiration. Rob was the problem, but I didn't know where he was. I knew what he wanted, and I knew what he was prepared to do to get it. I spun in my chair, adding up my assets, and watching the world rotate. Desk, wall, Lu's door, desk, wall, Lu's door. Lu's door...

Rob wanted to meet the Devil, to cut a deal. If Lu wasn't going to help me, maybe I needed to think like the man downstairs. I got up from my chair, a little dizzy, and walked into Lu's office. It had the same austere decoration as when it was occupied, but it was missing Lu's presence. I walked behind his desk and spun his chair, looking around to make sure he hadn't suddenly appeared. I sat down gingerly, lowering myself into what was the most comfortable office chair I had ever experienced. I let out a held breath, cringing slightly, worried that I was breaking an unwritten rule. Maybe I had, but I needed more of the perspective that Lester talked about. I've seen many printings of "WWJD?" (What Would

Jesus Do?) over the years, but never expected to be considering "WWLD?" (What Would Lucifer Do?).

At that point, I wasn't sure if Rob was sane enough to tell the difference between reality and whatever fantasy world he was living in. How could I neutralize him as a threat without doing something I would regret? I'd lied, cheated, and stole, but I hadn't killed and didn't plan to start with Rob.

Lied, cheated, and stole.

Lied and cheated.

Lied.

I had a plan.

I went back to my desk, silently thanking the inspiration in Lu's office, hoping that he'd never know that I sat in his chair. The first thing was a call to Jessica in legal.

"You need what?" She sounded even more uncooperative over the phone.

"I need a fake contract. Okay, not a fake contract." I felt manic, and pushing toward a conclusion was filling me with energy, "but I need it to do nothing."

"Nothing?" her voice dripped with distaste.

"Absolutely nothing," I concurred, "but I need it to be legit. It has to go through the motions, but everything he gives up he gets back, and everything it gives him it takes away." I stopped talking and held my breath, waiting for a reply.

"Do you know how much I get paid?" Jessica was clearly not in the mood for my shenanigans.

"No," I admitted, "but today you work for me. I need it in two hours."

"Fine," she relented, "*boss.*"

She was probably paid quite a lot, given that she got me exactly what I wanted in fifty minutes from desk to door. I was on the phone with Amy, giving her the rundown on my plan, such as it was, and there was a resounding thump on my desk.

"Here's your stupid contract, for your equally stupid plan." Jessica huffed at me. "I expect lattes for this. Many."

"Your diligence is noted and appreciated." I couldn't help but smile, paging through the contract. "Handshake deal?"

"Mmhm. Your M.O. apparently." She straightened the glasses on her face. "Good job being cliché."

"Ends and means," I replied. "Ends and means."

Jessica went back downstairs and I was already walking out of the office. I high-fived Lester on the way out, riding so high on having a plan at all. Now it just needed to work.

CHAPTER 25

The New Haven Green was beautiful in the moonlight. I had found a bench in the middle of the park to make my phone call. I needed a place public enough that I could expect good behavior, but secluded enough that he'd be willing to even show up. If there was somewhere I could be assured of solitude, other than the occasional panhandler, it was the Green.

"Is he ready to meet?" Rob's voice had a dangerous edge to it. I didn't hear Derek in the background. I hoped he was okay.

"Yeah, he's ready. Center of the Green, the war monument, between Temple and Church." I took a breath, steadying myself. "You bring Derek, then you let him go, and you'll get your meeting."

"No." His voice shook with suppressed rage. "You don't hold the cards here, Nick! This goes how I say it does!"

"Seriously?" I tried to sound as nonchalant as possible, though my veneer of calm was paper thin. "You're going to dictate terms to the Devil himself? I thought you wanted a deal, not that you had a death wish."

Rob seemed to think about this for a minute, breathing into the phone, before replying. "Fine, but I don't let Derek go until the deal is done."

"Acceptable." I hung up.

I wasn't sure how long it would take for them to get here. I didn't actually know where they were, but I had time. I tried to prepare myself for what would happen next, but there were only so many scenarios I could run in my head before I gave it up for a lost cause and reminded myself that I couldn't predict everything. Some of my best work, so far, had been improvisation. Why mess with what worked?

I began strolling around the flagpole, keeping an eye out in all directions, when I noticed Derek walking toward me from the road. Close behind him was Rob, wearing a stereotypical black trenchcoat despite the mild weather. I assumed he was armed in some way but, given what I knew of him, it would be something sharp that I could run from rather than something that went bang.

Waiting for them to get closer, I sat on the stone surrounding the WWI memorial, my messenger bag hanging off my shoulder.

"Where is he?" Rob spoke loudly, past Derek.

I stretched my hands above my head, trying to signal that I was unarmed and harmless. "He's not coming."

Rob closed the distance between Derek and himself in two long strides, grabbing onto the back of Derek's shirt. Derek's eyes widened and I could see the whites at a distance. Given the abuse I heard him take while I was on the phone, his worry was legitimate.

"Chill out, Rob." I stood and hopped down the memorial to sit on one of the stone benches, patting the spot next to me. "He doesn't need to be here."

Rob wasn't sure what to make of this, but he was confused by how casual I was. He marched Derek toward the bench but didn't sit. I hadn't lost him yet, I just needed to bait the snare.

I began my pitch. "He doesn't need to be here, because he sent me to negotiate on his behalf. You see before you an authorized representative of Lucifer." I bowed slightly at the waist, maybe it was a little dramatic but I had to set the tone. "You were entirely correct, and I'm working for the Devil. Luckily for you, that means

I am at liberty to offer you, and authorize, a deal." Before I left, I looked in my closet, recalling some outfits Lu had worn when he tried to get me on board. I dressed in my best black suit and decided to up the ante with a red shirt and black tie.

"Don't play with me." Rob pulled Derek closer to him, whose eyes bulged like he had a sharp point in his back. "How do I know you're not lying to me? Like you lied earlier."

"Your whole premise was that you figured out that I was working for the Devil, right?" I spread my hands in an honest gesture. "It would be a shame if you didn't believe me now, right when you're about to get what you want."

Rob relaxed a little but didn't let go of his captive. "Why deal with me now?"

"We managed to play you when you had Amy, but you outwitted me with Derek." I wanted to give him an ego boost. "So now we're ready to bargain. Lucifer likes people who take initiative. Creative thinkers. You impressed him when you didn't back down. First things first though, I need you to let Derek go."

I could see the crazy burning in his eyes. So close to the finish line, and he was definitely nibbling. He wanted to believe. No, he *needed* it to be true, that his self-described devotion had been worth it. I decided it was time to try and set the hook by taking the contract, padded extra thick by design, slowly out of my bag, and placing it on the bench between us. I made sure to ask Jessica for the twenty-four-carat deluxe package, the shinier the better for someone like Rob. The moonlight shone off the filigree, and I could see the gold reflected in Rob's eyes.

The hand holding Derek's shirt relaxed, and Derek bolted like an injured rabbit for the other side of the memorial. Once he was free, he looked over at me to gauge what my plan was. I gave him a wave of my head that said "get out of here" and he sprinted toward the edge of the Green.

Rob sat down on the bench opposite me, his hands shaking as he reached out to pick up the contract. I trusted Jessica's work, so I didn't worry when he started reading voraciously.

"How does this work?" he asked, sounding calm for the first time since this whole escapade started.

"First, you tell me if you accept the terms." The contract was pretty standard: money, power, influence, all the generic things people asked for. The verbiage was put together well, and the terms should have been airtight, so I trusted that Rob wouldn't find the loopholes while he drooled over the rest of it.

He took some time to go over it, though the legal mumbo jumbo made anyone but the most dogged lawyer skim rather than dig for content. His eyes got wider and wider as he flipped the pages and, by the end, he was nearly hyperventilating. I almost felt bad for taking advantage of his compromised mental state. Almost.

"Do you accept?" I asked him.

He put the pages down on the bench and looked back at me. "I get all this?"

"And more," I countered, trying my best to sound confident and mysterious. It probably sounded more like Bella Lugosi's *Dracula*, but I did my best.

"Where do I sign?" he asked. "There's nowhere to sign."

"No signatures required." I stood up and dusted off my pants. "I'm old-fashioned that way. You shake my hand and it's done."

Rob stood up, shakily, his hands trembling. I held out my hand and he stepped forward, grabbing it firmly. As soon as we touched, it happened again. My eyes blazed with a fiery glow and, for a split second, I couldn't see anything but the flames. That same instant the contract, sitting on the stone bench, disintegrated in a flash. Amy watched from somewhere close by and that was her signal to call the police and alert them to the presence of a kidnapper on the Green.

His eyes widened and, as our hands parted, he asked, "So what happens now?"

I turned and walked the other way, toward the center of the park. "The check's in the mail." Sirens wailed in the distance but sounded like they were coming closer. I didn't look behind me, trying to make a dramatic exit. I expected the police would be there momentarily. I did not, however, expect the stars that danced in front of my eyes as I lost consciousness.

So much for that plan.

Rob must have been carrying something heavy under that coat of his because it felt like a long time before I was able to think clearly. I woke up in a dark room. It was dusty and what groans I made coming back to consciousness echoed strangely, mostly absorbed by the walls. It felt like I was in a stone room, maybe a crypt.

Hell.

Inventory time. I wiggled my hands and feet. They were bound, and partially numb, but still there. Poor range of motion, because each arm was tied to something beyond it. I could move my feet, but couldn't make progress in any direction. Alright. My body, check. Eyesight? I didn't feel a blindfold, it was too dark to see. I was in a dark room, check. Not freaking out because at least I knew what had happened? Mostly check. Odds and ends? Probably got kicked at least once while I was down, my ribs were on fire when I breathed. They were at least bruised, but I'd never broken one so I didn't have a frame of reference for how bad it was. Adding insult to injury, I had a pounding headache from what was, almost certainly, a concussion. Full system check, and ouch dammit.

I had good news and bad news. The good news was that I wasn't dead. The bad news was that someone, presumably Rob, had felt threatened by my endgame and bashed me over the head with something, tied me up, and put me in some sort of stone room. The worse news was that Rob's knots were better than what he had done with Amy. I also had no idea how long I had been unconscious, or what day it was.

A door cracked open and light filtered into the room from above. I glanced around quickly, getting what details I could before it closed again and left me in the dark. The room was dark granite, probably ten by ten, and the walls had hatches on them, likely a family crypt. There was a staircase going upward, to the open doorway, so I was definitely below ground. The ropes attached to my wrists were secured to handles on either side of the crypt, holding me in the center. Looking down at my feet, I realized I had been placed in the middle of a large, blood-red, pentagram. I checked what parts of my body I could see and didn't notice any visible wounds. I exhaled in relief that it probably wasn't *my* blood at least. Some other ritualistic paraphernalia was scattered around the circle, but I didn't have time to take full stock. I looked back up to see a figure standing there, backlit by the light coming through the doorway. They were at the top of the stairs and closed the door behind them, shutting us both in the dark. It didn't last long this time, the flare from a match blinded me and was soon replaced by the warm glow of a lantern. As my eyes adjusted, the bobbing wick moved down the stairs and toward me. As they got closer, I confirmed my fear.

"You're an idiot," Rob said, placing the lantern on the floor at the end of the circle, "you know that?"

"We had a deal, Rob," I protested, trying to remain calm, "You sold your soul and got your deal, what more do you want?"

"Then why," Rob walked into the pentagram and slapped me across the face, "can I do that?"

If I hadn't been testing the length of my bonds, and been at the end of my range, I would have fallen over, and not just from the surprise. My face burned hot and I tasted blood. I spat crimson on the floor before I spoke. "I don't hold your contract, Lucifer does!"

"I don't believe you, Nick." Rob paced around the small room, lighting candles around the perimeter as he went. "I heard the sirens and saw the police cars coming to the Green. You played me."

"I–" I tried to defend the interaction, but Rob cut me off.

"STOP *LYING*!" he shouted, his voice echoing within the confines of the crypt. He charged over to me, slapping the other side of my face. At least I'd bruise evenly, if I lived through this. "First tool of the Devil, right? Father of lies. It's a test," his voice sped up as he launched into a rambling tirade. "He's testing me. You were sent to feed me those lies and I had to see through it. The police? They were there to punish me if I didn't see through the deception." He chuckled, which was a little unnerving. "I saw through it and knew what I had to do. So I took the Devil's puppet with me. The police were looking for one man, not a pair stumbling home together."

So the police didn't even see him, that certainly didn't play out like I had hoped. Murphy's law had been in full effect.

"So if you think this is all a big test," fear and pain apparently made me cocky, "what are you going to do now? Do you think you've passed?"

"The final test," he rubbed his hands together and walked around the circle, clearly checking to make sure things were in order, "is to summon Lucifer himself."

"And you think I'm the key to that?" I laughed, a little nervously. "He doesn't want you, Rob! Never did! Why do you think he never came to you? Why didn't he offer you anything?"

"He can tell me that himself. And you're not the key, Nick. Well, not all of you. It's your blood. Your death." He stopped in front of me and tried to lift my chin with his finger. I attempted to bite his finger, but he jumped backward laughing to himself. "Everything is in place to send the Devil's lackey back to him, and bring him here to me." He pulled a long, thin, dagger from somewhere and held it up to the candlelight.

Self-preservation kicks in pretty hard when you're tied up and someone pulls a knife. "Rob, let's talk about this. Do you really think Lucifer is going to be pleased with you? Killing one of his agents?"

"No deal, Nick," Rob giggled to himself. I wasn't going to get anywhere with him. "I'm done talking to the middle man." He walked up behind me and grabbed a fistful of hair, pulling my head back. The knife, reflecting the orange glow of the room, was held out to the side. Rob's voice was loud, even though he whispered, his mouth close to my ear. "Goodbye, Nick."

There's the cliché of life flashing in front of your eyes when you're about to die, but that didn't happen in my case. My future with all the possibilities that could have been, but would never be, exploded in my mind as I watched the blade move in slow motion toward my neck. I would never find out what would happen be-tween Amy and me. I would never see my parents again, likely they would never know what happened to me. What would happen to Odin? Would anyone mourn me? Would I be remembered? I didn't even know if I was going to go to heaven or hell. Worst of all? I wanted to know what kind of person I would become. So much had happened and, while it felt cliché to think, I had grown so goddamn much. I wanted to live, more than anything I wanted to see what happened next. You bastard, I thought pointedly at Lu, you gave me the tools but I still need you if I'm going to get out of this. But I still needed to know that I could stay myself, and keep the core of who I was. It was risky, but even in the face of imminent death, I didn't want to compromise who I was. "I don't know if you can hear me," I quickly whispered aloud, "but I accept, with conditions." I felt the edge of the knife, sharp as a razor, press into my neck.

"Let's not be so hasty," said a voice in the corner of the room behind me. I couldn't see who it was, but I knew the voice. The dagger stopped its path and my breath hitched and caught in my throat at my sudden reprieve. I breathed shallowly, trying to regain any semblance of composure, but it wasn't happening quickly. The good news was I didn't think anyone expected me to participate at this point. I was a bystander along for the ride.

Lu, dressed much like I was in the park, strode past me into view and turned to examine the scene. "What," Lu spat the words, "exactly do you think you're doing?"

Rob had moved to stand in front of Lu and dropped to his knees, bowing. "I seek to serve, master."

"*Master*?" Lu arched a contemptuous eyebrow. "Presumptuous, aren't we? And you dare to summon me?"

"I..." Rob faltered, "I didn't finish, sir. I was trying to. But, I mean, you're here."

"I am not a dog," Lu kneeled and lifted Rob's face by his chin, staring into his eyes, "I do not come when called." He stood again and walked the perimeter of the pentagram. "You should get with the times, all of this is very last century." As he completed the circle, passing in front of Rob, he glanced in my direction and winked. "What do you want, boy?"

"To serve you!" Rob's mania returned. "To have a place at your side, and do your will."

"Do you have a résumé? Curriculum vitae?" Lu paused. "List of useful skills?"

This line of questioning perplexed Rob, and his mouth opened and closed like a fish out of water. He stood up from his praying posture and tried to make words come out, but mostly just cleared his throat and said, "Um."

"So you've wasted my time." This was not a question. Lu tapped his foot impatiently.

Rob gestured frantically at me with his dagger. "I passed your tests! I knew his offer was false and that you'd come when I was ready!"

"You should have listened to Nick," Lu said, leaning against the wall, "I have no interest in your services."

"What?" Rob looked crushed, as if all life had drained out of him.

"What do you bring to the table?" Lu asked. "I mean, besides the obvious fanaticism and poor taste in interior decor."

Rob thought for a moment and then pointed at me again with the blade. I still felt wetness trickling down my neck, I assumed I was still bleeding from the gash he had started. I wasn't so far from my imminent demise that I was comfortable having that thing waved in my direction. There wasn't much I could do, still being tied up, but give everyone in the room the hairy eyeball. Whatever Rob had been expecting, it wasn't this, and he latched onto some of the subtext of Lu's questions like a drowning man grasping at a life preserver.

"I would be twice the servant *he* is–" Rob started to say.

"Half," Lu stated firmly, interrupting Rob, "you'd be half as valuable an asset as Nick here. At best. Also, he's not a servant. Well, I could probably get away with calling him that but *you* certainly shouldn't. Beyond that, I can't imagine what you could do for me that he wouldn't."

"I would kill for you." Rob turned, raised his hand, and lunged for me ready to finish what he had started. The look in his eyes was crazed, and Lu leaned against the far wall, too far to intervene. I expected to die with a look of surprise frozen on my face. Once Lu had arrived I expected to eventually walk out of there, perhaps a bit battered but no more the worse for wear. I closed my eyes and waited for the pain to come, and hoped it would end quickly, if nothing else.

Luckily, the surprises kept coming.

There was no pain. I opened my eyes and saw that the look on Rob's face had changed from crazed fervor to wide-eyed terror. One of Lu's hands restrained the arm that was holding the knife.

"Now, Rob," Lu tutted, "that wasn't very smart. Did Nick give you the rundown on the whole free will thing?" He didn't wait for an answer. "No, probably not. Cliff notes then, I don't want to bore you. Normally I can't interfere with a human's free will. You should, in theory, be free to kill my employee here. That, however, is where the distinction matters." The dagger clattered to the floor, Lu still keeping hold of Rob's arm. "Little known clause. Most people don't stumble across it, given that we're in the wish fulfillment business and our clients are usually very happy with us. You can threaten, torture, or maim all you like, but truly attempt to murder someone in my employ? Well, that lets me get involved. Personally, if I choose."

Lu released Rob's wrist and let him stumble away toward the wall, clutching his arm in pain. Lu snapped his fingers and the ropes holding my arms dropped to the floor. My hands were free to quickly untie my feet. I went to grab the dagger but Lu waved me back with a look that said, "Don't bother."

"Look, kid," Lu slowly stalked toward Rob as he spoke, "I tried to not hurt your feelings earlier, but what's the saying? 'The gloves are off now,' thanks to you. I know everything about you: why you became a Satanist, what your home life was like growing up, and how many people rejected you on your road to adulthood. I don't need or want your type of obsession." He reached the wall and leaned his hand against it, next to Rob's head, and leaned in closely. "I need people who are fast thinkers, responsible, good-natured, and dedicated. People like Nick. Truthfully? You hurt the brand."

Lu backed away from Rob, who sank to the floor, his face white as a sheet.

"Here's the deal, and this is all you're going to get from me." Lu crossed his arms over his chest, staring down at Rob. "I don't want your soul. I've told Nick it's a numbers game, but some just aren't worth the trouble of keeping them. What does that mean for you? It means you should probably play it on the straight and narrow for the rest of your miserable existence. If your soul ends up in hell with me? It's not going to be weekends on the beaches of purgatory, let me put that out there right now. So if you keep your nose clean, and try to make up for some of your most recent activities, you might just end up at the pearly gates. Don't forget, I'm proof of hell so you can expect the reverse to be true."

Rob made the first noise since he had tried to cut my throat. "You want me to be *good*?"

"You're missing the point here, Rob." Lu shook his head like he was explaining something to a simpleton, "I don't want you to be anything. I don't care about your existence. What I care about is that you've crossed a line that I care about, attacking one of my people with real intent to kill. I also hold a mean grudge, just ask the guy upstairs. I'm giving the best advice possible." Lu walked over to Rob again and crouched in front of him. "I'm telling you that you're better off trying to get into heaven because you don't want to end up in hell." Lu patted Rob on the cheek, then stood up and walked toward the stairs. "Coming, Nick?"

I got up, having rubbed feeling back into my hands and feet, and followed Lu toward the exit. We walked upstairs, leaving a shell-shocked and confused Rob behind.

As we walked up the stairs, Lu's last words for a while were, "I'm starving. Tacos?"

CHAPTER 26

He wasn't kidding about the tacos. I was still shaking from the adrenaline by the time we got to the restaurant, and once I had come down from the excitement it was the best food I had ever put in my mouth. Almost dying does that to a person.

I went over the finer details of my original plan with him, and he shared what he knew about what had gone wrong. Overall, he was pretty impressed with what I had come up with on short notice. A zero-sum deal to get Rob into the open and nearly guarantee that he'd be held in custody, likely because of his apparent mental instability, long enough to figure out how we'd deal with him longer term. Amy saw the signal and called the police, which got them moving on the Green. Once Rob suspected something he knocked me out cold with a piece of pipe he had squirreled away in his coat, and carried me off. Amy wasn't the only one who knew something about the old steam tunnels and Rob was able to transport me to the crypt, unseen after getting away from the park itself.

Lu had planned to be hands-off until I had sealed my next deal, ostensibly to give me space to handle things completely independently. You know, prove to myself that I was capable of something. When I shook hands with Rob, Lu took that as the completion of my second task, so monitored the situation again. It meant he was listening when I accepted his deal, though he couldn't get involved until my life was in danger. Which was why it took so long for him to step in. I wasn't sure if this meant I wasn't in any danger of actually being killed, but he didn't seem to want to talk about it. I took my good fortune for what it was.

By the time we ate, I was nearly unconscious in my chair, and the reaction to what had happened to me finally set in. I stared at the bruises on my wrists when Lu finally got my attention.

"I said you did pretty good," Lu reached out and snapped his finger in the air above the table, "but this sort of thing takes a toll on a body. Why don't I take you home?"

I faded in and out of awareness as we left the restaurant. Luckily, I wasn't driving so I eventually recognized that I was home. I still had my keys. Rob's intention had been murder and not theft, so he left my pockets alone since I didn't have any knives or tools. The door to my apartment opened and I stumbled through it, but realized very quickly that I wasn't alone. It was that feeling you got when you knew there was another person in your space, but couldn't see them. I didn't have much left in me, so I braced for the worst and came around the corner into the living room.

"You had to outdo me, didn't you?" Amy's voice was overflowing with emotion, defying the offhand nature of her comment.

"I..." My voice faltered, and for the first time since Lu rescued me, I let myself go. I lurched forward and clung to Amy, my whole body shaking uncontrollably. We stumbled toward the couch and landed heavily with my head resting on her chest. I just kept telling myself, "I'm alive. I'm alive. I'm alive," not quite sure if I said it aloud or just in my own head. The what-ifs that had danced through my brain all surfaced again as bright points of possibility, a future not yet written unfolding ahead of me. I shook, and Amy held me, stroking my hair and whispering reassuring sounds that I could barely make out.

I didn't remember falling asleep. I woke up to the smell of coffee and the sounds of internet radio coming from the kitchen.

Muzzy-headed, I came back to reality slowly. I was on my couch, a blanket draped over me, wearing the same clothes that I had come home in. I must have passed out, more than likely on Amy, and she was kind enough to cover me with a throw before sleeping somewhere else. I made my way into the kitchen on creaking joints and sat in a chair at the small table. Amy, the sweet saint of Caffeina, slid a full mug of java in front of me before sitting herself down with an identical cup.

"You were gone before I could do anything about it," Amy said without any preamble. "I ran after Rob, but he had already disappeared with you. The police couldn't do anything other than put out a bulletin looking for him."

"They wouldn't have found us," I croaked, sipping the brew to loosen my vocal cords. "He took me into the steam tunnels and into a crypt." I shook my head to clear it, trying to remember the details of the night before. "I can't even remember where we were when Lu and I walked out. What day is it?"

"Sunday." That meant I had been unconscious for the better part of a day. She continued, "I got a phone call yesterday when you were missing." Amy grabbed her phone off the table, which had been streaming her morning music, and showed me the call log. "From a guy named Lester. He sounded pretty worried himself but told me that you had a guardian angel who would be looking out for you. He said I should come here, so I could make sure you were safe once you were dropped off, and that the door would be open for me."

"Thank you." I raised my mug to her, "I don't know why I broke down so hard. I mean, you were kidnapped too, and handled it way better than I did."

"What happened?" Amy asked. "If it's not too raw, it might help you process it."

"Well," I began telling Amy about waking up in the crypt, bound and about to be sacrificed, and then about Lu and the confrontation with Rob. My heart raced when I told her about Rob's attempted act of devotion, but I steadied myself and finished the story. It had a happy ending, after all. I didn't tell her that I had accepted Lu's offer but planned to as soon as we talked about those conditions.

"I was pretty sure Rob wasn't going to hurt me, Nick." Amy put her hand over mine on the table, squeezing it. "He was just using me as bait. By the time he had you? You were like the anti-Christ. I mean, anti-Devil. Whatever. He had it out for you in a big way, and it sounded like you had a near-death experience."

"Yeah." I stared into my coffee, going over what Amy had said.

Then I started laughing. It started as a chuckle but slowly built into one of those cathartic, belly-aching, tears-running-down-your-face laughs. Amy stood up out of her chair, looking worried, but I waved her back down and tried to get a hold of myself.

"What?" Amy didn't understand what had gotten me going.

When I was finally able to speak again, I said through involuntary giggles, "Guardian angel."

She looked perplexed for just a moment and then started laughing herself. Not as hard as me, but she didn't need the release as badly. It got me going again too, so it took a while before we were able to breathe.

"He did save my life," I said, wiping my eyes. "The fallen angel on my shoulder came to my rescue."

"What does that mean now?" she tilted her head slightly when asking.

"You mean do I owe him?" I contemplated the bottom of my coffee cup. "I don't know. Probably."

The rest of the day passed in comfort. Lu didn't call, and I didn't call him. Amy spent the day with me, doing next to nothing. We watched movies, ate, and enjoyed each other's company. We didn't talk about anything that happened in the past week, or what would happen in the next one. On the seventh day? Nick rested.

I'd said before there was no rest for the wicked, and Monday morning refused to be denied. On top of everything that had happened, we were at a tipping point. I weighed recent history while I paired a shirt and slacks. I decided to dress to impress. I had a text from Lu telling me to come see him when I got in.

Fact number one: I had taken a man's soul in return for providing him creature comforts far away from his abused wife and son. The end result of which was a brighter future for the survivors, provided Sarah started having better taste in romantic partners.

Fact number two: I was supposed to be the leader of my own philanthropic venture, benefitting some lucky soul in the city. The end result was my girlfriend being kidnapped, Derek being kidnapped, and *me* being kidnapped, almost killed, and saved by Lucifer.

Fact number three: Walt, the priest and my friend from the soup kitchen, advised me that the whole business was a sham and the Devil just wanted my soul for himself. Lu, the Devil himself, reassured me that it was all in my best interest. It felt like an existential tennis match and my soul was the ball.

I had a hard time seeing the downside to my entanglement with Lu and his operation, other than the philosophical one. If I weren't involved none of this would have happened, which wasn't helpful when comparing the first two facts. I didn't know if he'd let me out of my agreement if he didn't want to meet my terms, but no point burning that bridge until we came to it.

I drove to the office, by way of the coffee shop, and stopped in at Legal on my way upstairs. Jessica gave me a rare smile when I dropped a latte off at her desk. I did my best to keep my promises, and she had done her part in my almost successful plan. One down, many to go.

Lu waited for me in his office. The door was open when I arrived, for the first time in my memory. I strode past my desk, which was exactly as I had left it the week before. He was leaning back casually in his chair when I walked in. I took the seat opposite him at the desk and assumed a fairly relaxed pose myself.

"You sat in my chair." Lu steepled his fingers under his chin and grinned at me. He didn't look upset, but I had the good decency to blush and adopt a sheepish smile myself.

"I needed some inspiration by osmosis." I defended my decision.

"I don't blame you." Lu leaned forward. "In fact, I applaud you." He lightly clapped his hands together, literally applauding me.

"It didn't work out the way I planned it," I sighed. "Rob caught on and I ended up in a mess myself."

"Let me remind you that I have had, from the very beginning, your best interests in mind." Lu held one hand over his chest. "No matter what you may think of me, Nick, I am not the monster that Rob wanted to serve."

"I wanted to thank you," I said, "for saving me. I don't know that I could have gotten out of there alive without your help."

Lu waved his hands. "No need to thank me, I was just doing what anyone with the ability to influence the situation would have done."

"But no one else," I countered, "could have influenced that situation. I was a dead man. I owe you my life."

"That's very sentimental, Nick," Lu smiled fondly, "and I appreciate the sentiment very much, but it was our business relationship that saved your neck. That's what I wanted to talk with you about today, in any case."

I expected to need every shred of confidence I could muster, given the expected topic of conversation, hence my sharp outfit for the day. "I figured that was it."

"Very true," Lu tapped the side of his nose, "and there are decisions to be made. First, let me say that despite the flaw in execution, I thought your plan was a good one. You needed inspiration and weren't afraid of my reaction to something as simple as sitting in my chair. Others would have committed seppuku before sitting in my chair, but not you. The chair is the simplest part of what you did, you used whatever tools were available to you to get this done. You saw the end and decided that the means would be justified. That's the kind of person I want on my team, Nick. Not just kowtowers and sycophants. I need thinkers and doers and people willing to take risks to get the job done. You did all of that and more."

I couldn't help but feel my pride swell when Lu gave me an attaboy, but it was tempered with what I had learned through my experience in the Devil's employ.

"Ah," Lu stood, and came around to perch on the corner of his desk, "but it's not just what you've done, it's what you've seen. What you've learned. There are monsters that walk among men, there are those willing to sell their souls for a penny. Also, unless I'm a figment of your imagination, there's a Hell. Subsequently, there's also a Heaven. So what was, before, a mental exercise in 'I wonder what I'll do in a few months when I have to make a decision,' is now a more informed but potentially conflicting reality. You accepted my offer, but you said you had... conditions. Why should I consider them?"

I crossed my legs, ankle to knee. "You trained me."

"True."

"You gave me an opportunity to help someone."

"Also true."

"You tried to give me a second opportunity to help someone, but in the interim, my girlfriend was kidnapped."

"Unfortunate," he nodded, "but still true. You did, however, have the resources to help her."

"Then," I continued, "a friend of mine was kidnapped and beaten. In trying to save him, I, myself, was kidnapped, beaten, and nearly killed."

"Extremely unfortunate," Lu added, walking back and leaning against the wall behind his chair, "but you also had the training, tools, and staff available to save your friend. You, however, landed in a situation harder to escape from."

"From which you liberated me," I mentioned, "after I agreed to sell you my soul–"

"Entrust," Lu insisted.

"Entrust," I amended, "my soul to you. I'm grateful, but I need some assurances."

"More than what you've already experienced? Though preferably without a relapse of the whole 'almost being killed' thing. What you've always wanted but never admitted until just a few months ago."

"Which is?" I knew but wanted to hear him say it.

"A chance to change the world." Simple words, but the weight of them was massive.

I brushed off my pants and stood up, looking Lu in the eyes. His were bright and full of hope. They reflected what looked like my own idealism. He also had uncertainty dancing behind his eyes, unsure what I was going to do but fully invested. If it was an act, it was a good one. Could I walk away if I wanted to? Did I even want to try?

I finally cleared my throat.

"Let me make you a deal."

EPILOGUE

It was a crisp fall day, but still temperate enough that many of the restaurants in the city still served on their patios and terraces. I looked down at my watch, it was nearly noon and my appointment should be there shortly. I picked a piece of fur off my blazer. Odin had expressed his displeasure at being locked out of the bedroom for another night by rubbing as much of himself on it as possible.

The wait staff of Café 126 bustled among the outdoor tables, preparing for the lunch crowd. When Amy heard where I was going for lunch, as I dropped her off at work, she made me promise to take her there for dinner one night soon. I was more than happy to agree.

A young man walked past the terrace three or four times before deciding he was in the right place. Finally, he noticed me sitting there, his nerves were plain on his face. I wasn't sure what he saw in my appearance, but he assumed correctly that I was the person he was there to meet. I gestured to the seat across from me, and he perched anxiously on the edge of the chair.

"Will?" I asked, extending my hand to shake his. "I'm Nick." His file was under my menu. I had been reviewing it with a cup of coffee while waiting for him to arrive. The green dot on the tab was the only thing showing. Green was for "good deed" and those files hit my desk first.

He shook my hand but was a little reluctant. "Yes, I heard you might be able to help me?"

"I believe I can, but I don't like to talk business before the main course." I smiled as I gestured to the menus in front of us. "Make sure you try the soup. It's life-changing."

ACKNOWLEDGMENTS

First, thank you kind reader for making it to the acknowledgments. This novel was a long time coming. I originally started writing it in 2006, then shelved it until National Novel Writing Month in 2014 when I completed the first draft. Life happened, so it sat for a long time until I picked it up again mid 2023. None of this would be possible without the support of a fantastically supportive group of local authors and friends.

I want to thank my first reader, Brandy, who waited with bated breath as I finished chapters and shipped them off to her in 2014. Thanks also to my partner, Kat, who listened as I read aloud often and at length during my extensive editing and rewrites. Special thanks to Nicole Mann, who provided a critique that helped the final product shine. My gratitude also to Ash B, David Niemitz, and the members of the local writer's Discord that I was invited to join. Thank you, Laurie, one of my oldest friends, for staying up late just to finish the book (and for all the helpful suggestions). Additional thanks to Tal Good for proofreading the final, final, no-really-this-time, final draft.

Finally, one slightly odd acknowledgment. I want to thank Tik-Tok (specifically BookTok I guess) and the wonderful women authors who read "terrible prose published by men." It reminded me that I had written a book that one time and it was at least better than that, so here we are.

About the Author

Ben Schenkman likes many things in his life: his 20-pound Maine coon cat, his family, his coffee, and his eclectic hobbies—not necessarily in that order.

Ben also likes to play devil's advocate in his urban fantasy books by exploring the gray areas of good and evil with questions like, "Does the end really justify the means? Or is it all simply black and white?" Ben leaves these questions lingering in the ether to challenge readers' conventional thinking and delve into the complexities of moral dilemmas.

As a writer and a native of Connecticut, Ben draws inspiration from his upbringing and college years in New Haven, where his urban fantasy novels take place. On the days he wants to escape being a writer, he's a massive foodie who goes on daring gastronomic adventures, an overachiever who collects degrees in Theater, Nuclear Engineering, and an MBA, or the manager-slash-performer of the fire dance troupe, "HVBRIS"—you know, the basics. No big deal.

To learn more about Ben Schenkman and his work, or if you simply want to invite him for a coffee and talk about cats, visit https://benschenkman.com today.

Thank you for reading! If you enjoyed this book, please consider leaving an honest review on your favorite platform.

Now Available
Dueling Shoulder Angels — The Devil You Know: Book Two
Too Many Gods in the Kitchen — The Devil You Know: Book
Three